Michelle Vernal lives  husband, two teenage sons and attention seeking tabby cats, Humphrey and Savannah. Before she started writing novels, she had a variety of jobs:

Pharmacy shop assistant, girl who sold dried up chips and sausages at a hot food stand in a British pub, girl who sold nuts (for 2 hours) on a British market stall, receptionist, P.A...Her favourite job though is the one she has now – writing stories she hopes leave her readers with a satisfied smile on their face.

Also, by Michelle Vernal

The Cooking School on the Bay

Second-hand Jane

Staying at Eleni's

The Traveller's Daughter

Sweet Home Summer

Series

Isabel's Story

The Promise

The Dancer

The Guesthouse on the Green

O'Mara's

Moira Lisa Smile

What goes on Tour

Rosi's Regrets

Christmas at O'Mara's

A Wedding at O'Mara's

Maureen's Song

The O'Maras in LaLa Land

Due in March

A Baby at O'Mara's

The Housewarming out November 2021

And... Brand New Series fiction, Liverpool Brides

The Autumn Posy

Book 2, The Winter Posy

Book 3, The Spring Posy

Book 4, The Summer Posy available 28 March, 2022

The Spring Posy

Liverpool Brides, Book 3

By

Michelle Vernal

Compendium of Liverpudlian words

Antwacky - Old fashioned or out of date

    Queen - A woman

    Bevvie - Alcoholic drink

    Ozzy - Hospital

    Cob on - To feel angry, agitated or irritated

    Boss - Describing something you really like

    Meff - A derogative term

    Arl fella - Father

    Brassic - No money

Part One

Chapter One

Liverpool, 1939

Lily

Lily Tubb clutched her mam's hand so tightly it hurt. Her oval-shaped face was sandwiched between two copper plaits coiling down from beneath the hat she'd wedged on her head before leaving the house. Her freckles were standing out like tiny brown pebbles scattered on a white sand beach, and her almond-shaped eyes that couldn't decide whether they were green or brown were wary.

Lily had always hated her freckles until her mam had told her they were footprints left by dancing fairies. After hearing that, she fancied they made her special, and she hadn't minded Mickey Kelly calling her freckle face so much. Besides, he wasn't in much of a position for name-calling with his nitty hair and grubby knees!

Mam always said she was special because they'd waited so long for her. Her parents had been in their thirties by the time she came along, which seemed positively ancient compared to her friends' parents.

A smile was playing at the corners of her mouth despite her stomach-churning. To smile when she was anxious or upset was a nervous trait of Lily's, and had seen her get in bother in the classroom more than once over the years. *'What are you smirking at, Lily Tubb?'* or, *'I'll wipe that smile off your face, young lady.'*

She wanted to dig her worry book out of her coat pocket. Perhaps if she wrote the words, *leaving Mam, what if I never see her again?* in the notebook, it might help ease her anxiety because, despite her smile, Lily was anything but happy. Instead, she was terrified as to what lay ahead and had dreaded this moment that was drawing ever closer—the moment when she'd have to give her mam a final kiss goodbye.

She wasn't ready. It had all happened too quickly. Lily didn't like change at the best of times, and this was anything but the best of times.

She was doing her best to be brave because she knew her mam needed her to be, and besides, at nearly thirteen, she was practically a grown-up as such tears wouldn't help. They wouldn't change anything. She wished she was fourteen because then she'd be working and wouldn't be able to go. Or, even better, that she had a baby brother or sister, which would mean her mam would be coming with her.

Around her, excited chatter filled the frigid morning air. It mingled with barked instructions and howls from the little ones who were overwhelmed by what was unfolding like Lily.

Her heart was thumping as rapidly as the poor sparrow's she'd found lying in the gutter on her way home from school the previous month. The sight of its broken body had made her sad, and she'd picked the tiny bird up, holding it carefully in the palms of her hands. Its heart beneath the downy breast was fluttering madly, and she'd closed her eyes to send up a prayer for the poor thing to be alright. Then, when she'd opened her eyes, the pulsing heart had slowed and finally stopped, so she'd sent up another prayer for it to be happy up there in heaven. It was the same prayer she said every day for her dad.

Lily wouldn't be surprised if her heart suddenly decided to stop because it was so exhausted by all the extra beating it was doing. On top of a racing heart, she was bilious to boot. It was down to fear about what lay ahead and having been woken shortly after five o'clock by her mam.

What a strange thing it had been to make their way to school, where they stood now, in the eerie pre-dawn light. The box containing the gas mask slung over one shoulder, her suitcase clasped in her hand.

She caught sight of Edith. She and Sarah were her best friends in the whole world, but there was no sign of Sarah. Sarah had said her mam wouldn't send her and her younger brother, Alfie, away. She refused.

Lily waved over at Edith, but her feet stayed planted to the asphalt because Edith was talking to her nemesis, Ruth.

Lily loved Edith like a sister, but she didn't like the way her friend couldn't stand being alone, not for a minute, and when Lily or Sarah weren't around, Ruth was the girl she turned to.

Ruth had a strawberry birthmark on her cheek she was terribly self-conscious of, and her face was plain with mousy, lank hair and dishwater eyes to match. She didn't like Lily or Sarah, for that matter, for the simple fact, she wanted to be Edith's friend. Her best friend.

Ruth liked to bask in the glow of Edith's blonde prettiness because being pretty meant you got attention and, you could get away with all sorts of things you'd get raked over the coals for if you were merely ordinary.

The sight of Ruth hanging off Edith usually annoyed Lily no end, and if these were normal circumstances, she'd go and make her presence known. These weren't normal circumstances, however, and she was reluctant to be parted from her mam.

Ruth's face she could see now the dark was receding was alight, and her eyes were dancing. Her little tow-headed brothers, Peter and George, were nearby. They were probably looking forward to this, Lily mused.

She knew through Edith that Ruth's parents shouted at each other a lot, especially since her dad had lost his job at the factory where Lily's dad had once worked too.

Unlike Joe Tubb, Ruth's dad enjoyed a drink. He'd a big red nose and spidery veins across his cheeks, and he wasn't very nice when he'd a belly full of it by all accounts. She'd have felt sorry for Ruth if she wasn't always so deliberately mean towards her and Sarah.

The bruise along Mrs Baldwin's jaw and how she behaved like a cornered animal with her nervous skittishness suggested things at home were a lot worse than Ruth let on to Edith.

She'd seen Ruth wince, and the sudden tears sprout when she'd put her coat on after school more than once, too.

Lily might not like Ruth, but she did know right from wrong, and she'd told her mam and dad that she thought Ruth was getting knocked about by her dad. Her dad had blustered that he'd like to go round there and give Clarrie Baldwin a taste of his own medicine. Her mam had told him he'd do no such thing. 'Leave it to Father Ian to sort, Joe,' she'd said. 'It's not our business.'

Edith's mam and dad had said the same thing when she'd told them her suspicions, but Mrs Carter, Sarah's mam, was the one who'd gone to the police. They'd done about as good a job of sorting Clarrie Baldwin out as Father Ian had Lily thought, now turning her attention to Edith.

Her friend's small heart-shaped face with its pointy chin beneath her hat was pale. Lily could see fear mirrored back at her in the deep-set blue eyes framed by thick curling black lashes all the girls envied. Her knuckles were white, clutching her mam's hand. Elsie, her livewire little sister with her mad mop already springing forth from the bunches her mam had tied them into, was hopping about excitedly.

Lily hoped she managed to get a seat next to them both on the train. She scanned the road, in the direction Sarah and her brother would be coming in if Mrs Carter had changed her mind, but there was no sign of them.

They were on the eve of war with Germany, and Lily understood this was why she and all the other children were leaving their home in Edge Hill. It was to keep them safe from the German air raids because everybody knew it was only a matter of time now before the bombs rained down on Liverpool. They were a prime target given the city's port. It was a frightening thought, but it also didn't seem real.

The build-up to this morning's exodus had been gradual. It had begun with murmurings about the children being sent from the city amongst the mams as they stood on their front doorsteps smoking their ciggies. Lily had thought this was just talk, and the news it was to happen, they *were* to be taken and deposited somewhere deemed safe had come with barely any warning.

It felt like months since they'd been sent home from school midway through the morning after an announcement had been made that the school was to close until further notice. It hadn't been, though. It was only yesterday that they'd been instructed to assemble here at the school gates for six o'clock the following morning.

Lily's mam was home when she'd burst through the door of their terrace house on Needham Road with this news. She'd left work early, having been issued with a list of what Lily was to take with her. She insisted on Lily ticking the items off as she packed them in the case calling out as she went.

'Underwear,' Sylvie Tubb stated as though she were a surgeon asking for the scalpel.

Tick, went Lily's pencil.

'Nightgown.'

Tick.

'Plimsolls.'

Tick. Her slippers were too small, but money was tight, and she knew her mam would be upset if she thought she was sending her off without the regulatory items. She could live without plimsolls, Lily decided.

'An extra pair of stockings?'

'Don't worry, Mam. I'll manage with the pair I've got on.'

Sylvie nodded before squinting at the list once more. 'Hankies,' she murmured more to herself than to Lily before disappearing out of the room.

Lily heard a drawer next door opening and closing, and then her mam returned with a pile of handkerchiefs.

They'd belonged to her dad, and her eyes smarted as she glimpsed the 'J' she'd embroidered for his birthday on the plain white one. She blinked the tears away in case her mam saw them, but she'd taken herself off to the bathroom to retrieve the last few things Lily would need.

She returned a beat later, waving them at Lily before wrapping her toothbrush, comb and some soap in a facecloth.'

Lily tick, tick, tick, ticked.

'And your coat. Where's your coat?' Sylvie's eyes, the same brown as her daughter's, flitted around the spartan but clean room anxiously. They might not have much coming in these days, and she'd learned how to make Monday's mutton stretch until Thursday, but she'd always prided herself on a clean home. Standards had not slipped on the home front.

'It's hanging up on the hook downstairs, Mam, and there's no point putting it in there.' She pointed to the open case at the foot of her bed. 'Because I'll be wearing it in the morning along with my hat.'

'Yes, yes, of course you will.' Sylvie shook her head and closed the case, her face wan in the afternoon light, which was fading to grey.

She'd lines etched into her fair skin that Lily hadn't noticed before, and her hair, once fierier than Lily's own rich copper mane, had faded and lost its lustre since her dad had died.

The click of the latches sounded final to Lily's ears, and she imagined there to be a mass clicking of suitcase latches all over Liverpool.

Now, as the final few stragglers made their way towards the school, she tugged on her mam's arm. Mrs Price, who taught the weekly hygiene class, was walking about importantly with a clipboard marking children off her list. They were all labelled like parcels with their names clearly pinned to their coats.

'Mmm, what is it, Lily?' Came the distracted reply.

'Do you think I'll go to the country? Edith thinks we're all being sent to Wales.'

'I don't know about that. I've heard Skem being mentioned.'

Skelmersdale was the closer of the two destinations, and Lily hoped this was where she'd wind up. It had been a mining town and, like its neighbours, was surrounded by brickworks. There was a river that ran through it and a paper mill. She knew this because her teacher had explained how paper was made and mentioned the mill by the River Tawd in Skelmersdale.

Skem was preferable to the country. She didn't want to go there again. Once was enough.

She'd been to a farm on a school trip when she was eight and hadn't much liked it. The smell reminded her of the May Day horse parade when the sun hit the steaming mounds of horse poo. She had enjoyed the bus ride there, though, because they'd all sung songs, and she'd liked the black and white dog who'd scampered down to the farm gate to greet them. His name was Shep, and he'd taken a shine to her.

'But what I don't understand Mam,' she said now, 'is why I've got to go. We've the shelter, haven't we? And there are lots of girls my age who're staying behind to help their mams. Sarah's not going.'

The ugly sheets of corrugated iron had arrived a few weeks back. They'd been stored in their strip of back garden. That had been the first hint that things were going to change again for Lily and her mam. Their already shaken world had begun to slip and slide once more as the inevitably of war loomed.

The talk of blackouts and rationing to come reached fever pitch, and then the van had pulled up in the middle of their street to distribute mystery boxes. Instead of dread, there'd been excitement in the air, and the boxes had been ripped open to reveal gasmasks.

The men had come five days earlier to put up their Anderson shelter, covering it with the dirt they'd dug up.

'Don't make this more difficult than it already is, Lily. You're making me feel vexed. What Mrs Carter decides to do with her two is her business.'

Lily knew her mam thought Mrs Carter, an odd woman. She did come out with strange things now and again, but Lily liked her. She always made her welcome.

'I have to do right by you for your father's sake. He'd have wanted me to keep you safe at all costs, and you're not the only one. Look, they're all going.' Sylvie's arm swept wide to encompass the milling group. 'We talked about this, and you promised me you'd make the best of things.'

Lily didn't think it would help any if she were to mention she'd had her fingers crossed behind her back when she'd made the promise. What was making this all the harder was the knowledge it wasn't compulsory. They didn't have to go. So why couldn't her mam be like Sarah's? Her bottom lip trembled. 'I could find work, Mam. I'm nearly old enough. I'd be better off doing something useful. You know I would, like the socks for the soldiers we've been knitting at Guides. Do you want them all to have cold feet?'

'I'm sure there'll be a branch you can join in with in Skem.'

Lily tried another tack. 'But, Mam, what use is an education when the world is at war, and we need the money?'

'Lily.' Sylvie's tone was sharp. 'Keep your voice down.' Money was a topic that was not to be spoken about in public. 'Your poor dad would turn in his grave at the thought of you not finishing your schooling. Look at them over there. They're not carrying on, and they're half your age.'

What was niggling at her, though, was if it wasn't safe for them, the children, to stay in Liverpool, then it wasn't safe for the parents either. She'd already lost her dad. If she lost her mam too, she'd have no one. She'd be an orphan, and the very thought made her breath judder out white on the dewy morning air.

'He's watching over us, you know, Lily,' Sylvie said gently. 'You won't be on your own. He'll be with you.'

Lily had felt him alongside her before, and the sentiment did make her feel a little better.

There was no time to dwell on this, though, because a whistle sounded. This was it. She swallowed hard. Her mam pulled her into an embrace, and she felt her breath hot against her ear.

'You're a good girl, Lily. Do as you're told and remember your manners. It's not forever, this horrid war will be over before we know it, and you'll be home with me where you belong.'

'Mam, I don't want to—'

'Quiet now; you've gorra go. I have to keep you safe.' Sylvie's eyes were dangerously bright as she planted her hands on her daughter's shoulders. 'Now then.' Her voice shook. 'You'll be back home with me before you know it. You'll see.' She turned her daughter around and gave her a gentle push towards the line that was forming. 'G'won with yer, Lily.'

Lily stepped into line behind Edith and Ruth, who scowled at her.

Operation Pied Piper had begun.

Chapter Two

Liverpool, Spring, 1982

Sabrina

Sabrina swept the mascara wand over her lashes, cursing as she blinked and left a smattering of black dots beneath what she considered to be her best feature, her brandy-wine-coloured eyes. Then, wetting a flannel and ignoring the mug in which Aunt Evie's false teeth were soaking in Sterident, she rubbed the black flecks away. Finally, sliding a glossy rose coloured lipstick over a mouth she thought was too wide, but which Adam said was made for kissing, and she was done.

She peered intently into the bathroom mirror as she did most mornings and wondered whether she looked like her mother. Did she have the same oval-shaped face with milky skin and freckles stamped across an upturned nose? She sometimes thought she could recall her face so like her own but didn't know if it was her imagination playing tricks on her or not. She'd only been three years old when she left her, and there were so many questions she desperately wanted answers to.

'You can't stand about gazing at yourself all morning, Sabrina,' she said to her reflection, banishing the ghost of her mother as satisfied she'd do; she made her way through to the kitchen.

She put the heater on to take the edge off the living room before moving into the kitchen. 'First things, first,' she muttered, switching the radio on before setting about fetching the pan and oats. She was in fine form given it was first thing on a Thursday morning, and she'd more than one temperamental bride-to-be due to be fitted before the day was done.

Her good humour was down to her having been to the cinema with Adam the night before. She couldn't remember much of the film other than it was called Blade Runner. It was more Adam's cup of tea than hers, not that he'd seen much of it because they'd been seated in the back row and had canoodled, as Aunt Evie would say, for the best part of the film.

Sabrina had succumbed to a fit of giggles when the usherette had pinned them with her torch after seating two latecomers. They'd sprung apart as though they'd a bucket of cold water thrown on them and her laughter earned her a look to rival Daryl Hannah's glare on the big screen from the man seated in front of them.

Rick Springfield's new hit, Jessie's Girl, was playing on the radio, and she was humming along, knowing all the words by heart. It was hers and Adam's song, and he made her laugh whenever it came blaring over the jukebox at the Swan by changing the lyrics to Adam's Girl. In her opinion, he might not be Rick Springfield in the vocal department, but he was every inch as gorgeous as the Australian muso. Her bezzy mate, Flo, was mad on Rick Springfield.

Sabrina fancied Flo would forget all about Tim Burns if Rick were to rock up and ask her out. The odds of this happening, though, were about the same as Tim giving Linda, his new girlfriend who bore an uncanny resemblance to Farrah Fawcett, the flick, so to speak.

Tim had met Linda when she'd brought her car into the garage where he worked for a service and had been instantly smitten. So, naturally, this wasn't sitting pretty with Flo. She'd a face on her like a wet weekend whenever she spied them together, which, given the Swan was their local was often.

She sighed as she sprinkled a pinch of salt into the porridge now beginning to bubble on the cooker-top. The path to true love was never straightforward, and in Flo's case, it was proving especially twisty. There was poor Tony, Adam's mate, who was mad on her, but she wouldn't entertain the idea of going out with him on a proper date. It was a shame she was digging her heels in because he was a nice fella, even if he did wear trousers that could have been sprayed on. He'd a good job too. By all accounts, he was going places at British Telecom, where he worked in engineering.

Flo could do a lot worse, Sabrina thought, knowing how well she got on with him, but she was adamant it was on a friends-only basis. At least she was happy enough to make up a foursome with them when Sabrina met up with Adam at the pub. It would have been awkward otherwise.

She tucked her iron straight, blondish-red hair behind her ears. There were three bowls set out on the worktop this morning because now spring was here, Fred was back. She'd not seen him for herself yet, but Esmerelda from the emporium a few doors down had swept in with her gin bottle at the ready last night to announce she'd seen the tramp shuffling off earlier that day from where he'd slept outside what had been the Christian bookshop.

A To Let sign had been hung in the window for months now and had sparked a conversation between Aunt Evie and Esmerelda about how Maggie Thatcher was trampling all over people's livelihoods.

Sabrina, who was tallying up the day's takings, had thought a little smugly that they'd be alright in the wedding business because no matter how tight things got, people would always get married. If they couldn't afford a new gown, well, a hand-me-down could always be rejigged. She enjoyed reimagining and repurposing old gowns with sentimental value. There wasn't much call for that, though. Most brides wanted new, and business, despite the grim headlines, was as brisk as ever for Brides of Bold Street.

She'd also been glad that she'd a date with Adam seeing as Aunt Evie and Esmerelda were obviously in the mood for putting the world to rights.

It was good news that Fred was back. She'd been worried about him, given she'd not seen him for weeks and hoped he'd slept in a shelter out of the cold during the worst of the winter months. She'd refused to allow herself to think of him frozen where he lay with nothing but an empty whisky bottle for company.

This was why she was taking extra care with this morning's porridge.

A surprisingly perky voice called out. 'Don't you be using the top of the cream on that vagabond's porridge, Sabrina.

I know you, my girl. You're too soft-hearted for your own good.'

Aunt Evie was all-seeing, Sabrina thought, staring at the unopened milk bottle in her hand from which she had indeed planned to scrape the cream. How she'd known this while she was still lying in her bed was a mystery.

'I'm saving that cream for my strawberries,' trilled the voice once more.

Ray Taylor had dropped a punnet of the berries in yesterday as a softener before asking Aunt Evie out. He was becoming more persistent, and how the strawberries had been sourced, given it was only April was another of life's mysteries. She'd wondered too how he knew they were Aunt Evie's favourite.

The humming of the old Singer sewing machine through which a pink bridesmaid dress was currently having ruffles attached had stopped at the magical, strawberry word being bandied about. Aunt Evie had appeared in the boutique with her glasses slipping down her nose and her hands thrust in the pockets of her orange shop coat seconds later.

A jolt of annoyance passed through Sabrina now as she placed the milk back in the fridge. She'd missed an opportunity yesterday. She should have casually dropped in that she was stepping out with Ray's son while they were both there. The moment she'd opened her mouth to speak, however, Aunt Evie had snatched the punnet out of her hands.

'She'll eat the lot, Reg, with that sweet tooth of hers,' she'd tsked.

She wasn't wrong. Sabrina's mouth had been watering at the thought of chomping into the plump, red fruit. She'd had to content herself with an Opal Fruit instead popping one in her mouth as she left them to it. She'd resumed her unpicking thinking that contrary brides-to-be were the worst of all, and as she chewed the orange sweet, she overheard Aunt Evie decline Ray's dinner invitation.

Clearly, the strawberries hadn't been enough of a softener.

Adam had seemed nonplussed when she mentioned Aunt Evie and his dad knowing one another. He'd brushed it off with a throwaway comment as to how his arl fella had had lots of business dealings on Bold Street. She wondered what Adam would say if he knew his dad was trying to woo her aunt and that the pair of them had a shared history. She'd get to the bottom of it one of these days, she determined. Easier said than done, though, as Aunt Evie clammed up whenever she broached the topic.

Sabrina stirred the plopping porridge.

She'd assumed her aunt had eaten all the strawberries yesterday, but instead, she must have hidden them. Aunt Evie could be cunning at times, she thought, scanning the kitchen shelves in the hope the berries might jump out at her. She'd have liked to have tried at least one.

'You won't find them, Sabrina.'

Sabrina scowled. *All-seeing, ahright.* 'I wasn't looking.'

'Yes, you were.'

'It's time you were up, Aunt Evie,' Sabrina snipped back, pouring porridge into two of the waiting bowls. She left hers warming on the stove. 'Your breakfast's on the table.'

Her head cocked to one side as she waited for the telltale squeaking of the bedsprings. 'And I didn't use the cream, for your information.' She pulled the hand-knitted cosy over the teapot. It would be brewed by the time she got back, and sliding her jacket on, she flicked her hair out from under the faux fur collar.

There was her morning ritual of switching the light in the stairwell on and off three times before she carefully made her way down the stairs with Fred's breakfast.

Still draped across the table in the workroom was the gown she'd been hand-stitching lace applique to the bodice. Debbie Parry's calico toile was draped over the headless mannequin, ready for her two o'clock appointment. It made for a spooky sight, and she didn't pause as in the dim light she traversed the obstacle course of mannequins and rolls of fabric on the boutique floor. It was a path she could have walked with her eyes closed.

The day would be a belter, Sabrina thought as, unlocking the door, she stepped outside. Flo would be pleased. It was the first get together of the Bootle Weight Watcher's jogging group this evening. Or, the Bootle Tootlers as they were officially called. The name was Bossy Bev, who headed up the weight loss group's idea, and she was even springing for T-shirts. Flo wasn't best pleased by the name or having to broadcast it by wearing the tee, but she was excited at having been put in charge of the group.

'I've never been in charge of anything before,' she'd told Sabrina excitedly. Before announcing she expected Sabrina to accompany the Bootle Tootlers on their maiden jog around North Park, she'd tasked her friend with bringing up the rear to ensure none of the members dropped by the wayside. 'Or decide to leg it home,' Sabrina had only half-joked when she'd finally agreed to take part. Flo had gone so far as to insist she make a Girl Guide promise she'd be there.

Bold Street was beginning to wake up with lights flickering on in the flats and businesses above the shops that didn't have To Let signs displayed in their front windows. Sabrina closed the door behind her, nearly dropping the porridge as a toot sounded and, spinning around, she scowled at the grinning lad in the lorry. He blew her a kiss.

The light was already on in Mr Barlow, the tailor's shop next door. He was getting an early start on the spring stocktaking by the looks of things, she mused. He looked up, catching her peering in and frowned.

Sabrina was tempted to poke her tongue out at the pompous little man. Would it have killed him to give her a wave? she thought huffily. They were neighbours, after all.

Above the tailor's was an entertainment agency and Sabrina was sure she'd seen Ian McCulloch from Echo and the Bunnymen heading up there the other day. She'd been tempted to rush home and get her autograph book, but that would have meant hanging about on the street waiting for him to reappear. Not an option given Cara Reid, a highly strung young woman whose wedding was on one minute and off the next, was due in for her final fitting. So she'd banged back into the shop with her nose out of joint at the missed opportunity, and when Aunt Evie asked why she'd got a cob on, she told her about having seen the lead singer from Echo and the Bunnymen.

'Who's Echo and worever you said when they're at home?' she'd asked with a shake of her head as she took her foot off the Singer's treadle. Her scouse roots raised their head from time to time, overriding the plummier tones she favoured these days.

'Bunnymen. And they're one of Liverpool's top bands. Ian McCulloch's boss. Wait until I tell Flo.' Her friend would be as disappointed as she was that she hadn't been able to get his autograph.

'It all sounds the same that rubbish you listen to. Now our Cilla, she could belt out a tune. Echo and the Rabbitmen indeed.'

Sabrina had almost been glad when Cara Reid walked into the boutique.

Shaking that conversation away, she did an about-turn and made her way past Esmerelda's Emporium to where she could see the familiar mound in the doorway up ahead. She could hear Fred's snores as she drew nearer, and as she reached the slumbering pile of coats and blankets, she cleared her throat and said loudly, 'Fred, it's room service.' There was no response, so she turned up the volume. 'Fred, wake up! Your porridge will get cold.'

A woolly hat was the first sign of life emerging, and it was followed by a red-nosed, whiskery Fred whose rheumy eyes blinked blearily up at her. His expression brightened as he dragged himself up so as he was sitting with his back against the wall.

'I say if it isn't my girl, Sabrina. What a sight for sore eyes you are, lass.'

'Ahright there, Fred.' Sabrina beamed. 'It's good to see you. I've missed you.'

'And I you.' He retrieved a bottle with only a few slugs of golden liquor left in it from under the ragtag blanket and coat he'd pulled over himself, eyeing it. 'Better than any fire or electric blanket and cheap at half the price, that is.' His teeth were yellow as he flashed her a grin before being seized by a phlegmy spasm of coughs. When he'd recovered, he stood the bottle out of harm's way.

'I dined like a king last night on a fillet of finest cod, Sabrina,' he said, gesturing to a grease-sodden sheet of newspaper balled up in the corner.

A fish 'n' chip supper, Sabrina thought, amused as he reached up with hands stuffed inside fingerless mittens to take the bowl from her. She watched as he spooned in the oats, scraping the bowl clean and smacking his lips when he'd finished.

'That, my girl, was just what the doctor ordered.'

If he had nothing else, at least he'd had that, Sabrina thought. 'How've you been, or more to the point where've you been?'

'I have laid my head at this hostel and that when the night's got too cool. A nomad of the city, that's me. Not always the most salubrious of establishments either, I have to say, Sabrina.' Then, as if to emphasise his point, he scratched at his arms. 'And tell me what you've been up to. How's that young man of yours? I take it from your peachy glow he is indeed your young man these days?'

'He is.' She couldn't help the smile twitching at the corners of her mouth at the thought of Adam. Her mind flitted over the adventures that even she had to pinch herself had happened, and if she were to tell Fred half of what had transpired since the last time they'd met, she'd be there all day.

'I'm sensing a but.'

'Fred, can I ask you something?'

He'd produced a packet of tobacco and was setting about rolling a whippet-thin ciggie. 'Ask away, my girl, ask away.'

She tried not to smile at his flamboyant delivery. He made simple remarks sound like lines from a play. He had to have been on the stage once upon a time before he'd wound up on the streets. When it came to the past, however, Fred, like her Aunt Evie, was tight-lipped. But, just as she had with her aunt, she vowed she'd get his story out of him one of these days.

She wondered too how many young women had a vagabond as Aunt Evie called him for an agony aunt. It wasn't the first time she'd asked him for advice, and she took a moment to formulate what it was she wanted to say. By the time she'd relayed her dilemma where Adam and Ray Taylor were concerned, Fred had located his matches and was puffing thoughtfully on his ciggie.

'The sins of the father springs to mind, Sabrina.'

'What do you mean?' Adam hadn't done any sinning.

'You're worried your aunt will take an instant dislike to your young man based on her opinion of his father. That she will assume he is, what did you say her catchphrase is?'

'A wide boy because Ray Taylor used to be in the Lime Street Boys when he was young, and you're right, I suppose I am.' It was more complicated than that, though. Aunt Evie made out she'd no time for the likes of Ray Taylor, yet her face lit up when he paid her one of his ever-increasing visits. She was offhand with him, but it never fazed him. Sabrina also had a feeling that her aunt would view his son as not being good enough for her. She had a saying about apples not falling far from trees she was fond of.

'He's not his father, and no good comes from keeping secrets.'

It was a little cryptic, Sabrina thought, bending to retrieve the bowl. She straightened as Fred added, 'You can't live your life for somebody else, Sabrina.'

There was a wistfulness to his tone, and Sabrina would have loved to have delved deeper, but if she didn't get back upstairs to the flat, she'd have to forego her breakfast!

'Thanks, Fred, I'd best be off. I'll see yer tomorrow.'

She set off back down the street, having resolved to tell her aunt about Adam that morning. What did it matter whether she approved of him or not? She was a grown woman, but even as she told herself this, she knew she was kidding herself because Aunt Evie's approval did matter. It mattered a lot because if it weren't for her Aunt, she'd have had nobody.

Chapter Three

Liverpool, 1939

Lily

Lily could barely see through the haze of tears as she made her way over to the other children who were lining up in readiness to walk to the train station. Edith grabbed her arm and dragged her in behind her. Ruth, her birthmark an angry red this morning, stood in front of Edith listening as Joyce Bunting told her all about the mussels she'd eaten cooked and straight from their shells on a long-ago holiday in Wales.

'Me mam put an extra apple and biscuit in me bag for you,' Edith said to Lily dipping her head towards the brown paper bag she'd a tight hold of. Her knuckles were white. 'We'll be ahright won't we, Lily?' She glanced at her friend fearfully before checking Elsie hadn't darted off. Her younger sister was waving excitedly over at her mam, eager for the off.

'Course we will,' Lily replied with a stoicism she didn't feel as she blinked away the tears. 'We've got each other, haven't we?' That much was true, she thought. Edith was with her, and as annoying as Elsie could be, she was as protective over her as Edith was. Who knew? Perhaps they'd all get to stay by the sea. That wouldn't be so bad now spring was here. So long as she wasn't expected to eat mussels or anything else straight from its shell.

The piercing whistle sounded again, and they were off with much waving, sniffling and flapping of hankies on the mams part.

Lily didn't dare look back, and she wished the sense of anticipation and adventure rife amongst her classmates was infectious. She couldn't help but think the cheeriness of the volunteer marshals with their armbands, clearly displayed as they walked alongside them, seemed forced, though. Mind you, her mam always said she was far too sharp for her own good.

That's when she saw the woman in the distance. She always stood far enough away that she couldn't make out her features, and she always wore a hat. She was watching her as she did from time to time. Lily didn't feel threatened by her, more puzzled. She was her guardian angel, and she'd never told a soul about her for fear she might vanish for good if she did.

By the time they arrived at Edge Hill Station, the sky was blushing pink, and the temperature had risen a notch. They piled onto the platform chaotically despite the warden's best efforts to keep them in line and milled about to wait for the train.

Lily's anxiety was growing with each passing minute, and her mouth had filled with saliva. She swallowed it down because she didn't want to be sick right here, where she stood on the heaving platform. It would not make a good impression if she were to arrive with the remnants of the morning's toast stuck to her front. It had tasted like cardboard going down, and she hadn't wanted to eat it, but mam had made her. She'd slathered the homemade peanut butter, one of the customers from the grocers where she worked had brought in for her, on it to fill her up.

To try and distract herself, Lily stared around the station, which was a hive of activity. Finally, her eyes alighted on a child standing far too close to the edge of the platform. What if he was accidentally shoved in the melee when the train pulled into the station?

She wanted to bite her nails with the worry of it all but couldn't as the hand that wasn't carrying the suitcase was entwined with Edith's. Edith, in turn, was desperately trying to keep hold of Elsie, who was beginning to wind up to another level as she got overwrought with excitement.

Lily worried about everything these days and with good reason. Bad things did happen. This was something she'd learned the hard way when her dad hadn't returned from the Meccano factory on Binns Road where he worked. It had been a year ago come November.

The thing was, Lily knew your day could start like any other, and then poof, just like that, your world could be upended.

The day her dad died, Elsie had been sick at lunchtime. This was because the dinner lady insisted she have the chocolate cake with white sauce for pudding. After all, her mam paid good money for her daughter's dinner.

Edith had stuck up for her little sister by telling the dinner lady that their mam had said she didn't have to eat it, but she'd been told to mind her own business. Poor Elsie had sat there for an age, working her way through that pudding only to throw it straight back up once she'd finally finished. The dinner lady had not been best pleased, but Edith, Lily and Sarah had agreed it served her right as she'd barrelled towards them with a mop and bucket.

She'd arrived home from school set to tell her mam this story, but she'd been busy talking to Mrs Dixon next door, the sheets she'd pegged out earlier in the basket at her feet. So, she pushed past her and made a beeline for the kitchen. The jam smeared doorstop her mam had left on a plate for her afternoon tea was soon demolished, and she'd headed out to play with the other girls from their street. She'd ignored her mam calling after her to put a cardigan on, or she'd catch her death far too eager to join in with the game of Double Dutch she'd seen getting underway.

Most evenings, she'd see her dad sauntering down their street as she turned the long rope while Margaret and Joan, who possessed the most prowess when it came to skipping, jumped it. Then, there he'd be along with the other dads, all eager to get home and have a hot meal placed in front of them. He'd have his lunchbox in one hand, a ciggie in the other and his cap pulled down low.

Lily would drop the rope or abandon the game of hopscotch to run over to walk the last few yards home with him. She liked to tell him about her day because he liked hearing about it.

The thing Lily loved most about her dad, though, was how he could always make everything alright. 'The Tubbs are a brave bunch, Lily. It's the Viking blood in us, you see.' Like magic, the scrape on her knee or Ruth's meanness, or the telling off from her teacher for talking in class wouldn't hurt so much.

They'd reach their two-up, two-down home where Lily had been born, and he'd hang his cap up on the hook on the back of their front door. Mam would appear in the doorway of the kitchen wearing a fresh pinny and a slick of lipstick. He'd greet her with a kiss, and on occasion, Lily had seen him grab her mother's backside. She'd swat him away with a flutter or her lashes and a giggle saying, 'Joe, there's a time and a place.'

Lily fancied the time, and the place was on a Saturday afternoon when she was sent off to the cinema along with most of the other children in the street. This was because Edith's older sister, Mavis, who was working and therefore old enough to know about these things, said all the mam's and dads were Saturday afternoon people. She'd then explained what she meant by that. When Edith, Sarah and Lily had recovered from their disgust, they'd found it very funny indeed.

That day last November, there'd been no sign of her dad, and when she thought back on it, she could remember the smell of fish. It was Friday, and the Moriarty family at number 12 always had fish for tea on Friday. By the time Lily's mam called her home, darkness was creeping in, and a fine mist was chilling the air. She stood there on the deserted street shivering for a minute longer in case he should suddenly bowl round the corner, but when her mam called her in again, her tone was insistent.

She found her in the kitchen making noises about the stew sticking to the pan. Her smile as she told Lily not to worry he'd be home any minute now was overbright and she'd lipstick on her teeth.

The knock on the door had come not long after that. Three sharp raps.

The policeman told them Joe Tubb had been on his way home when he'd stepped out of the way of an oncoming bicycle and into the path of a car. He'd died at the scene.

Lily recalled how the policeman stared at her with disbelief because she couldn't stop the smile from creeping over her face. It was like the nervous tick the fish-man had. Mam said he couldn't help it. He'd fought in the last war, she said, and that's what he'd brought home with him. Well, she couldn't help hers either and what that policeman didn't understand was he'd shattered her world.

She'd begun writing in her worry book after that. It helped to write her fears down.

The sudden flurry of activity dispersed the memories of that awful night as the train's whistleblowing signalled its approach. There was no time to think about anything as she was propelled forward. 'You're a Tubb, aren't you, Lily? And the Tubbs are a brave bunch. It's the Viking blood in us,' she whispered to herself as she boarded the train.

Chapter Four

Liverpool, Spring, 1982

Sabrina

'Are you alright in there, Rachael?' Sabrina called out from where she was tidying the pattern books away while waiting for the bride-to-be to appear.

Rachael had been in the fitting room for far longer than it should have taken her to slip into the bespoke ballgown style wedding dress. She was here for her final fitting and had brought along her maid of honour, Tina.

Tina was slumped over on the throne-like chair with Queen Anne style legs Sabrina had placed outside the fitting room. She was like a princess with bad posture and a penchant for hubba bubba gum, Sabrina thought, waiting for a reply.

None was forthcoming, but a muted grunting sounded, which caused Sabrina and Tina to raise their eyebrows.

'Rachael?' Sabrina called a little louder this time. 'Do you need a hand with the dress?'

She was startled as the pink velvet drapes were suddenly wrenched back, and Rachael with an 'a' as well as an 'e' flounced forth. She looked as though she were about to recite emotional lines from Shakespeare with her hands splayed either side theatrically. Her face was red with exertion, and her breath was coming in short puffs as she panted, 'It's me, mam's fault. I told her I shouldn't be eating sausage and chips with the wedding so close. The flamin' zip won't do up. Look!' She raised her right arm higher to show the side seam of the fitted bodice. An angry roll of flesh spilt out over the zip, which she'd only managed to pull a quarter of the way up. 'I wanted to take the dress home with me today too.'

The ginormous purple bubble Tina was in the middle of blowing popped at the sight of her bezzie mate, a distraught bridal apparition.

Sabrina wished the gum had gone splat all over her face like it had Flo's little sister, Shona's, that time. Shona had managed to get it in her hair, too, and Mrs Teesdale had snipped it out in the end. The poor girl had wound up looking like a Victorian-era street urchin.

Sabrina would have been only too happy to start snipping Tina's split ends if it meant she'd stop blowing bubbles because the sound of each pop was setting her teeth further on edge. It was the bubble gum equivalent of fingernails down a blackboard.

Now, the sight of Rachael, looking more Dolly Parton than demure which had been her go-to word when describing her dream dress at their initial consultation, was in danger of giving her lockjaw. She slammed the Vogue Spring Brides book shut, thinking Rachael had been at more than the sausage and chips. The amount of wobbling bosom exploding overtop of her sweetheart neckline would give her wedding an X-rating. How had she piled on so many pounds in the month since she'd last seen her?

Tina was busy pushing the wad of bubblegum into the side of her cheek, and once she had it sorted, she leapt up and began to try and yank the zip up while Rachael stood with her arms held out either side. The maid of honour's lips were set in a determined line. 'You'll be ahright, queen. We'll get you in it. It can't be worse than doing those jeans up you wore to the disco last Friday night. I thought we were going to have to cut you out of them at the end of the night. On the count of three, breathe in. One, two, three!'

'Stop, you'll rip it!' Sabrina ordered, hustling over to take charge. This was why she'd suggested a corset-style bodice. Rachael, however, had been adamant about not being be laced into her dress. 'I want to enjoy me meal, girl,' she'd said. 'And I won't if I can't sodding well breathe, will I?'

Tina had echoed, 'She won't, you know.'

Sabrina had wished the gum would go splat that time too.

'You put the undergarments you'll be wearing on the day on, didn't you?' Sabrina checked, giving the zipper one last wiggle. It wouldn't be the first time one of her customers hadn't followed her instructions to wear them to their final fitting. It was vital if the dress was going to sit as it should on her big day.

'I did, and they're strangling me and all.'

It was no good, she decided, having moved the zip half an inch. 'I'll have to let it out, I'm afraid.' And hope Rachael didn't decide to crash diet between now and next Saturday.

'Will that cost extra? Because the dress has already cost me as much as our honeymoon in Spain.' Rachael fixed blue eyes made up with matching eye shadow on Sabrina.

There were days Sabrina loved her job, and then there were times like this, she thought as she explained that no, it was all part of the service.

Rachael picked up her skirt and swept back into the fitting room to put her civvies on while Tina sat back down on the throne to resume bubble blowing in between, glowering over at Sabrina.

Oh, how she'd have loved to have said, 'It's not my fault she's put on weight.' But she was far too well trained for that. The customer was always right, and so Sabrina kept her expression neutral.

Fifteen minutes later, having made a further appointment for Rachael the following week and given her numerous assurances that the dress would fit her like a glove come her big day, the two girls made to leave. Rachael said to Tina as she opened the door, 'At least my Bazzer likes me with a bit of meat on my bones. He says there's more of me to love. I could murder a pie and mushy peas, me. I'm starvin'.'

The door banged shut, and Sabrina poked her tongue out at it before carrying Rachael's white gown out the back making noises about stupid meffs overeating. Aunt Evie she saw was mid cup of tea.

'Sabrina, I brought you up better than to use that slang,' Evelyn tutted, lowering her china cup with its delicate rose pattern. 'Why've you got a cob on? And why's that gown come back in. I thought it was her ladyship's final fitting?'

Sabrina laid Rachael's dress down carefully on the work table and told Aunt Evie all about Rachael having stuffed herself full of sausage and chips since her last appointment, which meant she'd now have to let the gown out. 'As if I don't have enough on me plate.' Their order book was chock-a-block. Spring was the wedding season, after all.

Evelyn gestured to the mishappen pottery mug. 'Ger that down yer.' She cleared her throat. 'You.'

Sabrina bit back a smile and picked up the mug of tea. 'Ta.' She cast around for something sweet. 'Where are the Garibaldis?'

'I didn't think you'd be wanting biscuits given you've joined the Bootle Tootlers.' Evelyn's mouth twitched. She knew Sabrina was joining the Weight Watcher's jogging group in a moral support capacity only for Florence.

'I'm not one of them, ta very much. I'm back up support, that's all.' Sabrina was indignant.

'If the shirt fits, and we're out of Garibaldis, I've put them on the shopping list.'

Sabrina had told Flo she wouldn't be wearing one of the T-shirts Bossy Bev had organised. 'I'm not an official member after all,' she'd told her pal.

'I won't be wearing the T-shirt, for your information.' She told Evelyn now.

'What T-shirt,' Evelyn was puzzled.

'Never mind.' Sabrina sat down with a sigh and picked up her mug. The tea at least was a welcome sight, and taking a decent swig; she felt her frayed edges smooth. The pips to signal the news came on, and she listened to the dismal broadcast full of unrest in the Middle East, more job losses here in the north of England and race riots in London.

'I'm going to turn the news off from now on.' Evelyn shook her head in a what's the world coming to manner.

Sabrina paid no attention to her because she threatened that most mornings. She did have a point, though. It was never good news.

'Why can't they ever tell us nice things?' Evelyn lamented, staring at the contents of her cup.

'Like who won the pools and how to beat the crowds in the January sales,' Sabrina added.

It wasn't exactly what Evelyn had meant, but it would be preferable to the doom and gloom broadcast they'd just listened to.

Sabrina remembered the promise she'd made herself earlier. There was no time like the present, and taking a deep breath, she adopted a light and breezy tone, 'Oh, Aunt Evie, I almost forgot.' She wondered if her nose had grown. 'You won't believe this.'

'Won't believe what?' Evelyn wasn't fond of sentences that began like this. In her experience, she could more often than not full well believe whatever she wouldn't be able to believe, and she usually didn't like it.

Out with it, Sabrina, girl. 'My Adam's only Ray Taylor's son.' She adopted a note of surprise as she added, 'It's a small world, ahright.'

Evelyn's teacup rattled in the saucer as she placed it down with a heavy hand. She was flummoxed. She'd not expected that, but now she thought about it, there had been something, something she'd not been able to put her finger on about that boy. Now she knew what it was, and in an un-Evelyn Flooks manner, she was also speechless. She remained on the stool at the work table for a moment and then pushed herself up to resume her position at the Singer.

She picked up the bolt of peach fabric she was in the process of transforming into a sleeve and inspected her handiwork, all the while her mind whirring.

Sabrina decided nonchalance was the best course to take. She swigged down the rest of her tea and picked up Rachael's dress. She'd make a start on the unpicking. She was all fingers and thumbs, though as she waited for a reaction other than Aunt Evie looking like she'd eaten an olive thinking it was a grape.

Evelyn couldn't entirely take it in. Sabrina and Ray Taylor's son? No, no, no, it wouldn't do. Ray was a womaniser and a wheeler and dealer who sailed far too close to the wind. The apple didn't fall far from the tree, which meant Sabrina would wind up with a broken heart, and she couldn't have that. Not her Sabrina, who was as good as her flesh and blood. She'd have a word with Ray when Sabrina was out of earshot. It was all too close for comfort. She gunned the machine into life with more force than was necessary.

The bell sounded, signalling a customer was waiting at the counter. Sabrina was glad of the excuse to put some distance between herself and Aunt Evie while she digested what she'd told her. Besides which, if she wasn't careful, she was likely to butcher Rachael's gown. Gathering herself, she plastered a smile on her face and walked into the boutique, feeling her aunt's eyes boring holes into her back.

'Good morning.' She beamed at the woman fidgeting at the counter. She looked to be about her age. Her fiery red hair cut into a cool, Suzy Q shag, but her outfit was the opposite of the singer's leather and denim style. Instead, she was wearing a white ruffle blouse with maroon knickerbockers and flat shoes. She'd the leather strap of her purse draped across her chest, and her shoes were ballet-style flats.

'Hello.' She smiled, and her face transformed from striking to beautiful. 'I'm Alice Waters. I've got an appointment with Sabrina. I spoke to her on the telephone.'

Sabrina had forgotten all about the appointment, but she wouldn't let her know that. 'Of course. I'm Sabrina. It's lovely to meet you, Alice.' She opened the drawer and retrieved her trusty notebook. 'I'll take notes in here,' she explained and opening the book, she flicked through to a blank page and wrote Alice Waters at the top. 'First things first then, Alice. What date's the wedding?'

'April the twentieth.'

Sabrina blinked, feeling a throbbing at her temples. She stared at Alice, who had the grace to look sheepish.

'I know it's short notice, but I already have the dress. All I want are a few simple tweaks made to it.' She held up a bag Sabrina hadn't noticed in her quick appraisal of her.

'My Mark's in the army, and he's being deployed to Belfast in early May. We want to be married before he goes.'

The way the pink went out of Alice's cheeks at the thought of her fiancé being sent to Northern Ireland didn't escape Sabrina, and she didn't have the heart to crush this young woman's dream of being wed before that happened either. Her attention had been caught too by the flash of green on her engagement finger. 'That ring's gorgeous. Is it antique?'

'It was me nan's mother's. So, yes, I suppose it is.' She held her hand out so Sabrina could inspect the pear-shaped emerald.

'Gorgeous,' Sabrina repeated. 'Was she a redhead too? Because it's perfect with your colouring.'

Alice nodded, 'She wor, yes.'

'Right, let's see the dress, then.' Sabrina smiled, deciding she'd make time for whatever alterations needed doing.

Alice flashed her a hopeful one by return before bending to retrieve the gown. She straightened, holding it up and giving it a shake.

Sabrina gasped as she took in the silk and satin white dress. It was a simple design with a crossover neckline, puff sleeves with cuffs and an A-line skirt. It was the simplicity that made it so exquisite. For all that, though, it was dated, and she could see in a flash how it could be brought up to date with a few nips and tucks here and there to ensure Alice was a beautiful spring bride. She instantly wanted to know all about the woman who'd once worn it too. She hoped she'd had a happy life.

'May I?' She gestured to the dress, and Alice nodded.

'Of course.'

Sabrina stepped forward and caressed the silk fabric of the skirt. She visualised a petite young woman full of hopes and dreams for her future standing opposite the man she was about to marry as she promised to love him always. Every wedding dress told its own story.

Alice pushed her shoulders back proudly, pleased by Sabrina's reaction. 'It's beautiful, isn't it?'

'It is. The fabric's like water running through my fingers to touch,' Sabrina affirmed.

'As I said, me nan and her mam before her wore it. Lily Waters was nan's name. She married me granddad Max back in nineteen forty-five. I've gorra photograph of their wedding day if you'd like to see it?'

'I would like to. Very much so.' Sabrina nodded, thinking how special it was that this girl, Alice, would have such strong connections to her late grandparents on her wedding day what with her ring and the dress. 'Here, let me hang it up for you.' She took the dress and carefully slipped it onto a padded hanger before hooking it up on the fitting room wall.

Alice, meanwhile, had opened the purse resting on her hip, and when Sabrina returned, she held out a small card embellished with creamy roses framed inside of which was a black and white photograph.

Sabrina took it, noting despite the frame, the picture was creased. The wedding party gathered on the steps of a registry office was still plain to see, though. The bride looked young, as did her new husband, and she voiced this to Alice.

'They were, Nan was barely eighteen, and me granddad had only just turned nineteen himself. They knew their own minds though. They were the loves of each other's lives.'

'How romantic,' Sabrina said, her eyes sweeping the rest of the clustered group. The bridesmaid looked to be around the same age as the bride. She was a pretty dark-haired girl dressed in a long dress with a ruffle around the bottom.

'Her bridesmaid was called Sarah,' Alice supplied.

'She's luvly,' Sabrina murmured as she glanced over the rest of the wedding party and then her eyes widened. She closed them for a split second and opened them again, not quite believing what she was seeing. However, the images frozen in time hadn't changed, and the blood rushed to her head like a rogue spring tide.

There, on the steps and visible behind the bride's shoulder, was a girl who looked exactly like her.

She stared at the photograph unblinkingly for a moment, her breath catching. Her hair was different, swept up in a side do. But it was her she was sure of it, but that wasn't what had her feeling as though the floor might turn to quicksand beneath her feet. Instead, it was the image of the man standing next to her.

It was Adam.

Chapter Five

Liverpool, 1939

Lily

The train journey from Edge Hill to Ormskirk wasn't a long one. Lily wasn't sure exactly how much time had passed, but she felt sure it hadn't been more than an hour and a half. They'd entertained themselves with sing-songs in between munching on the treats Edith's mam had packed. A glimpse out the fingerprint marred windows revealed buildings and green belt interspersed with the occasional early tinges of yellow, red and orange.

Lily wrote, *Will I see Mam again?* in her worry book and, snapping it shut, put the thought out of her head, joining in on the rousing rendition of Michael Finnegan being sung. Before she knew it, the train had screeched to a halt in the station, and they were disembarking. There was no time for lingering in the leafy surrounds of Ormskirk station as they were led out to the street and seen onto a waiting coach.

The singing resumed, but instead of pulling up beside the beach as the day at the seaside atmosphere on the rattling old coach would suggest, they parked outside an uninspiring sooty red building. Lily had seen the signs for Skelmersdale as they dipped down into the valley where the town nestled. Her mam had been right; this was where they were headed.

The sky was no longer blue. Instead, the clouds hung heavy and grey overhead as hesitating on the steps of the coach; she shivered. She ignored the nudge in her back from Edith in her reluctance to step down from the coach.

'Don't dilly-dally, children,' Mrs Price, warbled fixing Lily in her sights. She had a sharp tongue did Mrs Price and Lily didn't want to be on the receiving end of it, so she did as she was told and joined the others in the snaking line waiting to go inside the building. Once they'd all assembled and a final check to confirm nothing had been left on the coach completed, one of the volunteer marshals Lily didn't recognise led them inside. Mrs Price brought up the rear.

They entered a foyer with a cloakroom area and then filed into the hall leading off it. Women of mixed ages, one or two with babies dangling from their hips, were milling about chatting as though this were a cup of tea after church get-together. Lily kept her eyes fixed on the floor, which shone and smelled of wax and bumped into Ruth as she stopped suddenly.

The other girl spun around and hissed, 'Watch it.'

'No fidgeting, children,' Mrs Price bossed as she fussed around them. Jimmy O'Malley received a cuff across the back of his head and immediately stopped scratching. The children from Edge Hill formed a group at the far end of the room, and the hum of conversation began to slow and then it ceased altogether as curious eyes settled upon them.

A child was sniffling, and Lily heard Mrs Price tell Joan Storer she was a big girl now, and as such, she was to stop crying and make her mam proud. Poor Joan cried even harder at the mention of her mam, and Lily's hand snaked out to hold Edith's. Edith squeezed it hard. She wished Sarah were here with them too.

The frivolity of earlier was forgotten as worry about what would happen next spread like the chickenpox had at school the year before amongst the Edge Hill children.

A stocky woman with her short, grey hair set in tight curls was marching about self-importantly. She was wearing a dark green cardigan from under which the collar of a white blouse peeked, along with a dowdy skirt. In her hands, she was holding a clipboard from which she was working her way down a list ticking the women's names gathered off it. When she was done, she turned her attention towards the children at the top of the hall and nodded toward Mrs Price.

'When Miss Pinkerton calls your name, you're to step forward,' Mrs Price instructed them.

Miss Pinkerton made her way to the middle of the hall and cleared her throat before calling out Henry, Ronald and John Fitzwilliam's names. All three boys were beetroot as they stepped forward.

A woman of middling years with a hard line to her mouth stepped forward. 'These three will eat me out of house and home by the looks of them,' she muttered in a voice designed to carry before inclining her head. 'C'mon then, lads; we can't 'ang about 'ere all day now, can we?'

The waiting children's eyes were wide as the three brothers picked up their cases and followed the woman's purposeful stride from the hall.

One by one, the group thinned out, and when Edith's hand slipped from hers, Lily had to blink back, smarting tears. She watched as Edith and Elsie were bustled from the hall by a woman with a maroon hat and matching coat with a swan brooch pinned to the lapel. Her smile was kind. That was something, and Lily scanned the handful of careworn faces left, hoping she too would go home with a woman with a kind smile. She glanced to her side, wondering which of the remaining children she'd be billeted with and crossed her fingers it wouldn't be Ruth.

'Lily Tubb, Joyce and Yvonne Bunting.'

Lily and Joyce shot each other a quick smile; both girls were pleased with the arrangement. Lily liked Joyce even if she did eat mussels. Yvonne, her younger sister, was a happy soul who was constantly flashing her gappy grin. Lily hadn't realised she'd been holding her breath, and she exhaled in a big puff of relief she wasn't to be sent off with Ruth.

Her relief was short-lived, however, as a stooped old woman with her head covered in a scarf and wearing a navy coat which she'd buttoned right up to her chin, pushed her way forward. She'd wire-framed glasses on with a crack in one of the lens and Lily watched as she shoved those in her way aside with her walking stick. 'I told yer I could only take one of them.' Her voice was gruff with the throatiness that came from too many harsh winters.

Mrs Pinkerton referred to her clipboard. 'You did volunteer, Mrs Cox, and you're down for three. Your cottage has two bedrooms. We've all got to do our bit for the war effort, you know.'

Mrs Cox stood her ground, giving Mrs Pinkerton a withering stare. 'I said I could take one, and that's that.' She eyeballed Mrs Pinkerton, who looked uncomfortable as she studied the list on her clipboard once more.

A young woman with a plump baby with bright red spots on either cheek called out, 'I'll take them two that looks to be sisters, and the taller lass can go with Mrs Cox. How's that?'

Mrs Cox nodded as though the matter was now settled, and Lily turned panicked eyes to Joyce. There was nothing Joyce could do, though, other than stare back at her sympathetically. Even Ruth looked sorry for her. Lily's gaze swung pleadingly to Mrs Pinkerton, but the woman was already moving down her list.

'Are yer simple, lass? Get yer things.'

This time Lily couldn't help the tear escaping, and brushing it away, she picked up her case and followed the shuffling old woman out the door.

Chapter Six

Liverpool, Spring, 1982

Sabrina

Sabrina fanned herself with the notebook in which she'd written Alice's name. Her heart was thumping. The photograph Alice had produced sat on the counter between them, and Alice, bewildered by Sabrina's reaction, picked it up, studying it intently.

'How weird. Nan's bridesmaid looks just like you,' she said, looking up at Sabrina and then back down at the photograph.

'I know.'

'She must be related to you. I don't know what her name was, this girl in the picture.' She put the framed, black and white snapshot back down on the counter, angling it so Sabrina could see. 'Me nan passed away before I was born, and I never had the chance to get to know her.'

Sabrina caught the wistfulness slide over her face.

'Me granddad's been gone a few years now, but he used to talk about her all the time. So much so I feel as though she wor part of me life. Is this your nan then?' She gestured to the picture. 'What a coincidence, eh?' Her face suddenly lit up. 'Your nan might be able to tell me some stories I haven't heard about me nan when she was young! Ooh, I'd love that.'

Sabrina shook her head. 'No, sorry. She's not me nan.'

Alice's lips puckered. 'Are you sure? I mean, look at her.' She stared hard at the picture and back at Sabrina once more, frowning. 'She has to be related to you. I know it's a small photograph, but it's still plain as day. She could be your twin.'

'I just do know, and you wouldn't believe how I know if I wor to tell you.'

'Try me,' Alice challenged, raising her chin.

Sabrina hesitated and then decided it was best to say it and be done with it. 'I know the woman in the photo isn't me nan because that girl there,' she jabbed at the picture. 'Is me.'

'I don't understand?' Alice frowned and then took a step back, her expression guarded.

'Alice, I'm telling you that girl stood behind your nan is me.'

Alice snatched the cream card frame off the counter. 'Don't talk silly.' She shook her head and put the photograph back in her purse as though the matter was now closed.

'Listen, I promise you I'm not making this up and believe me, I'm aware of how mad this sounds, but I know it's me because me fella, Adam, he's in the picture too.'

Alice's lips twitched from side-to-side for a second or two, and then with another shake of her head, she strode over to the fitting room to retrieve her dress. 'I think I might have made a mistake coming here.' She didn't hang about stuffing the dress back into her carry bag. She wanted to put distance between herself and this shop. The girl was bonkers.

Sabrina sighed; she thought she was barmy, but it was suddenly vital that Alice hear her out because she wanted to know more about the couple in the picture, Alice's grandparents. 'Alice, don't go. Please, would you let me explain?' Sabrina knew if Alice thought she was odd now, then she'd think her barking by the time she'd finished.

Alice wavered. She'd been told by more than one of her friends that Brides of Bold Street was the place to go when it came to wedding gowns. So perhaps she should let her say her piece. It couldn't do any harm, she decided and besides, she hadn't a clue where else to go to have her dress altered at such short notice.

Sabrina seized on her uncertainty. 'Listen, why don't you let me make you a cup of tea? We can talk out the back in the workroom, and then if you still think I'm round the twist, you can go off about your business and tell everyone about the strange woman who works at Brides of Bold Street.' She gave a small laugh, but it sounded forced.

Alice gave a slow nod. Work at Bon Appetit, where she was learning the art of French cuisine, didn't start until two. First, she'd listen to what Sabrina had to say and see how she felt after that.

'C'mon then. I'll introduce you to me, Aunt Evie, who's beavering away out the back and make us all a brew,' Sabrina said. She needed a strong cuppa herself to settle her nerves after the shock of seeing herself and Adam in that old photograph.

Alice followed Sabrina's lead and smiled uncertainly at the woman in the bright coloured shop coat bent over an old-fashioned sewing machine. She reminded her a little of a parrot with glasses, she thought.

'Aunt Evie, this is Alice. Alice has a family heirloom dress to be altered for her wedding in two weeks.'

'Two weeks! You're cutting it fine, me luv. How do you do, Alice?'

'Erm, ahright, I think. Me fella's being deployed to Belfast. It's all happened rather fast, and we want to be wed before he goes, and Sabrina here's told me something dead strange.'

Evelyn tossed a questioning glance at Sabrina.

Sabrina pulled a stool out from under the table and gestured for Alice to have a seat. The bride-to-be perched on the edge of it, poised for flight if things got too weird.

'Alice showed me a photograph of her nan's wedding, Aunt Evie. Alice, would you mind showing it to my aunt?'

Alice dipped her head and undid her purse once more to produce the card containing the picture. She handed it to Evelyn, who pushed her glasses back up her nose before inspecting the image inside. The sharp gasp as the penny dropped was audible over the radio.

'What year was this taken?' Evelyn asked, still scrutinising the photograph.

'Me nan got wed in the spring of nineteen forty-five not long after her eighteenth birthday. The war had just ended.'

'And I'd not long reopened, she was one of my first customers. I remember her well,' Evelyn said quietly.

'You knew her?' Alice's greenish-brown eyes grew round.

Evelyn's head snapped up. 'Oh yes. I knew Lily.'

Sabrina's head was tilted to one side. She was as surprised as Alice.

'Lily and I worked together for a short time,' Evelyn said, filling in the blanks. 'I had to close the shop after conscription came in. There wasn't much call for bespoke wedding gowns at that time, and there was no fabric to be had anyway. My time was better served sewing parachutes. I heard young Lily had not long lost her mam, and I took her under my wing when we both worked at Littlewoods on Hanover Street.'

Sabrina was all ears. Aunt Evie had never talked much about the war years.

'We only worked together a few months before the factory was bombed in the blitz. After that, I moved to another factory and lost track of Lily until she called in here wanting her mam's wedding dress altered.'

'Like I've done today with Nan's dress.' Alice's cheeks reddened with excitement. 'Grandad told me she worked in a factory during the war and volunteered at the Royal Liverpool of an evening. She got into nursing not long after they married. It was her passion. I can't believe you knew her.' She shook her head. 'It's like fate brought me here.'

Sabrina and Evelyn exchanged a glance. It wasn't the first time they'd heard that.

'She wor a luvly girl who'd experienced a lot of sorrow for someone so young but she had her fella. They made a fine pair,' Evelyn said.

Sabrina was still waiting for Aunt Evie to twig who else was in the photograph, but Alice had begun talking once more.

'They were the luvs of each other's life, Lily and Max. They got married young but never regretted a second of their life together. Although Granddad was devastated when he lost her, he never remarried.'

Evelyn's eyes took on a faraway glaze. 'We lived with the threat of death every day during the war. When you don't know if you'll have a tomorrow, you don't waste your time on ifs and buts. Procrastination wasn't in our vocabulary. They were lucky to have the time together they did. I'm a firm believer that you only get one chance at luv. True luv.'

Sabrina gave her a quizzical glance. She'd never heard her talk like that before. Had she had her chance and missed it?

Alice nodded. 'I can imagine. It's why I don't want to wait to marry Mark. I never met me nan, but I feel as though I know her because Granddad talked about her all the time as if she was still with him. A photograph was taken on her twenty-first birthday that he kept in a silver frame on the sideboard, and he used to talk to that photo. 'Shall we have rice pudding, or tapioca, Lily me luv?' that sort of thing. I always half expected her to answer him! I'm wearing the dress on me wedding day because I want my Mark and I to be every bit as happy as me nan and granddad were.'

'It's a beautiful sentiment, luv,' Evelyn said.

'I've her ring too.' She held out her hand for Evelyn.

'The emerald suits you as it did, Lily.' Evelyn smiled.

Alice gave a sad smile. 'Grandad wanted me to have it, and I knew I wouldn't find anything else this beautiful. It makes me feel close to Nan. I don't get on well with me, mam, you see. She and me dad split up when I was young. So it wor me grandad who more or less raised me and it feels right to wear Nan's ring and dress.'

Sabrina nodded, trying to cool her heels. She was getting impatient now, waiting for her aunt's reaction to spotting her in the wedding party.

Evelyn, who was a wily old bird, hadn't missed a thing. She knew full well it was Sabrina standing behind the bride, and she knew what that meant. She knew a lot more than Sabrina did about matters of the past.

'Aunt Evie, look there, behind Alice's nan.'

This time the shock was plain for the two girls to see as Evelyn, who'd picked Sabrina out at first glance, registered who else was in the party.

'You know them too, then?' Alice asked.

'I do.' Evelyn nodded slowly, finally looking at Sabrina.

'You know what this means, Aunt Evie.'

She didn't reply. She'd never wanted Sabrina to mess about with the timeslip here on Bold Street. In her mind, you needed a long spoon to sip with the devil, and if Sabrina persisted in her quest to travel back in time, she'd need the longest spoon of all.

'Well, I don't, and if one of you could please explain in a way that makes sense, I'd appreciate it,' Alice said shortly. 'I haven't got all morning either, I'm due in work at two o'clock.' She shuddered at the thought of being on the receiving end of chef John-Paul's tongue. He couldn't abide tardiness, and even though he reverted to his native French when he was hot under the collar, he still managed to make his point clear through sign language.

'I promised you a brew, didn't I?' Sabrina didn't wait for a reply as she scooped up the tea tray from earlier and moved towards the stairs. 'I'll be back in a jiffy with a fresh pot.'

Evelyn raised the foot on the Singer and snipped the white cotton off before laying the gown she'd finished hemming down on the far end of the work table.

'Would you tell me what's going on?' Alice asked.

'I could, but you wouldn't believe me.'

It was the sentiment Sabrina had uttered earlier, and Alice felt annoyance pique.

'Tell me anyway.' Her voice was uncharacteristically short.

Evelyn cocked an ear, hearing Sabrina thudding about overhead. That girl was like a baby elephant banging about the place. She'd be a few minutes yet, and it was clear this young lady had had enough of waiting for an explanation as to their cloak and dagger behaviour. She sat down opposite Alice and laid her hands down flat on the table. 'Alice, there's something strange that happens to some people and not t'others, here on Bold Street.'

***

Sabrina was glad of the breathing space making the tea had afforded her, and by the time she carried the rattling tray downstairs, she was feeling calmer. She found her aunt and Alice sitting in the workroom in silence. The radio played The Tide is High by Blondie, and Sabrina thought fleetingly of Flo with her bleached mop. Debbie Harry had a lot to answer for!

Alice, she noted, setting the tray down, wore an expression of disbelief. Aunt Evie had told her then, she surmised pouring the tea. She put a teaspoon of sugar in Alice's cup, figuring whether she took it or not she could probably do with it.

'You've travelled back in time then?' Alice asked, scepticism lacing her question as Sabrina slid the cup and saucer towards her. 'At least that's what your aunt's told me.'

Sabrina nodded. 'It's true. I have. Twice now, and I wouldn't have believed any of it either if it hadn't happened to me.' Sabrina wished she'd a biscuit to dunk. 'What did Aunt Evie tell you?'

Alice glanced at Evelyn and then replied, 'That there's a portal here on Bold Street that sucks some people back to another time. She said it'd happened t'others; there are documented reports even.' She shook her shaggy red hair signalling her disbelief.

'As I said, it's incredible—'

'Ridiculous, more like,' Alice snorted.

Sabrina continued doggedly on, 'Worever. I know how it sounds but hear me out, Alice, please.'

Alice, against her better judgement, gave a slight nod.

'Ta. For most people, it's as if they turn a corner and find themselves in another time, and then they turn another corner, and they're back in the present. It's happened so quick they wonder if they've imagined it. But I get stuck where ever the slip takes me back to,' Sabrina said. 'Did you tell her about me, mother, Aunt Evie? Because that's where this all started.'

Evelyn shook her head; she'd thought it better to let Alice digest what she'd told her about Bold Street first. She was struggling as it was to take that on board.

Sabrina carried on. 'Aunt Evie found me lost outside Hudson's bookshop only back in nineteen sixty-three it wasn't a bookshop; it was a dressmaker's, called Cripps. To cut a long story short, nobody came looking for me, so she took me in and raised me. I always thought me, mam, for whatever reason, abandoned me here on Bold Street. Or at least I did until me fella, Adam—'

'The one who's in me nan's wedding photograph?' Alice interrupted, not knowing why she was still here other than, despite herself, she wanted to hear the rest of Sabrina's story.

'Yes.' Sabrina nodded, tucking her hair behind her ears. 'He told me his uncle used to bandy about a tale as to how he'd had a most peculiar encounter with a panicked woman looking for her daughter near Cripps back in nineteen sixty-three.'

'The year you were found?'

'Yes. The woman was bewildered and disorientated, and she was also adamant it was nineteen eighty-three. But, strangest of all was how she seemed to vanish into thin air.'

'And you think that woman was your mother?' Alice raised a sceptical brow.

'I do. I think we were separated by the timeslip somehow. I've been looking for her ever since in the hope I'll be pulled back to wherever she is because she must be looking for me too. Only, the first time I went through the slip, I found myself in nineteen twenty-eight. The second time, nineteen sixty-two. On both occasions, I was gone for months, but when I finally stepped back through to the present, hardly any time at all had passed since I'd left.'

'You said this woman looking for her daughter in the sixties thought it was nineteen eighty-three?'

'I did.'

'Well, that's only a year away. If what you've told me is true, and to be honest with you, I'm struggling to believe it, then you'll find your mother next year because if she lost you, her child, it would be all over the papers and on the tele.' Alice tried to imagine what this mysterious woman would think of an adult Sabrina turning up and claiming to be the three-year-old child she lost.

'Yes, that's why I didn't think I'd go back through the slip again. But having seen your nan's photograph, I know I must have because I'm there, aren't I? In nineteen forty-five and, for worever reason, Adam's there with me.'

Alice was quiet as she mulled through what Sabrina and Evelyn had told her. Her brain was fizzing with information overload. It was as farfetched as an episode of Doctor Who, but there was something in the earnestness of Sabrina's expression.

'What was she like, your nan according to your grandad, I mean?' Sabrina asked.

Alice drained her tea in one long gulp. 'He always said I wor a lot like her. She wor strong-willed and very determined.'

'She wor that ahright,' Evelyn murmured.

Alice looked a little sheepish.

'Both good traits to have in a woman,' Evelyn said, adding, 'You've her glorious hair too.'

Alice smiled. 'It skipped me, mam, and jumped straight to me.'

'What sort of wedding are you having?' Sabrina asked.

'Mark's mam wanted us to have a big do, but I put me foot down. She's not best pleased either, but I want to keep it small.'

'Your nan did too. She wasn't bothered about a big do.'

'No. Nan got married in a registry office as I will.'

Evelyn nodded. 'Your vows are your vows no matter where you say them.'

'I'd dearly love to alter your dress for you, Alice if you'd like me to, that is,' Sabrina volunteered.

Alice looked from Evelyn to Sabrina. Evelyn had known her nan. This woman with the owlish glasses had altered her dress for her special day, and Sabrina would do the same for her if she let her. Despite all the time travel malarkey, there was a connection between them she couldn't ignore.

'I'd like that very much,' she replied.

Chapter Seven

Skelmersdale, 1939

Lily

'Welcome to Skem, luv,' the bus conductor said, helping Mrs Cox aboard before clipping Lily's ticket. As he looked down at her, his smile was jolly. Lily, remembering her promise to her mam about her manners, rustled up a nod and smile of thanks. One foot was still planted on the pavement, the other on the open platform at the bus's rear. Her case was in her hand.

It wasn't too late. She could turn and run back to the hall. She could tell Mrs Price and Mrs Pinkerton that she'd go back home before going off with the witch-like Mrs Cox. She was about to step down and do exactly that when the conductor reached out and pulled her up alongside him. 'Best you take yer seat, luv, if you don't want to go flyin'. I don't want any broken bones on my run.'

The bus slowly chugged away, taking a belch of black exhaust with it; Lily's opportunity to run was gone. She turned back in time to see the last few children being shepherded from the building she'd just left. Mrs Pinkerton was locking the door behind her. She opened her mouth as though to call out, but no sound came, and she jumped hearing Mrs Cox snap, 'Stop making a holy show of yerself, lass, and sit down.'

'Don't worry, luv, she's all bark and no bite that one.' The conductor winked at her, but Lily couldn't find any reassurance in his words.

She made her way to where Mrs Cox had twisted in her seat, annoyance embedded between scraggly grey brows as she approached. As Lily slid in alongside the old woman, she thudded her stick down between them like a divider.

She smelled unwashed, Lily thought, wrinkling her nose. She stared straight ahead, trying to ignore the old woman's wheezing breath that whiffed of onions. Instead, she concentrated on the street they were pootling down. It didn't look all that different to Edge Hill. The rows of two-up, two-down sooty brick houses lined either side of the cobbled street. The smell of coal fires clung to the air despite it being the tail end of summer and not so much as a wisp of smoke coming from the chimneys. Coal was embedded in the very bricks of the buildings, Lily reckoned. It was the same at home. Her eyes alighted on the grocers noting the advertisements twinned those in the window of Peterson's near Durning Road where her mam worked.

She watched a bobby making his way down the pavement nodding his greeting to a woman pushing a pram. She clung to the familiarity of the scene, unaware she was gnawing on her nails until she received the sharp end of Mrs Cox's elbow in her side.

'Dirty habit, that, get yer hands out of yer mouth if you don't want worms.'

Hot tears sprang forth as Lily folded her hands on her lap, and all the while, the bus rumbled on stopping and starting as it disgorged its passengers on the residential streets, even the conductor had clambered off. Then it was only Lily, Mrs Cox and the driver remaining.

All of a sudden, the houses gave way to woodland and barren fields, and it seemed to Lily that they were at risk of leaving the town behind altogether. The thought of this made panic swell in her throat, and she worried it might close over. Poor little Katie Wandsworth must have felt like this when she'd had an allergic reaction to the bee sting on her foot the previous summer. The ambulance had come for her, and the talk had been it had arrived not a moment too soon. Ana something or other shock, they called it.

The road they'd bumped onto was surrounded by dense foliage. Lily imagined a witch's cottage deep in the woods like in the fairy tale book she had at home. *Where was she going?* She swallowed hard.

The bus's brakes screeched as it veered over to the side of the potholed road, and the driver called out. 'Ere we are Mrs Cox, me luv, home sweet home.'

Mrs Cox made a grumbling noise and nudged Lily, who was scanning both sides of the road hoping she'd see some signs of life in the ribs. But, instead, there was nothing other than a trio of rundown cottages.

'What are yer waiting for? You heard him. This is us.'

Lily shot up, not wanting to feel the sharp end of her elbow again and, picking up her case, she hurried off the bus.

'Are your hands painted on, girl? Can't you see I need help?' Mrs Cox glowered from the platform, and Lily, flushing, put her case down and held her hands out to aid the old harridan down the steps. When she'd safely disembarked, the driver tooted, and then the bus rambled on its way.

Lily watched it go feeling bereft. She also desperately wanted to wash her hands.

Mrs Cox, with her limping gait, hobbled the few paces to the cottages, opening the door of the middle one. It squeaked, indicating rusty hinges, and Lily, with eyes wide, followed her inside. It was dark, and it took a moment for her sight to adjust. The place smelled of old fat and ciggies with an underlying hint of damp.

'Born in a barn were yer?'

Lily shut the door. She was standing in the hall, and a glimmer of light shone in from the open kitchen door down the end of it.

Mrs Cox unknotted her headscarf to reveal silvered hair pulled back in a bun. She stuffed the scarf in her coat pocket and then hung her coat on the back of the door. 'You can 'ang your hat and coat on t'other hook.'

Lily took her hat off but hung back a moment, not wanting to discard her coat. It was chilly in here, but Mrs Cox was glaring at her, and once she'd divested herself of it, the old woman poked her stick at the closed door on her left. 'The sitting room's out of bounds, do you hear me? You're not to go in there under any circumstances.'

'Yes, Mrs Cox.' She was too intent on nodding to wonder why she wasn't allowed over the threshold to the front room.

'Your room's up there.' She lifted the stick and pointed to the stairs. 'The back bedroom. Take yer case up and unpack yer things, then you can come down to the kitchen and start earning your keep.'

Lily hastily retrieved her precious worry book and pen from her coat pocket and hurried up the stairs. The carpet runner was threadbare under her feet and the paper peeling off the wall, she noticed her stomach clenching at the thought of what she might find at the top of the stairs. Whatever lay ahead, she was desperate for a few minutes on her own to absorb all that had happened since she'd left Edge Hill Station that morning.

Despite the light being dim up here too, the floor was bare on the landing, and the boards creaked beneath her feet as she turned, with her hand still on the rail, to steal a glance in the direction of Mrs Cox's room. But, unfortunately, it was closed off to her as the sitting room had been, and she wasn't brave enough to sneak a peek.

However, the door to the bathroom was open, and she walked the few short steps towards it and, ducking her head inside, saw a yellowed sink with a mirror hung by a nail above it. A metal tub with handles on either side sat in the corner of the room. She breathed through her mouth because the tiny space smelled dreadfully of damp and needed to be aired. The window by the tub was closed, and as tempting as it was to fling it open, she didn't dare.

She moved across the landing to the room that was to be hers. She hadn't come from luxury by any means, but her mam kept a clean house, and she steeled herself for what lay beyond the door. Chewing her bottom lip, Lily pushed it open cautiously and stood there with her shoulders tensed as she took stock.

The space was hardly big enough to swing a cat and had a slanted ceiling beneath which a bed was pushed up against the bare walls. Spidering cracks laced the plasterwork, and a cobweb dangled in the corner above the pillow, but to Lily's relief, there was no sign of the spider who'd weaved it.

At least the bed was made up, she thought, eyeing the grey wool blanket folded at the end of it. She wouldn't think about who'd slept under that before her, she decided, shuddering, and she'd have to be careful not to bump her head of a morning, too, given the ceiling. She took a cautious step forward into the room, and the boards squeaked their protest as they had in the hall.

The only other furnishing in the room was a chest of drawers with a thick layer of dust sitting atop it, a mirror on a stand its only adornment. The room was cold and unlived in, and it too needed airing. As Lily moved forward, dust motes danced into the air, disturbed by her presence, causing her to sneeze several times and putting her worry book and pen down on top of the drawers, she made for the small window over the bed suddenly desperate for a gulp of fresh air.

She placed her case on the bed and felt the springs digging into her knees as she climbed on it. It took a moment or two of wrestling with the window sash before she managed to dislodge it, hefting it up. Given its stickiness and the musty odour of the room, she suspected the room had been closed up for a long time.

Lily stuck her head out the window and breathed greedily. Her room overlooked a narrow muddy yard with a gravel path from the kitchen door to the privy at the bottom. The washing line was empty, and a picket fence missing a few palings separated the yard from the field beyond where Lily could see freshly tilled soil.

The yards on either side were separated by a low fence and were identical in size, but to her right was an overgrown tangle of weeds with an abandoned air. 'Like me,' Lily thought glumly. Her eyes cut to the left, where washing snapped on the line. Then to the small shed alongside the privy, also at the bottom of the yard.

She'd best unpack, she thought reluctantly, closing the window and smoothing the wrinkled sheets as she scrambled off the bed and opened her case. Her fingers skipped over the meagre contents, and closing her eyes, she remembered her mam folding them and placing them in the case as she ticked the items off the list they'd been given. At the thought of her mam, a self-pitying tear rolled down her cheek, and she waited until it was about to drip from her chin before swiping it away.

She picked up her worry book, and the pen hovered over the page as she tried to formulate what was worrying her the most. *No kindness,* she began to write and then snapped the book shut. 'This won't do, Lily Tubb. It won't do at all. Pull your socks up, girl. Dad would want you to be brave,' she whispered to herself, and for a moment, she felt him beside her, willing her to be strong. It was of great comfort to feel him watching over her. He'd not let any harm come to her.

A sudden thudding on the floor beneath her feet made her jump, and she banged her head on the ceiling. It took her a moment to realise what the source of the noise was. Mrs Cox must be hitting the ceiling with her stick. Her way of telling her to get a move on.

There was no time to rub the sore spot on her head as she hastily put her nightwear and undergarments away in the drawer. She left her toiletries on the bed and then, closing the case, placed it on the floor, nudging it under the bed with her foot before hurrying back down the stairs.

'What took you so long?' Mrs Cox seated at the table, her walking stick in her hand, didn't wait for a response. 'It's not a holiday camp you've come to, girl.' She inclined her head towards the worktop where she'd laid out a turnip, potato, carrot and fatty piece of mutton. 'If you don't get that meat simmering, I won't be able to get my teeth through it.'

Lily was used to helping her mam in the kitchen, and she rolled the sleeves of her dress up, opening up a drawer in search of a knife to dice the meat when Mrs Cox brought her up short.

'Wash yer hands, yer dirty madam. I know what you lot from the city are like. Slovenly the lot of yer,' she wheezed before it turned into a phlegmy hack.

Lily wanted to throw the turnip at the old cow but willed herself to ignore her as she gave her shaking hands a good scrub with the soap before running them under the cold tap.

'And when you've got that stew on, you can give the privy a good going over for yer sins.'

Lily stared out the window in horror at the innocuous wooden building she'd spied from upstairs. It was clear to her that Mrs Cox wanted her here as a lackey and nothing else. The words she'd written in her worry book sprang to mind. No kindness. The best thing she could do was give the old cow no cause for complaint by setting about whatever chores she was given quietly. They'd been told in the hall earlier that they'd be attending a local school. At least that would be a reprieve, and she'd see Edith and all the other familiar faces from home.

'You're not afraid of hard work, Lily Tubb,' she told herself as drying her hands on a cloth draped over the oven door, she picked up the knife and sawed into the tough old meat. 'You'll show that witch what you're made of for Dad's sake. You can do this, girl. You're a Tubb, and the Tubbs are a brave bunch. It's the Viking blood in us, don't you know.'

Chapter Eight

Liverpool, Spring, 1982

Sabrina

Sabrina had not had a good afternoon. She'd pinned Alice Water's gown ready to be let out and taken in where necessary before she'd left the boutique. They'd agreed on some additional embellishments to give it a more up-to-date feel and made an appointment for her to come in to try the altered gown on early the following week. Sabrina had one hundred and one other bridal dresses to be stitching or altering, but she'd prioritise Alice given their unexpected link.

She'd waved the client responsible for completely upheaving her day off, knowing she'd done the same to her.

The thought of her and Adam having stepped back into nineteen forty-five had thrown her into a tailspin, and this was why she'd sewn faux seed pearls onto a gown that was supposed to have sequins around the bodice.

She'd made up her mind to leave things alone where her mother was concerned after the last time. She'd leave it to fate to sort out, she'd decided, and wait.

Now, however, she knew without a doubt she hadn't been able to let her quest to find her mother go. The proof had been staring out at her from that photograph.

It had taken her an age to unpick the sodding pearls, and while Aunt Evie might not have tutted out loud seeing her labouring over them, Sabrina knew her well enough to know she'd be doing so silently. She'd two things making her purse her lips in displeasure now, Sabrina stepping out with Ray Taylor's son and the knowledge she'd skipped off to nineteen forty-five with him.

Sabrina fidgeted in her seat, which was also annoying her aunt no end. She was desperate to confide in Flo about her encounter with Alice, and closing time couldn't roll around soon enough. Of course, she could take or leave the running part of the evening, but a promise was a promise. Her job would be to provide moral support for Flo and make sure none of the Bootle Tootlers did an erm, well runner.

This was why when she barrelled out the door shortly after they'd shut up shop for the day, she was clad in a lilac tracksuit outfit with blindingly white sneakers. She'd even picked up a towelling headband like Flo's to prove she was taking her role as backup Bootle Tootler seriously. Aunt Evie spying her new shoes as she legged it past her, had called out, 'You'll stop traffic in those.'

'Enjoy, Corrie,' Sabrina had shouted back up the stairs, not biting back. They were somewhat neon, she thought with a rueful glance down at her feet.

Just over half an hour later, Sabrina called out hello, having let herself into the Teesdales' house, which was a second home to her. She followed her nose through to the kitchen, inhaling a savoury aroma.

'Ahright there, luv? You look the part. My word, those sneakers are bright,' Mrs Teesdale blinked at the sight of Sabrina's snowy footwear as she looked up from the open cookbook she'd been peering at intently.

'They'll see you coming in those, queen,' Mr Teesdale muttered from behind the newspaper he was rustling as he sat at the kitchen table, a cup of tea half-drunk beside him.

'They're new,' Sabrina stated the obvious, tempted to run outside and rub them in the dirt, so they didn't look quite so glaringly so. 'And that smells gorgeous.' She forgot the shoes sniffing appreciatively and taking in the chaos of the kitchen worktop. 'What's for dinner, then?'

'It's French. Beef bourguignon.' Mrs Teesdale indicated the open cookbook. 'A Julia Child recipe no less. It even has wine in it.'

'Ooh wine, get you.'

'Waste of good wine that.' Mr Teesdale's head bobbed up over the paper this time. 'What's wrong with plain old British fodder? The French eat snails. Will we be having them for our dinner next?'

'Shut your gob. I know you, you'll be after seconds, and I'm serving it with mashed potatoes, Sabrina. There'll be plenty to go around if you fancy having your dinner here with Flo when you get back from your run. I dare say you'll be hungry by then. I can keep a plate warm for you both.'

'Ta. I won't say no.' She never did when it came to Mrs Teesdale's cooking.

'The potatoes are from my allotment,' Mr Teesdale added.

'Eee, there's no show without Punch, is there?'

Sabrina laughed. She loved Mr and Mrs Teesdale and knew they'd be lost without each other for all their bickering.

'Our Flo's in her room. Although why she's worried about her hair and make-up when she's supposed to be working a sweat up around North Park, I don't know.'

'Ah well, you never know who you might see along the way, that's why.' Sabrina gave them both a grin and then ducked off up the stairs.

A door creaked opened as she reached the landing, and two cheeky faces peeked around it. 'We're not allowed out of our room until Mam says,' Shona or was it, Tessa, Sabrina wasn't sure, supplied.

'What did you do?' she asked, poised on the top step waiting to hear what the latest misdemeanour by Flo's younger sisters, or the terrible twins, was.

'We were playing knock on the door and run away with grumpy old Mr Chiswell next door. It was Shona's idea.' Tessa shot her twin sister a look to say their solitary confinement was all her fault.

'You wanted to play too,' Shona retorted indignantly before adding, 'We reckon he's an evil wizard.'

Sabrina bit back a smile.

'Only Mrs Cummings from over the road saw us running away and told Mam. She went mad and chased us upstairs with the wooden spoon.'

Tessa nodded that this was indeed the case.

'Ah, well, I'm sure you'll be allowed down for your dinner.'

They both pulled a face. 'It's French, and Dad says the French eat snails.'

'Shona, Tessa, get back in that room until I tell you otherwise,' was bellowed up from down below.

The twins' eyes widened, and they slammed the door shut. This time, Sabrina did smile, hearing them scarper across the room to their beds. She gave Flo's door a nudge.

'I told you two to stay out of me room,' Florence snapped. She hadn't looked up from where she was arranging the towelling headband just so in her dressing table mirror.

'It's me, Flo.'

'Oh, hiya, Sabs. Sorry, those two are driving me potty. They're supposed to be in disgrace in their bedroom; only they keep tiptoeing across the hall and poking their noses in here to see what I'm up to.' Satisfied she was as close to Olivia Newton John's look in the Physical video as she was ever likely to get, Olivia being a natural blonde and all, Florence turned away from the mirror to check out her friend.

'I luv the lilac, girl.'

'Ta. Worra about the shoes, though?'

Florence frowned as she gave the sneakers the once over. 'They're super white, but a few laps of the park should sort them out after the rain last week.' She perched down on the stool in front of her dressing table.

Sabrina flopped down on Florence's bed and, raising her eyes, saw Midge Ure from Ultravox staring back down at her. 'That poster's new.'

'It was free with the album. I love Vienna, me.'

'Me, too.'

They both launched into *Ahhh Vienna* and then giggled.

'I don't know that I'd want Midge eyeballing me when I'm trying to go to sleep, though, Flo.'

'I quite fancy him, to be honest.' Flo grinned. 'He's grown on me, but I'd fancy him more if he'd shave that silly little pencilly moustache off. You know, if I squint, I can see a bit of Tim in him. I say goodnight to him before I go to sleep.'

Sabrina laughed at the image of Flo lying in her bed in her flannelette nighty squinting, saying, 'Night, night, Midge.' She couldn't see the resemblance between Midge and Tim, but if Midge's moody face staring down at her made Flo happy, so be it. 'If you tell me he says goodnight back to you, you'll have me worried.'

'No, he's the strong silent type.'

Sabrina snorted, making Flo laugh. Then Sabrina remembered everything that had transpired with Alice that day and sobered. She rolled onto her side, propping herself up on her elbow.

Florence stared hard at her friend for a moment. 'Come on then, what's happened? I can tell something has. Is it to do with your mam?'

'Yes, no, well sort of. How can you tell?'

'Sabs, you're me, bezzie mate. I know your face better than me own,' Florence stated.

It was the same for her, where Flo was concerned; she could read her like a book, Sabrina thought. 'Two things happened today. Firstly, I told Aunt Evie that Adam's Ray Taylor's son.'

'How did she take that?' Florence's expression was grave, but it was hard to take her seriously with that towelling headband, Sabrina thought. Then she remembered her own.

'She made that stewed prune face of hers, and I could tell there were a hundred things she'd like to say, but then this girl, Alice was her name, came in. She wanted her nan's wedding dress altered. Gorgeous it was too. Proper vintage, not at all antwacky. Her nan married in nineteen forty-five and she had a photograph of the wedding party outside the church and—'

Florence interrupted, 'I think I can guess where this is going and if you're going to tell me you were in the flamin' photograph, I'm going to put my hands over me ears.'

'You'd better put your hands over your ears then.'

'Ah, you said you weren't going to go back again! What I don't understand is why these brides-to-be all seem to find their way to your shop?'

'Boutique, not shop, and I don't know, do I? It's like it's fate or something. And it's not only me this time, Flo, Adam was in it too.'

Her brown eyes were like organ stoppers. 'Adam went back with you?'

'He must have because it was him in the photograph.'

'Oh my God, girl, have you told him?'

'I haven't had a chance to. Apart from Aunt Evie, who was there anyway and not best pleased, you're the first person I've told.'

Florence massaged her temples. 'Hang on a minute, wasn't the war only just over in nineteen forty-five?'

Sabrina nodded. 'VE Day was on the eighth of May, nineteen forty-five. I remember the date because when we learned about the celebrations with the big bonfires burning in history, I thought it sounded great fun, and because of your mam, of course.'

Florence mimicked her mother's voice. 'It's a lucky date to have been born May the eighth, VE Day.' Mrs Teesdale said this every year on the twins, birthday.

Sabrina grinned, but Florence didn't crack a smile.

'Well, that's settled then; you can't go back. What if you stepped back in the thick of the blitz? No.' She shook her head, and her bleached blonde, bobbed hair swung furiously, 'you can't go, Sabs. Adam or no Adam with you.'

'But Flo, you know how it works. If I'm there in the photo with Adam, it means we've already been back. It's already happened, and I can't change the past.'

'Yes, but what we don't know is whether you make it back to us this time. There's no guarantee of that now, is there?' She eyeballed her pal.

It was true, Sabrina thought, and it wasn't something she wanted to dwell on.

'I'd like to see Mystic Lou again and hear what she has to say.'

'Well, I don't want to see her,' Florence blustered. She'd not been impressed to hear her destiny was entwined with a man with a penchant for wearing tight trousers the last time the two of them had paid the psychic on Bold Street a visit.

'You don't have to have a reading with her, but please come with me, Flo? I don't want to go on my own, and I don't think I want to hear what she has to say on my own, either.'

Florence had a silent debate with herself.

'Flo, supporting each other is what bezzie mates do.'

Florence's eye's narrowed, 'Sabrina Flooks, that's blackmail.'

'No, it's not. It's a gentle reminder that I am supporting you by being your backup jogger this evening, so it—'

Florence held a hand up. 'Ahright, ahright, I'll come with you.'

'One evening next week?'

'One evening next week. Bloody hell, is that the time? Come on, Sabs, we can't keep my ladies waiting.'

Sabrina rolled off the bed and stood up in time to see Florence put something around her neck. Her mouth formed an 'O' as she twigged as to what it was. 'Oh, Flo, no!'

'What?' Florence feigned innocence.

'Tell me that's not a whistle.'

Florence grinned. 'Sabrina, all good coaches have one. It's in the coach rule book.' She gave it a blow for good measure, and with a satisfied grin at its shrill whistle, she thundered off down the stairs.

Sabrina rolled her eyes and followed her.

Chapter Nine

Skelmersdale, 1939

Lily

'We'd better enjoy this,' Edith stated as she unwrapped her cheese sandwiches. 'The ration books arrived yesterday, and Aunty Em said it won't be long until we're all having things like carrot sandwiches for our lunches.' She pulled a face at the thought of the obscure sandwich filling.

Lily was so hungry she wouldn't care what was squished between the two slices of bread, and she was grateful to her friend for sharing with her.

Edith and Elsie had been fortunate. Mr and Mrs Timbs, whose home they'd been billeted to, had welcomed them. The kindly couple had suggested they call them Aunty Em and Uncle Pete, and as for their two children, Bess and Lionel, they were of a similar age to Edith and Elsie and, as such, had been excited at the thought of extra playmates. Lily couldn't help but feel envious, and she missed Sarah and her mam terribly, too. The past three weeks had been the most miserable of her life, with the only respite being here at school.

Mrs Cox, or the old witch as she now thought of her, worked her to the bone. Lily was quite sure she'd keep her home from school if she felt she could get away with it. She was the unpaid help who was constantly reminded she had to earn her keep. The old witch had a way of thumping that stick of hers down. It made Lily flinch and loathe to do anything other than as she'd been told.

It wasn't even as if she got a decent meal at the end of the day as a reward for her hard work. By the time the old witch had ladled out most of the meat in the stews for herself, Lily would be left with nothing more than a bowl of vegetable broth.

Breakfast was a piece of yesterday's bread eaten dry and was only handed to her once Lily had taken down the card from the windows she'd put up the night before to comply with the blackout. The only room she didn't see to was the sitting room, which she presumed the old witch sorted herself.

Her ritual was to stuff the bread down and get on her way, eager to escape out the front door of a morning to pedal to school on the trusty old bicycle that a stroke of luck had seen come her way.

The stew and the bread weren't enough, and the hunger gnawed at her constantly. She'd felt faint in assembly this morning, and the ground had swayed beneath her. She'd had to lean on Edith until she'd managed to steady herself.

The only kindness she'd been shown since arriving at the cottage was from Mr Mitchell next door. It was him that had given her the bicycle to use, without which she'd have struggled to make it to school on time each day.

He'd seen Lily in the backyard hanging out the washing on the first Saturday morning after she'd arrived. The old witch had informed her Saturday would be wash day from hereon in. When she'd that done, she could see to the windows with newspaper and vinegar, she'd sniped, buttoning her coat up.

Lily tried not to mind too much, but it did seem unfair that she was to spend all of Saturday doing chores. She knew Edith and Elsie were off for a picnic with the Timbs family, making the most of autumn before winter came calling. They'd been excited leaving school the day before, chattering on about there being the possibility of a cake filled with butter cream.

The old witch had taken herself into town, and Lily had heard the bus moaning to a stop as she sorted the pile of laundry dumped on the kitchen floor. She didn't mind. She was grateful to be left on her own without the caustic, constant complaining in her ear. A sigh of relief had escaped her lips as the bus rumbled on its way, and her shoulders had relaxed, knowing she was gone.

Lily had set to with the washboard and the lemon soap like she'd seen her mam do, and by the time she stepped out the back door, the sky was blue. The sun appeared to dry up the remnants of a damp winter, and a fresh breeze blew. It was what her mam would have called a good drying day, Lily thought with a pang, beginning to peg out the washing. She'd spent the early part of the morning scrubbing the sheets and other sundries on the washboard in the metal tub, and her hands were red and chafed. Still, there was satisfaction in watching the sheets billowing, she thought, gingerly picking up a pair of the old witch's undergarments between her index finger and thumb.

Mr Mitchell next door had leaned on the fence, his cap pulled down low, and a pipe sticking out the corner of his mouth to call out a cheery greeting as she'd pegged the smalls to the line before introducing himself to her. There'd been a tinge of satisfaction at the thought of the old witch's holey undergarments on display for her neighbour to see.

She'd been glad to pause in her task to chat to the old man, eager for company, and had instantly taken a liking to his dancing blue eyes. Eyes were the window to a person's soul she'd read once, and she reckoned this was true. You could tell a lot about a person by looking into their eyes. The old witch's were the colour of stewed tea with not so much as a glimmer of warmth in them.

Lily had breathed in deeply as Mr Mitchell puffed away on his pipe because she liked the smell of pipe tobacco. Her dad had smoked a pipe, and it was comforting to inhale the pungent, spicy-sweet smell. It brought back happy memories.

'How's she treating you, lass?' he asked, taking the pipe out of his mouth to tamp it down with his yellowed forefinger.

Lily had been taught not to tell tales, but she'd also been taught to tell the truth, and she hesitated, uncertain as to what to say.

Mr Mitchell didn't look up from his task as he said, 'I thought as much. She's a hard woman, lass because life's dealt her a bad hand.'

Lily thought it must have been a truly terrible hand to make her so cruel.

'I worked with her husband, Ernie, at the paper mill These 'ere they were the factory cottages back in the day.' He made a sweeping gesture at the row of cottages. 'Ernie, now he was a good man, and she wor different back then.'

'What changed her then?' Lily asked, keen to hear more and happy to abandon the washing a while longer.

'He died, leaving her to struggle alone raising their three young lads. It wor an accident at the mill.' He shook his head. 'Terrible thing. He tripped and fell through a trapdoor onto the machinery below. Torn to pieces.'

Lily's eyes widened in horror, but he hadn't finished.

'Then she waved her boys off one by one to fight in the Great War, and not one of 'em came home. Three sons, she lost in that fight, and now here we are at war again.' He pondered the sadness of it all for a moment. Then, added, 'Sent her mad for a while and she weren't ever the same again after that. It wor enough to turn any woman bitter all that loss.'

Lily felt a frisson of pity for the old witch, but it didn't make the way she treated her alright.

'My dad died in an accident a year back. He was hit by a car on his way home from work.'

'Eee, lass, I'm sorry to hear that, I am.'

They were both silent as a tractor rumbled past in the field behind the yards. Mr Mitchell waved out to the farmer.

'Do you live alone?' Lily asked.

'I do since my Gladys passed a few year back. Me son and daughter are married with families of their own now.' He puffed away again on the pipe.

Lily watched the smoke curling upward. 'Does anybody live in the other cottage?' she asked, pointing in the direction of the empty yard behind her.

'That wor old Bill's place. I worked with him an all. He's been gone a year now. The place has been left to go to rack and ruin. No children, you see, and it's a right shame. He could have fed all of Skem with the vegetable patch he kept out the back there. It was his pride and joy, but it's a wilderness now. Sally, his wife, well, she'd be turning in her grave if she could see the state of the place. The mice will be making themselves right at home, mark me words, lass.'

Lily grimaced at the mention of mice, but she wasn't surprised to hear the cottage was empty.

They'd chatted on companionably enough, and then Lily remembered what had been worrying at her. 'Mr Mitchell, I'm to go to school on Monday, but I don't know how to get there. Can you tell me?'

Mr Mitchell explained the route she'd need to take, and Lily's face grew longer and longer. 'It will take me forever to walk there.' She didn't think it likely the old witch would give her money for the bus or let her off getting the dinner ready before she left in the morning to ensure she'd time to get there on foot.

An expression of pity passed over his face, and then he brightened. 'Wait 'ere; I've had a thought, lass.'

Lily watched as he shuffled over to the shed and returned after a minute or two, looking pleased with himself, bumping a bicycle over the patchy grass.

'It wor me son's. He won't be needing it, not with his fancy job in St Helens.'

Lily stared over the fence at the bike in delight, and then her face fell. 'But I don't know how to ride one.'

'Well then, lass, it's high time you learned in't it?'

She hung the last of the washing out and met Mr Mitchell on the road outside his cottage. 'There's nothing to it, lass; you've got to get on it and pedal for all you're worth.'

Lily looked at him doubtfully, but she swung a leg over and hoisting herself onto the seat, she placed her feet on the pedals. Mr Mitchell instructed her to pedal while he kept a firm hand on the bicycle, shouting instructions at her to avoid the potholes as he pushed her along. She didn't realise he'd let go until the bike began to wobble madly, and over she went winding up in a heap on the side road.

'Any broken bones, lass?' Mr Mitchell shouted down the empty road.

Lily took stock, relieved she'd not torn her stockings before picking herself up. The only injury was to her pride, and she wheeled the bike slowly back towards the cottages. 'Can we try again, Mr Mitchell?' she asked when she drew level with him. 'Me mam says I'm a quick learner. I'm sure I'll get it this time.'

He'd smiled broadly, hearing this and revealing a missing tooth Lily hadn't noticed before. 'I'd well believe it, lass. C'mon then, on you get.'

Lily had taken a deep breath and, with a frown of concentration, waited for Mr Mitchell to give the word. This time when he let go, after a few hairy moments, she managed to keep the bike upright. She grew bolder as she pedalled along, enjoying a sense of jubilation as the wind rushed past her ears.

She'd cycled back to a round of applause from Mr Mitchell, and they'd agreed between them to keep the bike down the side of his cottage. She could come and get it each morning and leave it there of an afternoon. It was unsaid but understood that Mrs Cox didn't need to know about the arrangement.

Lily had leaned the bike up against the cottage's stone wall as they'd agreed she should. She was about to venture back inside the old witch's cottage, knowing there'd be hell to pay if she hadn't managed to clean the windows with the newspaper and vinegar when she froze. Her spine was tingling, and her scalp was pricking with the sensation of being watched. Mr Mitchell had taken himself off inside, and his door was shut. There was no sign of anyone on the road, and her eyes turned warily towards what had been old Bill's cottage. She thought she saw the raggedy net curtain twitch but couldn't be sure, and spooked, she hurried inside, closing the door firmly behind her.

'Here,' Edith brought her back to the here and now, handing her the piece of sandwich she'd broken off.

'Ta, Edie.' Lily tried not to snatch it from her.

'Lily, look at your hands!' Edith recoiled in her seat as though she might catch something.

Lily flushed. They were scaly and red, scratched until they'd bled in places between her fingers. 'It's from having them in cold water all the time. I try not to scratch, but it itches like mad.'

Edith shook her head and opened her mouth to say something but shut it again, seeing her friend's closed expression.

Lily didn't want to pursue the conversation; she was too hungry, but still, she did her best not to eat the bread and cheese too quickly. She knew she'd feel fuller if she ate slower.

Her eyes flicked over Elsie seated at the table alongside them. She was stuffing her sandwich in like she hadn't eaten in a week, although she was well fed at the Timbs' house by all accounts. It was less about hunger and more about running off outside to play with her new friend Lily surmised, noticing her jiggling about on the seat like she'd ants in her pants.

'You'll get a tap on the shoulder from miss over there if you're not careful, Elsie,' Edith warned. Her little sister had got a smack on the back of her hand the other day. She didn't need another one. All three pairs of eyes flitted over to Miss Ellis, who cut a lean, stern figure prowling the room.

Elsie settled down in her seat and took a daintier bite before lisping. 'Tell us about the ghostie next door, Lily.'

Lily managed a grin. Elsie loved this tale, not that there was much to tell other than Lily had seen the curtain fall in the empty cottage next door more than once. She was sure she'd heard footsteps through the wall too. It was unsettling, but Lily was too busy scrubbing and dubbing to feel frightened most of the time. She relayed this to Elsie once more who listened while she finished her lunch at a more sedate pace before scampering off.

'Will you come outside today?' Edith asked, hopefully brushing the crumbs from her skirt. Ruth would keep her company, but she'd rather Lily did.

'I can't, Edie. You know I've got to wash up the teachers' lunch things,' Lily said, getting up from the seat. 'Thank you for sharing with me.'

Edith, who'd had a decent breakfast of porridge and toast, was indignant at her friend's circumstances. 'It isn't right, Lily, you not getting fed properly by the old witch. She's getting money you know for your keep.'

Lily flushed. 'Shush.' She gazed about, but most of the children had disappeared outside eager to stretch their legs before the afternoon classes began. Lily had admitted to Edith the reason she'd volunteered to clear up after the teachers was to eat their leftovers, and it wasn't something she was proud of. It also rankled that Ruth would pounce on Edie as soon as she made her way into the asphalted play area. She'd link her arm through hers with that superior air of hers.

Things were worse than she'd told Edith. She was too embarrassed to mention she'd been charged with emptying the old witch's chamber pot of a morning. This morning she'd taken the loathsome thing down the stairs, and its yellowed contents had sloshed on her dress. She'd done her best to sponge it off but still felt tainted. She knew it was in her head, but she couldn't get that acrid smell out of her nostrils and had been terrified arriving at school this morning that she might smell of wee.

'You've got to say something,' Edith urged. 'I told Aunty Em how awful she is—,'

'Edith, you promised!'

Edith was unrepentant. 'She said you should speak to Mrs Young.' She'd been disappointed by this response, having hoped the Timbs' would rescue her friend, but it would seem adults were all the same when it came to other people's business.

Mrs Young was the rather formidable headmistress, and she wasn't young. She was at least as old as the old witch, and

Lily had no intention of confiding in her as to how horrid her living circumstances were because she knew she wouldn't find sympathy there either.

She pulled a face. 'I don't want to make things worse. What if she were to have a word with the old witch? She'd make my life even more miserable then. Besides, I promised Mam I'd make the best of it. I'd send her a letter if I'd money for a stamp.'

Edith could see her point where Mrs Young was concerned, but as for her mam, she felt sure she'd not stand for Lily being treated like so if she knew how bad things were. She tilted her head to the side for a moment, saying, 'I know. I heard there's to be a Wednesday night youth club meeting for us Edge Hill kids. The vicar's cycling out here to see us so as he can take messages back to our mams and dads. You could tell Father Ian. Your mam's sure to make things right when she hears how bad it is for you.'

Lily felt a surge of hope and determined she'd get away next Wednesday night even if she had to climb out her window and shimmy down the drainpipe.

Chapter Ten

Liverpool, Spring, 1982

Sabrina

Sabrina looked down at her chest where the words, 'Bootle Tootlers' were emblazoned in black against the cheap yellow stretchy fabric that left little to the imagination. It was a good job it wasn't cold, she thought mutinously, or their headlights would all be on full beam. So much for not wearing the T-shirt. She'd almost got away with it too.

Flo had remembered the shirts Bossy Bev had organised at the last minute, racing back up the stairs of the Teesdale home just as they'd reached the front door. She'd called Sabrina back up to her room, insisting she put hers' on, trying to tell her that given Sabrina wasn't an actual member of the Bootle Weight Watchers branch, she was fortunate to have been allocated one. In the end, Sabrina couldn't be bothered arguing. She'd slipped it over her head, and she and Flo had laughed at one another in the one size fits all, too small, shirts before doing a couple of Charlies Angels poses in the mirror.

The twins had giggled their heads off, spying them in their matching tops and made buzzing bumblebee noises as they breezed back down the stairs. Flo had stuck her head around the kitchen door on their way out to tell her mam to sort them out. Her dad had also chuckled at their expense, and Mrs Teesdale rushed outside after them to take a photograph. She wanted to test out her new-fangled camera that spat the picture out before they made their way to the park.

Now, as she stood on the path by the Marsh Lane entrance to North Park where Flo had arranged to meet up with the rest of the Bootle Tootlers, she wished she'd put up more of a fight. The yellow clashed dreadfully with the lilac track-bottoms. At least the odds of seeing anyone she knew here were slim, she thought, wincing as Flo blew her whistle.

Chit-chat in the gathered group ground to a halt.

The members who hadn't telephoned Flo earlier to say they were sick and unfortunately couldn't make it stood to attention. There were ten women in total ranging in age from Sabrina and Flo's twenty-two years through to sixty plus, all proudly squeezed into their new yellow T-shirts. Down below, some were clad like she and Flo were in tracksuit bottoms, two or three had braved shorts, and one, for some unknown reason, had wriggled into Spandex like the Nolan sisters.

Sabrina hoped they'd all got a decent bra given how well blessed the majority of the Bootle Tootlers, Flo included, were. She didn't like to butt in, though, as their team leader checked nobody had any pre-existing medical conditions or injuries she should know about.

Sabrina didn't know what Flo thought she'd do if they did because she wasn't a nurse, and their first aid training was limited to wrapping a bandage around each other's ankles back in their guiding days. She held her breath, waiting to see if anyone would raise a hand, but all hands remained firmly by their sides; that was something at least.

It was a balmy evening by early April standards, and with the clocks having gone forward an hour, Sabrina reckoned they'd a good few hours of light left before darkness descended. Plenty of time to do the loop Flo had in mind, she thought as her pal launched into a warm-up routine.

Florence, seeing Sabrina standing about daydreaming, glared over at her, and she quickly followed suit, raising her left arm over her head and bending at the waist to her right before repeating it on the other side. Hands-on hip lunges swiftly followed the side bends, and heads swivelled at the sound of breaking wind, but no one in the group owned up to it.

A pep talk followed the warm-up, and Sabrina's eyes narrowed as she recognised a few lines. Flo had pilfered them from the dance teacher on that fab, new tele series Fame. The Bootle Tootlers didn't seem to mind being told that if they wanted to lose weight, then they were going to have to pay because weight loss costs and right here in North Park was where they were going to start paying in sweat! When Flo had finished her impassioned speech, they'd all begun shouting 'Yeah!' and punching the air.

Once the furore had settled, she announced, 'Right then, ladies, before we head off, I'd like to invite each of you to share what your motivation is for turning up this evening and to take this opportunity to congratulate each of you for doing so. Sabrina, would you like to start?'

No, she flamin' well would not, she thought, scowling at Florence, but as the Bootle Tootlers turned their attention to her, she cast about for something to say. 'Erm, hi,' she gave a little wave. 'I'm Flo's. I mean Florence's bezzie mate, so I'm here to help out erm in that capacity.'

'Sabrina's our backup runner. She'll be keeping an eye on you all, making sure nobody decides to pack it in halfway round,' Florence informed them. 'And she's also here because—'

She'd bloody kill Flo later, Sabrina thought, not knowing how she'd get on if she had to manhandle any of these women should they decide they'd had enough halfway round. She realised they were all waiting for her to answer, and she blurted, 'I'm also here because my favourite jeans, they're Calvin Klein's, you know, like the ones Brooke Shields wears, they're getting a little snug around my middle.'

There were nods of understanding and a smattering of applause, and to her surprise, Sabrina felt better for having owned up. They *were* getting tight. It was the fish and chip suppers she and Adam were partial to, and a gentle jog was not going to do her any harm whatsoever. She smiled shyly.

Florence thanked her for being brave and sharing.

By the time they'd all finished saying their piece, their muscles would have seized up, Sabrina thought, politely clapping the woman who was receiving hugs from the group for having shared she wanted to see her toes again when she stood in the shower.

Finally, Florence announced it was time to get the show on the road. She put her mouth to the whistle and blew, which saw a man wrestling with his dog who was determined to hare towards her. Then, she was off!

Her arms were pumping and her stride bouncy. Florence was settling into an achievable pace as they jogged past the

Vauxhall dealership set back on their left, the trees splitting the park in two up ahead.

The mood was jolly for the first while. Some of the Bootle Tootlers waved out to dog walkers and fellow runners or chatted amidst themselves. As they pounded on down the park's gently winding path through the trees to where there was talk of a fancy leisure centre being built, however, the chatter dried up. It was replaced by gasping and panting. Sabrina was beginning to feel it, too and knew her face was glowing red with exertion. Not an attractive combination with the yellow shirt. Bossy Bev hadn't splurged on the tees because the fabric felt sweaty and clingy.

That was when she saw them.

Adam, Tony, and Tim. They were sitting astride their motorbikes on the Hornby Street side of the park; it was them, Sabrina thought, taking in the leather jackets as the trio ribbed one another laughing. She wished the ground would swallow her up. Under any other circumstances, her heart would sing at the sight of Adam, but today in her yellow and lilac ensemble, the poor lad would be blinded. Perhaps they wouldn't notice them? she thought, hopefully keeping her head down but realising there was fat chance of that given they were like a swarm of plump bumblebees invading the park.

Florence hadn't seen them, Sabrina realised as her friend jogged on, oblivious to the fellas nudging each other across the way. A cheer went up from the direction of the motorbikes, followed by a wolf whistle as piercing as Florence's efforts. It all happened quickly after that.

Florence, shocked at seeing Tim and the other two lads, had tripped over her own feet and gone head over heels. Janice, directly behind her, hadn't been able to stop in time, nor had Gina, and so it went like skittles being bowled. The only woman remaining standing was Sabrina because she'd already stopped and was watching the carnage unfold in what felt like slow motion.

A hand shot up from the pile of bodies a split second later, and a voice from the depths called out, 'I'm ahright.'

Sabrina began plucking the Bootle Tootlers off her friend one by one. Then, finally, she looked up to see Adam and Tony running over. Tim was still sat on his bike, roaring with laughter and Adam and Tony were doing their best to look serious as they raced towards them.

'Florence, girl, give me your hand,' Tony said as he reached them. 'I'm in charge of first aid at werk; you'll be ahright.'

Florence did so, and Tony helped her to her feet. 'That was quite a tumble you took. Do you need me to check you over?' He smiled at her eagerly, and the tenderness beneath his sandy shock of hair was there for all to see. All except Florence, who pulled her hand away and shook herself down like a dog at the beach.

'I don't, ta very much.' The last thing she wanted was Tony feeling her up on the pretence of checking for broken bones. Her eyes snaked over to where Tim was still in fits of laughter. Why, oh why hadn't he been the chivalrous one getting off his Triumph to come to her rescue? Life wasn't fair, she thought and turning her attention back to Tony, she gave him a weak smile. He meant well. Then, as the rest of the group sorted themselves out, she remembered she was in charge. 'Ladies, do we have any injuries?'

The ladies had made a speedy recovery and were busy checking out Tony's jeans which he could have been sewn into. How he got in and out of the things was one of life's mysteries, Sabrina thought amused.

'Ladies?' Florence asked again, irritation flaring.

Janice dragged her eyes away. 'What? Oh right, no injuries, ta, you wor a soft landing.' There was a murmuring of agreement.

Sabrina couldn't help the grin that crept across her face as she caught Adam's eye and saw him doing his best not to crack up at the unfolding scene. Then remembering they were responsible for the tumble the Tootlers had taken, demanded, 'What are you lads doing here?'

'We were headed to the Swan for a pint, but Tony here suggested we come down and give you some moral support first. Flo was telling him about the running group the other night at the pub. Didn't you hear us cheering you on?' He rubbed his ear. 'Tony was yelling right in my ear.'

'I heard the wolf whistle.'

'That was me.' His grin was sheepish.

Florence had recovered her equilibrium and wanted to put distance between herself and Tim, who by the looks of him bent double on his bike would be dining out on what had happened for weeks. She was also feeling a tad annoyed with the Bootle Tootler's behaviour where Tony was concerned. They were undressing him with their eyes which, granted, would be easier than trying to get him out of those jeans in real life. It would serve her girls far better to put their energy into the rest of the circuit. 'Well, we can't stand about chatting; that's not going to burn the calories, ladies.' She blew the whistle extra loudly and hobbled off.

'I better go with them,' Sabrina said, reluctant to leave Adam.

'I like the T-shirt, by the way.' He grinned, not looking at her eyes. 'Fits you well that does, sweetheart.'

'Cheeky sod.' She swatted him away, laughing.

'Meet us down the Swan after?'

Sabrina nodded. 'I've got something to tell you.'

Adam's expression was panicked, and she slapped his arm gently. 'I'm not preggers! I'll tell you later.'

'That's not fair, Sabrina, don't leave me hanging.' A lock of dark hair fell into his eyes, and Sabrina reached up and pushed it aside. She breathed in the scent of leather from his jacket and spice from the aftershave she'd bought him. It had made her feel properly grownup buying her man aftershave.

'I'll tell you at the Swan, and it's nothing to worry about.' That wasn't entirely true, she thought, but the group was getting away from her.

'At least gi's a kiss.'

That she could do, she stood on tippy toes and planted a quick kiss on his soft lips before charging after the others. She was well aware he was watching her backside, and when she turned to see him staring after her, she gave him a wink before picking up her pace.

The rest of the loop went without incident, with the group rejuvenated after their halfway break. As they drew close to their starting point, they saw a woman loitering with a flag. She looked as though she were going to wave cars in at the end of a race, and as they neared the start of the path, she began flapping her flag in earnest.

Sabrina heard the word go round; it was Bev, the team leader at their Weight Watchers branch.

'Well done, girls,' Bev trilled, abandoning the flag to give them a clap. She had a box at her feet, and bending down, she grabbed the little cans of branded baked beans and began passing them out. 'A freebie for your efforts,' she beamed.

She paused when she reached Sabrina, on the fence, about whether she could give a non-member a can of Weight Watchers beans. But, in the end, she decided to spring for it, and Sabrina took hers with a thank you.

'Who's he?' Janice asked as she spied a man with a cigarette dangling between his fingers. He was leaning against a battered brown Ford Cortina with a camera slung around his neck. It was apparent he was watching them all.

Bev beckoned him over. 'We're ready, Steve. That's Steve from the Bootle Times; he's come to take a group shot of us all. Come on, ladies, gather round and if you could all hold your beans up when he takes a photograph.'

Steve ground out his cigarette and strolled over.

'I don't know why she's got to be in it,' Florence whispered, eyeballing Bev as she got into line next to Sabrina. 'It's not as if she ran around the park.'

'She's after a free plug.' Sabrina whispered back, holding up her beans and waiting for the nod to say cheese. She wasn't happy about this; they'd look like poor excuses for Page 3. Girls in their yellow T-shirts. She whispered as much to Flo.

Florence laughed, adding, 'With a penchant for baked beans.'

Bossy Bev shot them a look, and they quietened down, but once the flash had popped, Sabrina elbowed Florence and said, 'You owe me big time, Florence Teesdale.'

'A pint at the Swan do it?'

'You're on.'

Chapter Eleven

Skelmersdale, 1939

Lily

Lily was on her hands and knees, giving the kitchen floor a scrub. With its busy pattern, the worn linoleum hid many sins, and the water in the bucket was almost black. She'd washed up after their meal and stuck the blackout cardboard to the windows in all but the sitting room. Her irritated hands were burning, but she intended to finish the task the old witch had set her.

She wanted to give her no cause for complaint because she had a plan. She'd formulated it carefully and had written it all down in her worry book because it made her feel braver. She'd fallen into the habit of writing in her worry book each evening before she put her light out. The pages were filling up rapidly.

It was Wednesday evening, and from seven o'clock, the youth group would be gathering. They were to meet at the centre where she and her fellow schoolmates had been taken when they arrived here in Skem. Lily was determined to get back there tonight night to speak to Father Ian about sending word to her mam as to how unhappy she was.

She didn't think she could stand it much longer. She was beginning to suspect the old witch was quite potty.

Once she'd finished the floor, she was going to feign a headache and take herself off to bed. The old witch liked to sit in the front room Lily wasn't supposed to venture into after dinner, and she was determined she wouldn't hear her sneak back down the stairs. Nor was it likely she'd check to see how she was, and her plan was to duck past the front windows. Then, she'd sneak around the corner of Mr Mitchell's cottage to collect the bicycle and get on her way!

Lily had leaned, her ear to the door of the sitting room the other night before heading up to bed. Her curiosity had been piqued because she could hear the old witch talking to someone in there. Her tone was unfamiliar and soft, and she'd thought this odd given she hadn't heard anyone knock at the front door.

What the old witch did for the hours she shut herself away in the room had been a mystery until Saturday. Then, Lily had used her absence to investigate what secrets the space held for herself.

She didn't know what she expected to find. Still, surveying the front room, she was disappointed nonetheless to find it was rather ordinary and, like the rest of the cottage, it smelled of damp. The odour was insidious akin to dirty socks.

The only point of difference was how clean it was in here compared to the state the rest of the cottage had been in when she'd first arrived. The old witch was determined Lily should give the place a top and tailing while she was here. This wasn't something Lily would have begrudged had any kindness been sent her way. She wasn't frightened of hard work.

In the sitting room, however, the hearth had been swept, the carpet, although threadbare in places, was spotless, and there was no sheen of dust coating the sparse furnishings. Instead, there was a shrine-like feel to the space.

Net curtains yellowed by age hung in the window facing the road outside, and pale green drapes patterned with roses hung from the pelmet above the frame. Lily spied the blackout cardboard laid out on the floor in the corner, ready to be put back up that evening. With its fading green leaf swirls, although beginning to peel in corners, the wallpaper gave the room a cheery feel. It would be a cosy space in which to while away the evening, she thought, her eyes sweeping over the furniture.

A chair was covered in the same fabric as the curtains near the fireplace and there was another plain green armchair with a white, embroidered antimacassar draped over the back. A rug separated the space on either side of the fire between them. An oak sideboard was the only other piece of furniture in the room. It had spindly turned legs, and sitting upon lace doilies on top of it was a pile of envelopes and a cluster of photographs.

On the wall above the sideboard were four identical oval frames. With curiosity outweighing caution, Lily moved closer to inspect them. The first image her eyes alighted upon was of a couple in their wedding finery. She thought their outfits were antwacky, staring up at the sepia photograph inside the oval frame.

It was hard to equate the young, serious bride standing formally next to a moustached stern groom with the nasty bite to whose care she'd been given over, but it had to be the old witch. It made her feel strange to think of her husband on his wedding day, so unaware of the horrible death fate had in store for him. She felt a chill dance up her spine, and she glanced back over her shoulder even though she knew she'd hear the door if the old witch came back.

A young man in uniform with carefully combed hair was depicted in the next frame, as were the other two hanging on the wall alongside it.

Her son's. All of whom had died in the great war.

Her fingers touched upon the pile of opened envelopes on the sideboard, and she picked the top one up, carefully sliding the letter out.

Dear mam, she read before placing it back in the envelope. The cluster of photographs alongside them were grainy shots of the Cox boys as younger lads perched formally in a photographers studio.

Lily's breath caught as it dawned on her who it was she'd heard the old witch talking to.

The ghosts of her husband and sons.

She talked to the photographs and read and re-read the letters she'd been sent from her boys while they fought for their country. She dwelled in her memories.

It was terrible what had happened to her family. Still, Lily found it hard to rustle up sympathy given the way she'd been treated. She'd done nothing to deserve it, and she backed out of the room, putting what she'd seen from her mind.

As she continued swirling the rag around on the floor, she heard the familiar thudding plunk of the old witch's walking stick making her way towards the kitchen. She put extra elbow grease into her cleaning.

'I'm nearly finished, Mrs Cox,' she said without looking up from her task.

'Not until it's been polished with the wax, too. Did your mam not teach you anything?' Her voice was as coarse as her words were sharp.

Lily could hear the clock ticking. Time was marching on. She needed to be on her way, and soon. Panic swelled. 'Please, Mrs Cox, could I do that tomorrow? I've a terrible headache. I think I'm sickening for something.' It wasn't a lie. Her head was beginning to pound.

Mrs Cox keeping her distance, leaned heavily on her stick. The girl's cheeks did look flushed. She'd no wish to pick anything up. 'Yer to have it finished before you leave in the morning, do ye hear me? I won't have a job half-finished.'

'Yes, Mrs Cox. Thank you.' Lily nodded gratefully, feeling the fear that she'd be too late to make her way into town abate.

The old witch didn't say anything but made a wheezing harumphing sound before turning and shuffling back to the front sitting room.

As soon as Lily had painted herself into the corner, so to speak with the wet rag, she got to her feet and brushed herself off before heading upstairs. The deliberate thump of her bedroom door closing was loud enough to reverberate downstairs but not so loud to earn her a telling off. Next, she stuffed the pillow under the covers and made a mound-like shape with it before unlatching the window in case the old witch decided to lock the front door. There was always a first time for everything, and she wasn't leaving anything to chance. How she'd clamber up to the second storey, she didn't know, but where there was a will, there was a way.

Then, satisfied she'd done what she needed to do, she let herself out of her bedroom, quietly closing the door behind her this time.

She stood poised for a few seconds at the top of the stairs listening out. All was quiet, and so with stealth, she put a foot down gingerly on each step testing it out before putting her full weight down. She could hear the old witch murmuring quietly in the sitting room and holding her breath as the floor creaked under her feet; she waited. The one-sided conversation didn't falter. Satisfied she could make her escape Lily unearthed her coat from beneath the old witch's and shrugged into it. She opened the front door, pulling it gently behind her.

The evening air was considerably cooler than the day that had been slapped her, and she was glad of her coat as she took a moment to survey the street. It wasn't dark yet, and despite the curtains being drawn over the blackout paper in the windows, she ducked down and made her way past Mr Mitchell's cottage and around the corner.

The bike was where she'd left it, but as she wheeled it up to the road, she noticed it was hard to push, and the tyre was making a thwumping sound. She glanced down at them, and her heart sank. The tyre was flat as a pancake.

She moved across to the other side of the road a little way down from the cottages as she tried to think of what she could do. Mr Mitchell would have a pump, but he wasn't home. She'd seen him go out earlier and had no idea when he'd be back. Tears of frustration welled.

'Where are you off to?'

The male voice behind her made her yelp with fright, and her hand flew to her chest as she spun around, eyes wide with fear. A young lad stood there.

'Shush,' she held her finger to her lips and gazed towards the cottages holding her breath as she waited to see if the door she'd not long exited would be flung open. She counted to ten slowly and then relaxed.

'Sorry. I didn't mean to startle you,' the boy whispered.

He looked to be the same age as herself, Lily deduced.

'I'm Max. Max Waters.' He held his hand up in a conciliatory manner, she noticed a hole in the elbow of his blue sweater. His shirt hung out the bottom of it, and his shorts looked too big for him. Hand-me downs from an older brother, no doubt. She could see the piece of string he'd tied around his waist to hold them up, dangling down. His knees were grazed, Lily noticed. She moved back to his face. He'd a cap on. The face beneath the peak was grubby, but there was a liveliness to it too.

'Well, you did,' she said in no mood for chit chat. Where had this Max come from? The road had been empty when she'd stepped outside. Had he been lurking in the woods? And if so, that could only mean he was up to no good. Was he planning to rob Mr Mitchell or the old witch?

'You're wheel's flat.'

'Obviously,' Lily retorted, careful to keep her voice down.

Max didn't seem bothered by her tart tone.

'Where were you off to anyway?'

'None of your business. And where did you come from?'
She squared up to him.

'None of your business.' He flicked back quick as a flash.

They eyed one another, his blue eyes refusing to budge
from Lily's brownish-green ones until Lily sighed. There was
no harm in telling him what she'd had planned, she
supposed.

'I'm Lily Tubb. I was billeted there to the cottage in
the middle,' she pointed across the way and this time, she
whispered, so Max had to lean in to hear what she said.
'There's only the old witch who lives there and me. I'm off to
a youth group in town because I need to tell our vicar how
awful she is. Father Ian's cycling up from Edge Hill where I
come from to see us kids tonight and take any messages back
to our mams.'

'An old witch, aye?'

'An old witch,' she confirmed. 'Who thinks I'm asleep in
bed because if she knew what I'd planned, she'd have stopped
me going out.'

'How old are yer?'

'Thirteen nearly fourteen.' Lily placed a hand on her hip.
'I answered your question now it's your turn.'

Max nodded. 'Fair enough. I turn fifteen soon. I'm due
to start work at the paper mill, only I'll be long gone before
then. I go to the empty cottage sometimes when I've had
enough of things at home. I don't do anything wrong,' he
added hastily, seeing Lily's wary frown. 'I like being on my
own is all, and nobody can find me there.'

'How do you get in?' She asked, understanding now there was no ghost in the cottage next door, only a boy who didn't belong there.

'There's a window down the side I climb in. There's a lot of shouting goes on in my house. I like the peace and quiet in the cottage, that's all. It's full of mice, though, you know, so I'm not alone. Not really.'

Lily pulled a face at the mention of mice. Another question occurring to her, 'How did you know the cottage was empty?'

'Everybody knows everything about everybody in Skem.'

'Have you lived here all your life then?'

'I have, but I want to move to my brothers and his wife's flat like I said. They're not far from Edge Hill themselves.'

'Why?'

He shrugged. 'I don't like it much here.'

'Me either.'

A silence swelled between them. All that could be heard was the running water of the River Tawd off in the distance and the rustle of leaves beside them.

'I could take you into town. I've gorra bike, it's how I get here. I hide it in the bushes up the road, so nobody sees me going in and out of the cottage.'

Hope flared on Lily's face, and Max grinned a slightly crooked smile.

'G'won, put that back,' he inclined his head to her bicycle. 'And I'll meet you back here with it in a few minutes.'

Lily watched him run back up the road for a second, and then she wheeled the bike back to its hiding place. She'd have to get up at the crack of dawn tomorrow to get the floor waxed and leave enough time to ask Mr Mitchell if he'd pump the tyre up for her so as she could get to school.

She waited under the whispering leaves, and true to his word Max pedalled up alongside her in no time at all.

'Hop up on the handlebars,' he said, placing his feet on the ground to hold his bike steady.

Lily smiled. The road was full of potholes, and if he were to go down one, she might go flying. Cuts and bruises would be hard to explain come the morning.

'What's so funny?' Max was bemused.

'Nothing, I'm not sure getting on there's a good idea is all.'

'Then why are you smiling?'

'It's something I do when I'm nervous or scared, I can't help it.'

'Oh right. I stutter when I feel like that.'

Most people didn't understand, and Lily felt a kinship with this strange lad, but still, she hesitated.

'Listen, Lily, I know this road like the back of me hand. You'll be safe as houses with me, I promise.'

She had two choices. She could hop on or go back to the cottage, and the latter wasn't an option. So she hopped on and held on for dear life.

Chapter Twelve

Liverpool, Spring 1982

Sabrina

Sabrina and Florence had said goodbye to the Bootle Tootlers and ducked back to Flo's. Both girls were starving after their run. Mrs Teesdale had left their dinner warming in the oven, and they'd agreed between them that French fare was tasty as they'd wolfed down the beef bourguignon and mashed potato.

Florence, uncaring that the buttery mashed spud was breaking her Weight Watchers programme, mumbled through a mouthful, 'I deserve this after what happened tonight.'

Sabrina wasn't sure whether she was talking about the tumble she'd taken or the fact they were all going to be in the local paper.

Florence raced upstairs to get changed once she'd all but licked her plate clean while Sabrina washed up. She could hear the television playing in the front room and was about to pop through to tell Mr and Mrs Teesdale how they'd got on when Florence reappeared. She was wearing a new maroon rara skirt, tights and flat shoes, which she'd teamed with a high collared, ruffle blouse. Her fringe had been re-gelled and was suitably spikey. Fresh makeup, too, had been applied.

'Wow. You look fab, girl. I love the skirt.' Sabrina gushed, having yet to splurge on one of the new mini-skirts hitting the high street shops. Seeing Flo modelling one now, though, she wished she had.

'It's not too much, is it? We're only off to the Swan, but I wanted to wear it, being new and all.' Florence glanced down. 'Do me legs look like tree stumps?'

Sabrina laughed. 'No and no.' She knew why Flo had gone to town, and it had everything to do with Tim having seen them in all their yellow T-shirt glory at the park. She wanted to knock him out and replace the memory of her going head over heels with an updated and much-improved one. She'd given up on trying to get through to her friend where Tim was concerned. Flo was going to have to learn the hard way.

Florence, happy she didn't look as though she should be stood alongside the oaks in the park, shouted out a 'we're off' to her mam and dad. Then, pulling Sabrina along behind her, said, 'Come on, if we get cornered by them, we'll never get out of here and Dad will only go on about the length of me skirt.'

They got the bus from Marsh Lane back to Bold Street, and Sabrina let them into the flat, where they found Evelyn settled in her armchair, slippers on her feet. She'd a cup of tea on the side table next to her. She leaned forward in her seat, telling the Sharon Gaskell character on Coronation Street off for being cheeky to poor Rita.

By the looks of things, Sabrina mused. Aunt Evie was letting her annoyance at her out on Sharon on the television screen.

Hearing the door go, Evelyn turned to greet the girls blinking behind her thick lenses at the sight of Sabrina squeezed into her yellow Bootle Tootler T-shirt. 'I'm surprised you didn't cause an accident wearing that,' she said curtly, then she turned her attention to Florence. 'You're looking swish tonight, Florence. I like that blouse on you. It's very chaste but a word of advice.'

Florence raised an eyebrow waiting.

'Don't be bending over to tie your laces in that skirt.'

She grinned. 'I won't, Aunt Evie.'

Sabrina bristled as she glanced down at her T-shirt. 'It wasn't just me wearing it. We all were, Flo included, tell her Flo.'

'We were, Aunt Evie. I think Bossy Bev, she's the head honcho at the Bootle branch of WW where I go, scrimped getting them made because some of the girls have already ripped the seams of theirs. They get awful whiffy quick too.'

Sabrina frowned, hoping she wasn't implying she smelled.

Evelyn's mouth twitched, but then she remembered she was annoyed over the Adam Taylor revelation, and it returned to a firm, flat line. Her attention turned back to Sharon on the television set.

Sabrina had had enough. She hated it when her aunt was out of sorts with her. So, not caring that she was talking over the top of her favourite programme, she launched, 'I'm sorry you disapprove of me going out with Adam, Aunt Evie. But I love him. I won't stop seeing him because you, for worever reason, have a problem with his dad. Adam's not his father, he's his own man, and it's not fair you lumping them together.'

Evelyn opened her mouth to interrupt, but Sabrina wasn't stopping.

'And as for him and me going back to nineteen forty-five, you know full well there's nothing I can do about that. The past has already happened.' There, she'd said her piece, she thought, her hands unconsciously having settled on her hips as she drew breath.

Florence fidgeted nervously at her side, unsure where to put herself.

Evelyn shook her head, causing the grey curls she had shampooed and set every week to bounce. 'There's no need to take that tone with me, Sabrina, me girl,' she huffed back. 'I worry that's all and not without good reason, might I add.' She wished she hadn't smoked her ciggie earlier because she could do with a puff right about now. Evelyn, however, was a creature of habit and ten a week was all she allowed herself.

Sabrina had it all wrong too. It wasn't that she disliked Ray. He couldn't be trusted with a woman's heart, was all, because a woman's heart was a delicate thing, easily broken. Not that he'd broken hers, she'd never have let him. Not him or any other man. She'd seen plenty whose hearts he'd trampled on, though, and worever Sabrina said, Adam *was* his son. How was she supposed to stand by and watch him break Sabrina's?

Sabrina softened. 'I know you do, but I'm still here, aren't I? This time I'll have Adam with me, and he's a lovely lad, Aunt Evie. He'll look after me. Give him a chance. Please.'

'He is luvly, Aunt Evie,' Florence confirmed. 'And he adores Sabs. Thinks the sun shines out of her.'

Sabrina flashed Florence a grateful glance.

'Well, someone has to, I spose,' Evelyn muttered, thinking for a moment. There was nothing she could do to stop Sabrina from travelling back in time once more. Not given it had already happened. That much was true.

Evelyn knew Sabrina better than the girl knew herself, and if she'd made her mind up, Adam was the one for her, then she'd be wasting her breath trying to change it.

She looked from Florence and back to Sabrina. *Good, grief, that T-shirt!* This time she couldn't help the chortle that escaped, and Sabrina exhaled, feeling the tension in the air dissipate.

'This is the last time I'm wearing this shirt, Flo,' Sabrina huffed, taking herself off to her bedroom to get changed.

She reappeared five minutes later in a sweater she knew Adam liked and her Calvin's. 'I think they feel a little looser already,' she announced happily to Florence, who'd taken up residence on the sofa.

'Let me watch the end of this, Sabs; it's all happening on Corrie tonight.'

Sabrina settled in next to her, not rising to the bait when Evelyn mentioned a little bird had told her she and Florence were future cover girls. However, she did elbow Florence and mutter, 'You better not have told her you'll get her a copy of the Bootle Times.' She knew by Florence's silence she had done just that, and when the familiar tune signalling the end of the long-running soap opera began to play, she hauled her friend out of her seat. 'C'mon, Judas, the pub will be shut by the time we get down there.'

'Night, Aunt Evie,' Florence said, picking up her shoulder bag from where she'd tossed it on the table.

'Don't forget the newspaper next time you come, Florence.'

'I won't, Aunt Evie.'

Sabrina glowered at them both, then leaned down to give her aunt's soft, powdered cheek a kiss. She was pleased they'd made peace, and she caught the faint whiff of the Woodbine ciggie she'd have allowed herself after her tea.

'Goodnight, luv,' Evelyn said. There were things she'd like to tell Sabrina to help her understand her wariness where Adam was concerned. The words wouldn't be appreciated, though. So she said nothing, reaching up to pat her arm instead. 'Behave yourselves,' she added. 'Making the papers once in one evening is enough, do you hear me?' Her tongue was firmly in her cheek.

Sabrina and Florence left Evelyn for her evening in front of the tele, and Flo waited patiently for Sabrina to flick the lights three times. She understood her friend's compulsive habit lay behind a fear that something terrible would happen if she didn't do it and didn't comment. Then, once Sabrina was satisfied all was as it should be, they took to the stairs. The back door beside the workroom disgorged them onto Wood Street, where, a little further up, was the Swan.

It was getting dusky dark now, and linking arms, they clip-clopped their way over the well-worn cobbles to the pub they called their local, giggling about Bossy Bev and the cans of baked beans. They could see the light beaming out from inside the pub each time the door opened and closed, revealing the row of motorbikes lined up outside. This signalled Adam and his mates were inside. An old Led Zeppelin number was thumping and drifting down the quiet street, filling them both with anticipation of a good night ahead.

The door opened as they reached the pub, and a lad who hadn't realised flares had gone out at the start of the decade held it open for them to pass through, giving them both an approving once-over.

Not forgetting her promise to Sabrina earlier, Florence made her way to the bar to get the bevvies in. At the same time, Sabrina scanned the heaving pub for Adam. She spotted him, Tim, Tony and a few of the other lads they got round with, taking up several tables near the jukebox. A haze of cigarette smoke floated overhead, and their helmets were in a pile on another table.

The silly smile she got whenever she spied Adam played across her lips, and Sabrina fluffed her hair before making her way towards him. Sometimes she could pinch herself that they'd wound up dating. It didn't seem all that long ago her eyes had first alighted on him walking into the pub here with Tim Burns. She remembered how gorgeous she'd thought he was with his dark eyes and blue-black hair curling at the collar of his shirt. He'd worn his battered leather jacket and jeans well, and she'd been smitten at first sight.

Adam put his pint down, an identical silly smile spreading across his face as he saw Sabrina. He got up from the table at which he, Tony and Tim, who had his new girlfriend, Linda of the Farrah flick hanging off him, to greet her with a kiss.

'Gerra room, you two,' a lad called Lenny called out as someone else way-hay-hayed.

Adam grinned over at them and told them they were jealous when they broke apart, and Sabrina reached up and wiped the lipstick off his mouth. 'Not your shade.' She grinned.

'Ta.' He winked and then took a step back to appraise her. 'You look gorgeous, girl. Although I did like you in the yellow.'

'I know what you liked, and it wasn't the colour,' she said, brushing past him to squish in at the table. She was sat on the edge of the seat with her back to the wall. Behind her, a black and white print of Liverpool of old was hung. Adam pulled a chair around next to her before resting his hand territorially on her leg. Tony was already up scanning the pub for a spare seat for Florence.

Sabrina looked to the bar to see how Flo was getting on with the bevvies. She was chatting away with Mickey, the bartender whose polished head and gold tooth shone each time they caught the light. It was a few minutes before she made her way towards the table with a face on her like she'd trod in dog poo when she spied Tim with Linda.

Sabrina would have liked to have kicked Tim under the table, seeing him whisper in Linda's ear, making her toss her blonde hair and laugh before they both turned to look at Flo.

Florence had seen the exchange and was doing her best not to spill the pints she was carrying. Her face flushed pink, knowing she was being talked about, but she held her hands steady.

'I hear you've taken up jogging, girl,' Linda said, a sly look on her over-made-up face as Florence set the glasses down on the table. Tim dragged on his ciggie and exhaled lazily, waiting to see what Florence's reaction would be.

'Yeah.'

'Not good for your health from what I hear,' she tittered and then took the cigarette from Tim's hand and dragged on it deeply.

'Neither's that,' Florence retorted, pointing to the cigarette. 'And jogging won't give you a mouth like a cat's arse either.'

Sabrina snorted into her pint glass, and Flo, head held high, sat down, turning her back on Tim and Linda.

'Well said, Flo,' Sabrina whispered, leaning close to her friend, feeling proud of her. Tony and Adam were laughing, and Sabrina was pleased Florence had missed the flash of admiration that had passed over Tim's face at her snappy comeback. She didn't need any encouragement where he was concerned.

'I put your favourite song on the jukebox,' Tony said to Florence edging his seat closer to hers.

Flo inched hers away as De Doo, De Da Da by The Police came on.

Sabrina would have to get Adam to have a quiet word with Tony about behaving like an eager puppy. If he was going to win Flo over, he would do far better to try an uninterested—she couldn't think of the right sort of dog and realised Flo was talking to her and the others.

'Mickey says, Georgie Best's upstairs at the Steering Wheel.'

A conversation buzzed as to who'd seen who venturing up to the exclusive club. But, of course, it was closed to the likes of them. However, the girls had on occasion managed to wangle their way in there.

Having finished sulking over Flo's getting one up on her, Linda studied her polished red fingernails, feigning boredom. She told them she didn't know what the big deal was. She'd been to the Steering Wheel loads of times, and if you'd seen one celeb, then you'd seen them all. Tim butted in at that point to inform them that Linda had dated several footballers. Sabrina nudged Flo with her foot, sensing another remark about to slide from her friend's lips. She didn't want a full-on catfight to pull apart.

She needn't have worried, though, because as Devo's Whip it Came blaring out, Linda squealed and began wiggling in her seat as though she'd filled her pants. 'Timmy, come and dance with me.' She stood up all fitted top and skin tight jeans as she pouted at him until he got up from his seat, running a hand through his dirty blond hair.

'Timmy?' Florence mouthed at Sabrina incredulously before accepting Tony's offer to dance so as she could accidentally on purpose stand on Linda's foot. The four of them moved to the area reserved for those who fancied dancing.

Adam squeezed Sabrina's knee. 'Come on then, what did you have to tell me?' he asked over the music.

Sabrina swivelled to face him, 'You won't believe this Adam—'

Chapter Thirteen

Skelmersdale, 1939

Lily

The wind whistled past Lily's ears as she perched on the handlebars of Max's bicycle. His hands were on either side of her, steering them in a straight line towards town.

Under any other circumstances, she'd have been embarrassed by their close proximity. Still, these weren't normal circumstances, and she'd been too worried about falling off her precarious perch to be anything but grateful Max was holding the bike steady.

It had taken a good few minutes to stop clenching her jaw and trust Max at his word because he did know this road well. They hadn't gone over a single bump.

They heard the low purr of an engine long before the slotted covers over the headlights, deflecting the light downward, alerted them to the car's approach.

Max slowed the bike and then came to a stop. Lily jumped down as they melded into the trees. Neither of them wanted to be questioned about what they were doing out here. They watched the car glide past and once it was a safe distance down the road, carried on their way.

Aside from the car, there were no signs of life until they reached the town, and in an unspoken agreement, they were silent as they sailed along the cobbled streets. The houses were a long line of rectangles with stark chimney pots on either side of them. A bored dog's, bark was the only alert to their presence.

'Nearly there,' Max called out softly, swerving and muttering under his breath as a cat suddenly streaked out in front of the bike. He managed to keep it upright, but Lily's heart pounded at the near-miss, and her jaw tightened once more. Her heart was banging, and she was grateful they weren't far off now.

The cars idling slowly home were few and far between, and a dustbin lid rattling echoed loudly on a still night. They didn't encounter anyone, except a man whose face was hidden by a hat as he mooched down the street until they reached the community centre. It looked like a grey box in the dim light. Not so much as a chink of light showed from its windows. The thumps of children running about emanated from inside, though.

How could it have been over a week since they'd arrived here from Liverpool by bus? It felt like a lifetime, Lily thought, jumping down from the handlebars and rubbing her backside surreptitiously through her coat.

The air was growing damp with fog, and she didn't see the young couple until they were almost upon her. They'd their arms linked, and the man was clutching an open newspaper parcel of chips. The woman giggled over something he'd said.

Lily's mouth watered at the salty, greasy smell, and her legs felt weak. Her mind flew back to sitting with her dad, watching the boats navigate the busy port of Liverpool. Squalling seagulls circled above them as they munched on a parcel of fish 'n' chips. The memory was so vivid she could taste the vinegar-soaked, hot chips with their crispy exterior and floury middle. Her stomach rumbled as she gazed after them longingly. She flushed as Max coughed, wondering if he'd heard it.

'I'll wait for you here, shall I?' He was still seated on the bike with his feet planted on the ground.

Lily couldn't read his expression, but she'd understood what he'd said. 'Don't be silly. You'll get drilled if anyone sees you loitering about. Come in with me. There'll be too many kids running around for anyone to notice you're not one of us Edge Hill lot,' she urged.

She was desperate for him to venture in with her because he might get tired of waiting and go home if he were to stay out here. 'There's sure to be supper,' she added, hoping it would be enough of a sweetener to sway him because she didn't want to walk back on her own in the dark. It worked, and from the way he leapt at the offer, she sensed that, like her, he knew what it was to go to bed hungry, only it wasn't an experience that was new to him like it was her.

The thought of telling Father Ian of her treatment buoyed her, and she fidgeted, eager to get inside. At the same time, Max clambered off the bike and wheeled it to rest against the side of the building. They followed the thumping clues letting the sound lead them to the main doors. These opened up into the semi-darkness of the foyer, but there was a sliver of light under another door.

Lily shed her coat and hat, hanging them up along with all the others in the cloakroom area and then pushed the door to the hall open. It was hot and stuffy and smelled of bodies, she thought as she and Max stood blinking against the light. The curtains covering the windows on the outside wall were firmly closed. Once their eyes had adjusted to the light, they saw a handful of children. They were charging about in a game of tag.

A harassed Father Ian was trying without success to rein in the children racing about. Still, his attempts only seemed to excite them further as though it were part of the game. Over in the far corner of the hall, a much more sedate game of ludo was underway with four earnest faces bent over the board. A group of little girls were drawing away at a table, and a bunch of lads were spinning a top for all it was worth.

The older children milled about awkwardly. They were too old for games and too young for much else. All, however, were eager for the supper that was being laid out on a trestle table.

A matronly woman shooting disapproving looks at the mayhem unfolding was setting down a tray of triangle sandwiches with meat paste squishing out the sides. At the sight of the butterfly cakes with their whipped buttercream icing upon which the sponge wings perched, Lily's mouth watered. As for the sandwiches, she planned on stuffing as many as she could get away with, taking in her pockets. They'd do nicely for lunch tomorrow.

'Lily!' Edith came rushing over, a beret on her head and her blonde plait draped over her shoulder. Her cheeks were pink with pleasure at the sight of her friend. Ruth, who she'd been chatting to, stood back glowering at the sight of Lily and a strange boy.

Edith's gaze swung quizzically from him to Lily once she'd let her friend go.

'Edith, this is my new friend Max. He brought me here on his bike.' Lily enjoyed the incredulous look that passed over Edith's and Ruth's faces.

Max gave Edith a nod, and she said a shy hello.

She wasn't ordinarily shy, and her coy reaction didn't escape Lily's attention.

Her blue eyes with their curling lashes widened as Lily filled her friend in on the adventure she'd had getting here. She felt very grown-up compared to the other children in the room all of a sudden, and if Ruth's face could have turned green, she was sure it would have.

Max hadn't begun acting foolishly like most boys did when they were in Edith's presence, and Lily was pleased. It would have been a letdown if he had. She'd also noticed that the face she'd pegged as lively was, under the bright lights of the hall, handsome. Now that he'd taken his cap off, she could see his mid-brown hair, and his eyes were an unusual ice-blue. The contrast was arresting. It was his eyes she liked best, and that lopsided grin she decided, sneaking a surreptitious sidelong glance.

He'd a way about him that Lily recognised because she'd seen it in her reflection that morning when she'd told herself to hold her head high because she was a Tubb. It was in the way he carried himself. His posture whispered of courage.

Yes, she loved Edith dearly, but she was glad he wasn't swooning all over her.

Edith, who took the reaction others had to her prettiness for granted, was a little taken aback at the lack of attention as she toyed with the hem of her sweater uncertainly. She chattered about the picnic with the Timbs going on about having seen a swan with its cygnets.

Ruth had edged over closer to listen to her story, and there was no chance of anyone else getting a word in.

Edith was trying to impress Max, Lily realised, but it wasn't working because his attention kept drifting towards the lads engrossed in their game of whip and top. He waited politely for a break in her monologue and then took himself over there to show them how it was done.

Edith stared blatantly after him, and Lily was stabbed by annoyance. He was *her* friend. She was the one who'd brought him here, and this was one occasion she wouldn't let Edith take over.

Ruth didn't miss the cloud that crossed Lily's face or the interest on Edith's as she watched Max walk away. She liked to squirrel away scenes like this. She wasn't sure why; she just had a feeling she might find them helpful to revisit one day.

Lily tried to shake off the unfamiliar pique with her friend. She needed to focus on what she'd come here for, and she cast about for Father Ian. He'd collared Elsie, she saw, who had been the one leading the charge where the game of tag was concerned. The sight of her blonde head bowed but by no means cowed by the telling off she was receiving made her smile. Beside her, Edith sighed heavily, well used to the sight of her little sister in bother.

Now would be as good a time as any to have a word with him, Lily decided, telling Edith her plan.

Ruth listened in on her story with disbelief. What did Lily have to go running to the vicar about? She had to do a few chores and didn't think there was enough meat in her stew. Well, bully for her. Where Ruth and her brothers were concerned, being sent to Skelmersdale was the best thing that had ever happened to them.

She knew Lily had lost her dad, and that had been sad what happened to him, but she still had her mam. Ruth would give anything to have a mam that put her and her brothers first the way Lily's mam did her. She didn't know how lucky she was, and she'd no clue what hardship was.

Lying in bed with your brothers squeezed in beside you with your hands covering their ears, so they didn't have to listen to the sound of their father's roaring and their mam's sobbing night after night. That was hardship. Her blood boiled as she watched Lily make her way importantly over to the vicar. She'd better not spoil things for the rest of them with her whining.

By the time Lily reached their young parish vicar, he'd let Elsie go on the promise she'd behave. She bit her bottom lip uncertainly, unused to having one on one conversations with a male adult.

An exasperated expression on his freckled face, Father Ian ran a hand through his sandy hair seeing Lily standing there. His housekeeper kept dropping hints his hair needed a trim, but he'd yet to find time, and he wasn't letting Mrs Murphy near him with her clippers. Her poor husband had a bald patch where she'd been too heavy-handed. 'Lily Tubb, how are you getting on then?' he asked, affixing his piercing gaze on her.

The tears that sprang forth took her by surprise, and Father Ian, not used to dealing with weepy young ladies, took a step backwards. He sought help, but Mrs Hamilton, who was in charge of the supper, had her back to him and was shooing away a little boy. The cheeky lad had been trying his luck at getting in early with the sandwiches.

'Homesick are you?' Father Ian finally offered up, and his tone was sympathetic.

Lily nodded and wiped the tears away with the back of her hand.

Father Ian winced, seeing the state of her hands. 'That looks nasty. Have you something to put on it?'

'No.' She'd scratched the dermatitis rash to the point of weeping.

'You mustn't scratch at it, or you'll get an infection. I'd get your billet mother to take you to the doctors or at the least the chemist.'

'She won't take me,' Lily murmured.

'I'm sure she will, Lily.' Father Ian pinched the tip of his nose. It was a habit of his he wasn't aware of.

'No,' she spoke up louder. 'She won't, Father Ian. She isn't kind.'

'Now, now, Lily. You're not the only one missing your mam, but in times like this, we've all got to make sacrifices. It's not safe for you in Liverpool. You're better off here.'

If Lily had been of a different temperament, she'd have stamped her foot. But, as it was, she had to clamp her mouth shut to stop the 'shurrup' that was poised on the tip of her tongue. From what Lily had heard, there hadn't been so much as a sniff from a German plane. Liverpool was still standing, but she'd fade away if she had to stay put here in Skelmersdale.

'Please, listen, Father Ian.' She tried to stay calm and quell the rising panic that he wouldn't do anything to help her.

'I am listening. Tobias Finch, how many times! Stop running. This isn't a race track.'

'I'm not being fed properly, and I'm being treated like a skivvy.' His lashes were transparent, Lily thought as he finally gave her his full attention. 'I said, I'm not being fed properly. I feel faint at school of a morning, and she works me to the bone. That's what caused this.' She held out her hands. She would not tell him about the chamber pot. She'd never tell anyone about that.

Father Ian rubbed his chin, frowning and Lily noticed even the backs of his hands were freckled. 'You're not being given enough to eat, you say?'

Lily nodded. 'Please, will you tell me, mam? I've written a note for her, and I'd be ever so grateful if you'd pass it on to her. She'll send for me when she reads it and finds out how bad things are for me here.'

'You're not exaggerating, Lily? I know it's hard to be away from your home, but your mam wants to keep you safe. She can't be with you all the time now, can she? And here you can go to school. I could perhaps have a word with Mrs Pinkerton to see if there's not somewhere a tad more suitable you could be moved to.'

'I don't want to go somewhere else; I want to go home. Please won't you give me mam the note?'

Father Ian took the note and gave her a nod as little Mary Smith tugged at his trousers. 'Father Ian, can I show you the picture I've drawn for me, mam and dad?' He smiled down at the little girl who was missing her two front teeth. 'Of course, Mary.' He turned back to Lily. 'I'll pass it on.' He gave her a smile she was sure was meant to be reassuring but did little to comfort her.

She'd said her piece and given him her note. Now she had to hope and pray extra hard that she'd be sent home.

She felt a tap on her shoulder and turned, expecting to see Edith. But, instead, it was Max, and his expression was grave. 'They don't listen properly, do they? Adults, I mean. They only hear what they want to hear. They're supposed to help us, and they say that's what they're here for, but then they don't do anything.'

Lily didn't know what to say, but she hoped with all her heart that on this occasion Max was wrong and that Father Ian had listened. She didn't know what she'd do if he hadn't.

Lily didn't see Ruth have a quiet word in Father Ian's ear about how Lily was prone to storytelling. On account of her being an only child, you see, Ruth explained to the young minister. She was an attention seeker. Everybody knew that.

Before he journeyed home that evening, Father Ian balled up the folded note. He tossed it in the bin, having decided poor Lily's mam had enough on her plate without worrying unnecessarily about her daughter.

Chapter Fourteen

Liverpool, Spring 1982

Sabrina

Sabrina threw her jeans-clad leg over the back of Adam's pride and joy, his nineteen seventy Triumph Bonneville. She scooted up, so her body was pressed hard against his back and wrapped her arms around his waist. She could feel the juddering of the engine beneath her as Adam, with his booted feet on either side of the bike holding it steady, let it turn over at a fast idle.

He reached down and squeezed her gloved hands. She'd learned the hard way that it could be cold riding pillion and never forgot to wear her gloves when they ventured out, even when the sun was shining like it was this afternoon. Gloves and sunglasses. She'd no wish to look like Alice Cooper when they arrived at Blackpool ta very much. Been there, done that!

'Ahright?' His voice was muffled behind his helmet, as was hers as she shouted back, 'Yeah.'

He waited for a break in the Saturday afternoon match traffic before pulling away from the kerb outside Brides of Bold Street, where the closed sign was displayed in the window.

It had been a chaotically busy morning with a steady troop of brides-to-be, bridesmaids and mothers of the bride piling in the door. Sabrina would have been worried if it had been any other way, given the time of year.

Aunt Evie had left half an hour before, all wrapped up in her red and white Liverpool colours to catch the number 17 bus to Anfield as she did every Saturday. She never erred from her routines. Wednesday evenings, she put the world to rights with Esmerelda. Friday night was reserved for bingo with the long-suffering Ida. The season ticket to the football was her one luxury. She never missed a match come rain or shine, and it was on a Saturday she smoked the balance of her ciggie allowance.

Sabrina hadn't elaborated on her plans with Adam because she knew her aunt would worry about her going all that way on the back of his bike. Aside from that, she'd a cob on because it was Ida who'd taken home the rolled beef roast from their Friday night bingo. There'd been mutterings of foul play and cheating on and off for the best part of the morning. How you could cheat at bingo was beyond Evie, but she knew better than to make mention of this.

Adam steered the bike deftly around the traffic, making the lights ahead of the cars jammed up behind one another. They roared through Bootle, Crosby and Formby, following the A565 through to Southport. Sabrina loosened her grip around his middle as they blatted along. She was far more relaxed on the back of the bike these days, although she'd never go so far as to call herself a biker girl!

She was excited about their outing that afternoon. It had been Adam's idea that they visit the popular seaside resort town of Blackpool. So naturally, she'd leapt at the chance to forget about her encounter with Alice Waters. For a few hours at any rate. Adam had said it would do them both good to go and have fun. After all, he'd elaborated, whatever would happen, would happen. They couldn't change it.

Que será, será, Sabrina had echoed because he was right.

As such, she fully intended to let her hair down. She might even go up the Tower despite being dubious when it came to heights, and she was definitely bringing a stick of rock home. She'd promised Flo one too. But, unfortunately, they wouldn't see the famous illuminations today because the lights wouldn't come on until September.

She hadn't been to Blackpool in years. The last time had been as a teenager with the Teesdale family. She smiled as the wind whipped cold against her cheeks, recalling how she and Flo had spent the best part of the day trying to shake off her mam, dad, brother and the twins because they were cramping their style.

They'd failed miserably as Mrs Teesdale was determined they wouldn't be left to their own devices. 'It's a family day, girls,' she'd said more than once. Sabrina and Flo had heard the unspoken message that they weren't to be parading up and down the prom showing off to the local lads in the boob tubes they'd worn under their jackets.

Shona had thrown up on the new Tidal Wave, pirate ship ride and Tessa had nearly been abducted by a donkey with a mind of its own on the beach's wet sands. In one of the penny arcades, they'd lost Flo's older brother, Gerard, and spent a good hour searching for him. Dinner had been vinegar-soaked fish 'n' chips, after which they'd watched the famous Blackpool Lights come on. They'd all been open-mouthed by the magic of the illuminated spectacle.

The day had been rounded off with a ginormous piece of candied rock to suck on the way home.

A perfect family day out.

Sabrina cherished those times with the Teesdales because being around the boisterous family made her feel normal. She loved Aunt Evie with all her heart and knew she'd done her best by her, but it had always been just the two of them. She was torn between her aunt and loyalty for a mam she barely remembered, and she longed to know whether she had siblings; so many unanswered questions.

Adam slowed his speed, and they put-putted down terraced house streets with the paint flaking from their front doors thanks to the salt air. They weren't far from the Golden Mile as the stretch between the North. South Piers was known when he spied a narrow parking spot beside a green Ford with a sticker in the window saying I Love Jesus, and he nosed the bike in deftly.

Sabrina clambered off the Triumph and stretched before removing her helmet. She gave her hair a surreptitious fluff and pushed her sunglasses up onto her head. Adam waited, hand outstretched, while Sabrina discarded her gloves and shoved them into the pocket of her bomber jacket. She took his hand, and they meandered down the sloping street towards the promenade.

'The last time I was here was a stag night.' Adam grinned, regaling Sabrina with a story as to how the poor groom had wound up minus his eyebrows thanks to Tim.

'Well, he better not do anything like that to you on your stag night.' She coloured, hoping Adam hadn't taken her comment to mean she was assuming they might one day get married. A girl could dream, though, and Adam didn't loosen his grip on her hand.

They reached the road and waited until it was clear before crossing over to the promenade, where a stream of people in all shapes and sizes were wandering. Laughter and chatter overrode the thrum of vehicles passing by loaded with daytrippers and early holidaymakers. Sabrina paused for a minute to inhale the fresh air carrying its whiff of seaside fodder.

The sand was a golden-brown expanse with the Irish Sea in the distance. Sabrina watched the white horses dancing as the waves rolled in, leaving a wet arc behind as they were sucked back out.

It wasn't a day for sunning yourself on a striped deckchair, though, not with the stiff breeze whipping down the promenade, she thought, glad of her jacket. However, hardy children were still playing in the sand, being watched over by parents rubbing goose-pimply arms. They were probably wishing they hadn't been lulled into a false sense of summer having come early!

A red kite flew high, a bright stain against the blue sky, and the wind carried the sound of the penny slot machines cashing out from the arcades. The atmosphere was festive and relaxed. It was contagious, and Sabrina felt as though she were on her holidays. Not that she'd had much experience of such things.

'What do you want to do?' Adam asked as she began to walk once more, her step light as she kept pace with him.

'I want to go up the Tower. I wasn't brave enough last time. What about you?' They sidestepped a large family with a tot in a pushchair hidden behind an enormous pink frothy swirl of candyfloss.

'The Doctor Who exhibition.'

She should have guessed what with Adam being a fan of all things sci-fi. He nudged her and inclined his head towards the beach. 'I reckon you could get away with looking like you're under sixteen if you fancy it.'

Sabrina looked towards the soft damp sands upon which colourfully bedecked donkeys were parading children up and down. She grinned, 'No, ta. You can't trust them.' She told him what had happened to Tessa on her last visit to Blackpool. 'It took off at a canter with her. They can move when they want to, you know. I wouldn't mind one of them, though,' she pointed to the ice cream van down on the sand.

'Your wish is my command.'

True to his word, Adam returned with two "99" flake ice cream cones a few minutes later.

'My favourite, ta.' Sabrina took hers, licking the bottom before it melted and ran down the cone. They walked the short distance to Central Pier perched on its mesh of stork legs and making their way through the excited rabble nabbed a spare seat from which to watch the world go by. A seagull perched nearby on the rails surveyed the scene with disdain. Sabrina enjoyed what was left of her cone as the waves rolled in beneath them.

'I used to sit here with me, mam and dad when I was a kid, eating ice cream. We came to Blackpool every year. Never missed,' Adam said, biting the bottom of his cone and sucking the remainder of his ice cream through it.

Sabrina watched him, amused but didn't say anything. He didn't often talk about his childhood, and she wanted to hear what else he'd say.

'They were good times. We had a lorra laughs on those days out. It's the place, I think. It's not real, is it? You come here to have fun and forget about all the other stuff at home. Me mam always seemed,'–he frowned searching for the word–'I dunno, carefree I suppose when we were here. I liked seeing her like that.'

'Tell me about her. What wor she like?' Sabrina wanted a sense of the woman she'd been.

'She wor lovely me, mam. You'd have liked her, and she'd have liked you.'

She hoped so. She hoped Mrs Taylor would have approved of her and not seen her as a stray whose mam had abandoned her. She looked at Adam from under her lashes, seeing a tenderness had settled on his face. 'What did she like? You know what interested her?'

'What made her tick, you mean?'

'Yeah.'

His arm had snaked across the back of the white, iron fretwork, and his hand rested on Sabrina's shoulder. 'Well, she loved music. All kinds of music and dancing. When I got older and came here, I'd bring a mate, and me mam would make the arl fella take her dancing at the Tower Ballroom. She loved that; she did. She'd gush about the polished mahogany floor and the frescoed ceiling all the way home in between complaining about how many times me, dad had trod on her toes.'

Sabrina laughed, and he flashed her a smile.

'She wor always making things too. Dad would tell her she could go and buy worrever she wanted for the house, but it wasn't about that. She liked the satisfaction of knowing she'd made it.' His face was animated now with memories. 'She'd turn her hand to anything. She re-covered all the furniture one year, and I remember her going through a macrame phase. We had that many hanging macrame plant holders. Dad said it wor like livin' in the flamin' botanical gardens.' He laughed, staring out beyond the people strolling past, lost in his memories. 'She spent more time hammering away or painting or worrever in the garage than he ever did.'

Sabrina sensed a shift in his mood, and she glanced at his face watching his smile fade.

'I don't think she should have married me, dad. I think they only got wed because she wor expecting me.'

He'd told her his dad had taken a back step when his mam had been dying. The reality of it was something he'd been unable to cope with, and her care had fallen to Adam. There was resentment wedged between father and son as a result.

'I heard her talking to her sister, Aunty Jean, once. She told her she always thought his heart belonged to someone else.'

Sabrina felt clammy. 'He was having an affair, you mean?'

Adam made a disparaging noise. 'Knowing the arl fella, I think he had plenty of those but no. I don't think that's what she meant. I think she meant he loved someone else, properly loved them, I mean, and what's worse, isn't it?'

Sabrina nodded, slowly, unsure what to say. She couldn't shake the thought the woman Ray Taylor had loved was

Aunt Evie. How would Adam react if she told him her suspicions? Would it taint the way he felt about her? It was best to say nothing. She'd no evidence her suspicions were correct anyway. It wasn't worth risking the best thing that had ever happened to her on a feeling she had.

'Come on,' Adam said, shaking her out of her reverie as he stood up. Her shoulder felt bare without his hand resting on it. He shoved his hands in the pockets of his leather jacket, a closed book once more. 'Let's go up that Tower.'

Sabrina followed after him feeling instead like the sun shining down on her day had disappeared behind a cloud.

Chapter Fifteen

Skelmersdale, 1939

Lily

It had been two long, dreary days since Lily had pleaded with Father Ian to get word to her mam, and nothing had changed. Well, that wasn't entirely true, she thought, pedalling down the long stretch of road. Today had been different insomuch as she was annoyed with Edith over the way she'd been drilling her about Max whenever she had the opportunity:

'How old is he, Lily?'

'Nearly fifteen.'

'Where does he live?'

A shrug.

And so on.

Lily had thought hard about this, and she couldn't recall ever having felt properly annoyed with Edith before. She wished Sarah were here to talk to. Lily hadn't even taken the sandwich half Edith offered her today, preferring to act the martyr and go hungry. She'd regretted that choice all afternoon as she sat at her desk with her arms wrapped around her tummy trying to ward off the hunger pangs.

It seemed unfair that Edith should set her sights on Max. She thought herself worldly at times did Edith, especially since she'd started her courses. Thirteen was too young for her to be thinking about a boyfriend, though, and Max was *her* friend not Edith's. She'd met him first. She didn't know why she felt so protective of him because the feelings were all new to her.

He'd pedalled back to the cottages with her after the youth group had disbanded the night before last. Thrillingly, he'd shown her how he stole in and out of the abandoned house with no one noticing. He'd dared her to go inside with him, and Lily, not wanting him to think her a scaredy-cat, not even when mice were involved, had shimmied in the window after him.

She'd wondered as to what sort of a family he had if his mam didn't notice he wasn't home.

Max might not have been a ghost, but the cottage felt full of them, and she'd sat down on the floor, pulling her legs up under her chin and wrapping her arms protectively around them. It was freezing.

Lily had shivered inside her coat before turning her head to rest her cheek on her knees. She'd watched Max's shadowy shape as he'd produced a match and lit a stubby candle in a holder, careful to keep it low to the ground.

'What if someone sees the flickering light?' Lily had asked.

'Pull the curtains,' Max had suggested, shrugging. 'And so what if they do? The place is empty. It isn't as if there's anything to rob. They'd probably think it was down to a ghost.'

He'd laughed softly as Lily dragging the curtains together, relayed how she'd thought the strange noises she'd heard coming from the place were thanks to a ghost.

'Your hair's like fire,' he'd said, suddenly staring at her copper plaits.

'It's the Viking blood in me,' Lily had replied without thinking, although the red hair came from her mam's side. She'd found herself telling him about her dad and what had happened to him.

'Everything changes when yer dad dies,' Max had said when she'd finished talking.

Lily had nodded. It was true.

'Just be sure if your mam decides to marry again, she picks a good-un.'

'Oh, she won't marry again,' Lily had said, her mam would remain a widow.

'People marry for all sorts of reasons, you know. It can be because they're lonely or because they need food putting on the table. Me mam needed food putting on the table, but he, me stepdad, barely manages that. His wages are all but spent at the pub each week. I can't wait to leave.'

'Your brother's near Edge Hill?' Lily asked, remembering what he'd told her earlier.

'Yeah, Toxteth.'

He'd been easy to talk to, and Lily had opened up to him in a way she hadn't been able to her friends. They'd whispered back and forth until, yawning, she'd fancied it must be at least midnight. Then, finally, she'd got to her feet, brushing herself off and told Max she had to go. He'd blown the candle out and clambered out the window after her. He'd watched in the shadows as she let herself silently back into the cottage. She'd been terrified she'd be rumbled, but it had made her feel a little better knowing he was outside.

She needn't have worried. The cottage was in darkness, and the only sound was that of the old witch's grumbling snores drifting out from under her closed bedroom door. As she climbed the stairs, Lily wished her bedroom overlooked the street so she could watch Max cycle away.

Now her mind returned to Edith. It was unfair too that today, she'd go home with Elsie to a house where there was laughter, kindness and most of all, enough to eat. Yet, at the same time, Sabrina would suffer at the hands of the old witch for yet another night. She'd written all this down in her worry book first thing this morning but hadn't felt any better afterwards.

The sense of trepidation she felt each afternoon as she made her way back to the cottage intensified with every turn of the wheels.

Lily was lost in her thoughts, and the grass verge was nearly upon her, she realised blinking and managing to swerve in the nick of time. Stay on the road Lily Tubb, she told herself, knowing coming a cropper wouldn't help matters.

She prided herself on being a level-headed sort of a girl who could focus on whatever she set her mind to. Lately, though, she found it impossible to concentrate on anything. It was hard to pay attention when she was permanently hungry. It was a constant gripe that had only been staved off by the supper at the community hall and the secret sandwiches she'd stashed in her coat pockets the other night. She still had crumbs in them.

You couldn't stockpile food in your belly, though, and now it was empty once more. Lily had been told off more than once today for not getting on with her work. How could Miss Lewis possibly understand how hard it was to do your sums when all you could think about was steak and kidney pudding, and the like?

Adults, she'd realised in her brief time but what felt like a lifetime here in Skelmersdale only saw what they wanted to see. Her hands were evidence that something wasn't right, and she flexed them now as they cramped holding the handlebars of the bike. Her skin was openly weeping, and she'd seen Mrs Lewis's lip curl with distaste, but she hadn't asked her if she was alright. Was this why Ruth's dad got away with the way he treated his family? And Max, too, had hinted at hardship on the home front.

It wasn't right. It was the adults job to see what was going on. Her eyes watered both from the cold and frustration. She resolved on that empty stretch of road to never ignore what was right in front of her eyes when she was a grown up.

It had been freezing that morning, and the chill had barely lifted. Her cheeks felt icy, and she knew they'd be stained red from the cold. The temperature had been positively freezing first thing. If she wasn't sent home or, at the very least, moved from the old witch's, then she could add being chilled to the bone to her woes. She didn't relish the thought of weathering winter in the stone cottage.

The condensation had run in rivulets down her bedroom window when she'd opened the curtains, reluctant to leave her bed first thing. The inside of the curtain was blackened with mould specks, and she'd traced Lily Tubb was here with her finger onto the pane. She'd been consumed by an irrational fear she'd be forgotten about. Inside her worry book, she'd written with stiff fingers, *I might be forgotten if something happens to Mam.*

A motorcar puttered past, and she jolted. She'd not heard its approach, and the bike wobbled for a precarious second, but again, she managed to straighten the wheel and steady the bike. She'd fully expected a knock on the classroom door at any minute these last couple of days. She'd pictured an indignant Mrs Pinkerton appearing demanding Lily Tubb be excused. She'd the scene set clear in her mind. She'd be bustled into a motorcar and driven back to the cottage to fetch her things. She'd toss her meagre belongings in her case, hearing the old witch being berated for her shameful neglect beneath her.

Oh yes, she'd thought. She'd close those suitcase latches with satisfaction and walk down the stairs with her head held high.

Lily had two versions of this particular scenario. In one, Mrs Pinkerton went so far as to call the old witch a traitor to her country in its time of need. Even she'd fancied this was a little farfetched, though. So, in the end, settling on the old witch being told her behaviour equated to abuse and that she was lucky she wasn't being prosecuted.

She had no scenario for what she'd do if Mrs Pinkerton didn't come.

Her mind had drifted to Father Ian. Had he passed her message on? Then, drawing near the cottages, she braked and hopped off, pushing the bike the final few yards to its hiding place down the side of Mr Mitchell's.

There was no sign of the old man, and if she wasn't rescued and taken home in the interim, she'd see him the following morning when she tended to the washing. She'd like to thank him again for his kindness in loaning her the bicycle. Lily stood beside the cottages a few seconds longer, hoping to see another car because perhaps it would be Mrs Pinkerton come to take her home. The road, however, was deserted apart from a stoat. It zipped out of the woods on one side, disappearing into the foliage on the other.

Lily's sigh was dredged up from the bottom of her belly as she let herself in the door of the old witch's. The smell of onions, carrots and the fatty meat she'd diced and put in the pot earlier hit her. Despite the unappetising aroma, her stomach rumbled loudly. She shrugged out of her coat and hung it on the back of the door over top of the old witch's. Then, she made to retrieve her notebook from her coat pocket. It wasn't there. It must have slipped her mind to bring it down with her when she'd left for school.

The door to the front room was shut, and the house was silent. Lily didn't think about what she did next. It was as if she were on automatic pilot as her legs carried her through to the kitchen.

Retrieving the soup spoon, she lifted the pot's lid, plunged it into the steaming stew, and filled it up. She carried it over to the sink, careful not to spill a precious drop and blew on it until she was satisfied she wouldn't scald her mouth.

The blow when it came saw the spoon fall from her hand, and Lily coughed and spluttered orange flecks of carrot and stock into the sink.

'Steal from me, would yer!'

Lily's eyes were streaming, and she tried to catch her breath as she got her coughing under control. Her shoulder hurt where she'd been struck by the old witch's walking stick. Rubbing it, she turned around. 'I'm s-sorry, Mrs Cox. It was wrong, I know, but I was so hungry.' It was then she saw what she had in her hand. Her worry book.

The old witch waved it at her. 'And the lies in 'ere about me. You're a wicked girl you are.' Spittle oozed from her mouth. Lily stared at her, horrified. She was like a rabid dog.

'Wicked, I say.'

Something inside Lily snapped. 'I'm not wicked. It's you who's wicked. You're a wicked, evil old witch,' she spat back, her heart thudding as adrenalin surged. 'And you've no right to treat me the way you have. Or read my private things!' She snatched her worry book back. 'You'll get your comeuppance, you'll see.'

''Threaten me would yer, girl?' Mrs Cox snarled. She raised the stick and brought it down on Lily's shoulder before she could dodge it, with surprising force for someone so frail.

Lily crumpled this time, and the blows began to rain down on her back. She crouched with her hands over her head, her worry book hidden beneath her.

'That's enough!' Max's voice sounded. 'Stop hitting her.'

Mercifully the blows ceased as there was a moment of silence, then Mrs Cox, wonder in her voice, said. 'Billy?' Is that my Billy come home at last? Oh, I've missed you, son. Are yer brother's with you?'

Lily squinted up in time to see the old witch reach out her hand to pat Max's cheek. He sidestepped her and then took the walking stick from her. Her eyes were cloudy as she stared at him, seeing someone from the past. All the fight had gone out of her.

Lily clambered to her feet. She hurt all over, but she'd mend.

'Get yer things,' Max said calmly. 'You can't stay here.'

The old witch was murmuring to herself now, her hands clutched in front of her lost in another time.

Lily didn't hang about. Instead, she fled up the stairs and grabbed her case, flinging the few things she had in it.

Max was standing in the kitchen doorway when she ventured back down; keeping guard and shrugging back into her coat, she pulled her hat down low on her head. Finally, Lily put the worry book back in her pocket where it belonged. Then, she and Max stepped outside. He took her case while she retrieved the bike from down the side of the cottages. Then he fetched his own.

As they pedalled off, Lily heard the old witch's plaintive cry, 'Don't go, Billy. I've missed yer, son.'

She didn't look back.

Chapter Sixteen

Liverpool, Spring 1982

Sabrina

'How are you, Florence? I didn't hear you come in,' Evelyn said, appearing in the shop. She'd turned the radio off in the workroom, and without the steady thrumming of the Singer, the shop was suddenly quiet. Both her hands were in the pockets of Monday's green shop coat, and her glasses had slipped down her nose.

'I'm alright for a Monday, Aunt Evie.' Florence blinked at the verdant green colour of her shop coat. 'I have to say you're looking spring-like. The green looks well on you.' She had come straight from the docks where she worked as a typist for a shipping firm. Thus, she wore a boring cream blouse with a chaste bow at the neck and a navy skirt. She also suspected her carefully spiked fringe had flopped between leaving the office and arriving here at Brides of Bold Street thanks to the soft drizzle outside.

'Thank you, Florence.' Evelyn preened. Monday's coat was one of her favourites. She'd chosen green for Monday because she'd once read that the colour symbolised energy among a host of other things. She needed all the help she could get some Mondays! 'I'll get Sabrina wearing one, one of these days.' She fixed her wily gaze on Sabrina, who closed the till with a flick of her hip, having finished tallying up for the day.

'Here she goes, Flo.' Then, Sabrina adopted a bold tone, 'I can carry my pinking shears, a tape measure and the kitchen sink in these pockets, I'll have you know.'

Florence giggled and then sobered as she was on the receiving end of Evelyn Flooks's stare overtop of her glasses.

'Mock me as you may, Sabrina Flooks, but did I spend half my morning looking for the scissors and the pins?' She didn't wait for an answer. 'No, I did not. I knew where everything I needed was.'

Sabrina rolled her eyes. 'Come on, Flo. We'll get on our way.' She stuck her hand in her pocket and produced her packet of Opal Fruits.

'Gi's one.' Florence held her palm out, and Sabrina dropped the orange wrapped sweet into it before peeling one open for herself.

'Where are you two off to then?' Evelyn pushed her glasses back up her nose. She was looking forward to her ciggy and a nice cuppa. As for dinner, she fancied she might keep it simple if Sabrina was going out. Scrambled eggs on toast would do nicely. She'd a piece of bacon she might fry up as well. Her mouth watered at the thought of a crispy rasher.

Sabrina paused mid-chew, jumping in before Florence could land them in it. 'We're off to see a film. I don't know what's showing, but Monday's cheap night, so we thought we'd make the most of it.'

Florence's cheeks reddened at Sabrina's fib, but she didn't say a word, smiling and nodding as though the cat had suddenly got her tongue.

Sabrina held her breath. Not much slipped past Aunt Evie, and Florence looked like a guilty beetroot shifting from foot to foot. Her friend had never been able to get away with fibbing because she wore her heart on her sleeve.

Sabrina didn't like not being truthful with her aunt either but needs must, and she'd made her feelings about the clairvoyant a few doors down clear. The words, 'worra lorra rubbish,' sprang to mind from the last time she and Florence had paid her a visit. But, her disparaging remarks aside, Sabrina didn't want her worrying about what she might be told tonight. While Aunt Evie might disapprove of Mystic Lou, she'd still like to know all the ins and outs of their visit.

Evelyn, however, had her mind on her Woodbines, not Florence, and she shooed the girls out the door, telling them to get on their way and enjoy their film.

'What was all that about?' Florence asked once the door was shut behind them.

'I don't want Aunt Evie grilling me about our visit to Mystic Lou because she'll only fret regardless of what she has to say. Alice Waters called in today for a final fitting. She took her dress home with her.' With the alterations having been made, her grandmother's dress, now Alice's, had fitted her like a glove, and she'd looked a picture in it.

'The girl who showed you the wedding photograph of her grandparents?'

Sabrina nodded. 'She's swinging between thinking I'm completely mad and wanting it to be true. She said she'll call in again even though there's no need now she's got her dress.'

Florence was listening, but her attention was caught by the front window of Esmerelda's Emporium. 'Eee, look girl, Esmerelda's changing her window.'

The two girls came to a halt outside the emporium to watch the spectacle of Esmerelda wrestling with a mannequin in the front window. She was decked out in fuchsia pink with a matching turban and fingernails. Her requisite Silk Cut cigarette was firmly in place in the long black holder dangling between her fingers.

'She'll burn that dress if she's not careful,' Florence said, watching the glowing tip get dangerously close to the batik print mini dress. Esmerelda was attempting to pull it down to a decent length over the mannequin's legs.

'No, she won't. She's an expert,' Sabrina assured her pal, and indeed she was right.

The show was over, and the girls were set to carry on when the woman herself appeared in her emporium's doorway. She'd her arm posed at an angle, and her cigarette was nearly burnt down as it smouldered away in its holder. 'You two are just the girls I want to see.'

'We are?' they chimed.

'You are,' Esmerelda confirmed, batting heavily made-up eyes. It never ceased to amaze Sabrina how she managed to find the exact shade of lipstick to match her outfit, which was guaranteed to be outrageous and flamboyant. Behind her, the tantalising whiff of joss sticks hinted at the exotic goods to be found inside the emporium. 'I need fashion models.'

The words 'fashion' and 'models' had a transforming effect on Sabrina and Florence. They instantly straightened as if they'd books balancing on their heads for deportment lessons and sucked their stomachs in.

'Us?' Florence finally stammered.

'Yes, you two. I've a fabulous array of summer garments on the way as we speak, and I want to showcase them by holding a fashion show here in the emporium in a month.'

Sabrina's first thought was how on earth would Esmerelda find room for a runway? You had to pick your way through her treasure trove of incense, candles, love potions and other bizarre items to get to the counter as it was.

Esmerelda produced a portable ashtray from the voluminous folds of her caftan. She flicked the ash from her cigarette into it before inhaling what was left of it. She exhaled upwards and leaned towards them. 'The show will be an intimate soirée for my best clients on a Friday evening. We'll rearrange the shop floor so the runway can be down the middle and guests can be seated around the edges of it. I'll expect it to be all hands on deck, and I can offer you a silk scarf by way of payment. Are you up to the job?'

Florence, her eyes resembling milk chocolate buttons, spoke up for both of them. 'We are.'

'And do you have friends you could recruit? Because I'll be needing more than two models.'

'We do.' Florence replied again. She wasn't going to miss her modelling spotlight moment for anything. She'd rally up someone or other.

Esmerelda held out a vein-lined hand which they both solemnly shook before saying goodnight to her.

'I can't believe it, Sabs, me and you, we're going to be models!' Florence linked her arm through her pals as they opened the door leading to the staircase, which would take them up to Mystic Lou's rooms. Sabrina gave her mate an indulgent grin, but her mind was on what the psychic upstairs would have to say.

Chapter Seventeen

Liverpool, 1939

Lily

Lily would dream about Skelmersdale from time to time. But, unfortunately, they were never good dreams, and she'd wake in a sweat thinking she was still in the room upstairs in the cottage.

The blood would thunder through her veins, and it would take her a few seconds to realise she was safe back in her own bedroom. Her mam had promised no matter what happened, she'd not send her away again. They'd weather this war together.

In her mind, the old witch had morphed into the evil queen in the film Snow White, the part when she looked in the mirror and saw her long scraggly hair and wart covered nose; she had the black robes on and all. She'd seen the Disney film a few years back with Edith, and they'd both agreed she was terrifying. But, of course, they were far too grown-up for animated films these days.

Mrs Cox had been terrifying.

She'd been home with her mam for two months now, and Christmas was around the corner. As for the war, not a single bomb had fallen on Britain—unlike the snow. Plenty of that had been dumped. In fact, it was the coldest winter in years, people were saying as mist puffed from their mouths, and they huddled inside their coats, trudging through the wet, white drifts.

Sarah had been pleased to have her friend home, saying she'd felt like the child left behind in the Pied Piper story. Lily had been delighted to see Sarah too. She'd confided everything that had happened to her in Skem, even the part about the chamber pot.

She'd seen the woman in the hat only once. Her guardian angel. She'd been at the end of the road watching, waiting for her to leave school one afternoon. Lily had raised her hand and waved. To her surprise, the woman waved back before hurrying away.

Her mam said she should put her experiences in Skem behind her, and Lily did her best not to feel angry over having been sent away in the first place. She was old enough to know that there was no certainty as to when the Germans would strike, but that month of mistreatment at the hands of the old witch seemed like such a terrible waste of time now. The only good thing that had come from it was meeting Max. Although, she wondered now if she'd ever see or hear from him again.

Most of the other children who'd been evacuated were now home too. Edith and Elsie had returned, as had Ruth and her brothers. Although Edith had told Lily on the quiet, Ruth would have preferred to stay in Skem.

Edith and Ruth seemed to have forged a tighter bond in Lily's absence which perturbed Lily. She didn't trust the other girl, although she did feel sorry for her. Knowing the sort of home she'd been returned to, Lily had thought her mam must be a selfish woman to put up with her husband

and allow her children to be treated like so. She'd voiced this opinion to her mam, who'd told her that until she'd walked a mile in another woman's shoes, she'd no place commenting. That had told her!

Despite the blanketing of snow, life was carrying on much as it always had. Lily knew for the other children their time away had been relegated to an uninspiring holiday. School had reopened. Guides, where she was off to now, had been up and running again for the last three weeks.

Things had changed in subtle ways for Lily, though. She'd started her courses or the curse, as Edith called it, for one thing. She'd had it twice now, and it made her feel as though she'd joined a particular club.

Her mam was different too. She was working more, having increased her hours at Peterson's Grocers while Lily was away. Mrs Peterson was bedridden although Lily didn't know what ailed her, her mam had been annoyingly vague. Whatever it was meant, Mr Peterson needed Sylvie Tubb in the shop more. All the supplies arrived loose these days and had to be packaged up, which in itself was a full-time job. Some evenings she didn't get home until after eight complaining her feet were killing her.

Her increased hours meant more responsibility for Lily. It was up to her to light the fire and get the dinner on. All of which she was perfectly capable of. She missed not arriving home to a warm house each afternoon, but the extra money meant they'd plenty of coal for the fire.

It hadn't escaped Lily's attention that her mam was taking trouble over her appearance these days either. She'd even taken to wearing lipstick when she went to work, and the melancholy air that had hovered over her like a pea-souper since her dad died had dissipated.

Instinct told Lily not to delve too deeply into these changes because she might not like what she uncovered. She enjoyed seeing her mam happier, though.

She'd not mentioned any of this to Edith because she always read far too much into everything. It was a funny thing, but since she'd met Max, she'd stopped telling Edith lots of things. She'd not told her she missed Max, pined for him in fact because Lily knew it would sound silly given she hardly knew him. She had told Sarah, though. Just as the old witch had taken on the persona of the evil queen, Max had become her knight in shining armour. If it wasn't for him, who knows what might have happened that awful day when she'd helped herself to the stew.

As the sleety snow continued to fall, Lily's mind flitted back to the moment she'd pedalled away from the cottage. She'd been oblivious to the throbbing pain where the stick had landed on her back as she made her escape, wanting to get far away from the cottage.

With Max leading the charge, her suitcase dangling from his front handlebars, they'd ridden to the police station in town. He'd seen her inside the building, which was just as well because she didn't know if she'd have been brave enough to say her piece to the po-faced constable on the front desk otherwise.

Mrs Pinkerton had been called down to the station. A kerfuffle had ensued after that culminating in a red-faced Mrs Pinkerton driving her back to Edge Hill. Her face was even redder by the time her mam had finished with her. The words disgraceful, I trusted you and, shame on you had been hurled at her. Then Lily had been shepherded inside and the door shut firmly in Mrs Pinkerton's face.

Lily had turned around before she left the station to look for Max, to thank him, but he'd gone. She'd so much she'd wanted to say to him but knew the words would have come out in a jumble. He'd made her feel safe when he'd stepped in that evening and confronted Mrs Cox. She hadn't felt safe since her dad died. Perhaps it was just as well he hadn't hung about. She'd have only embarrassed herself and him had she had the opportunity to say her piece.

She'd made up her mind that evening as she lay safe in her own bed with her mam sleeping next door that one day, she'd marry Max Waters. She felt certain when she did, she'd not need her worry book anymore. She was only weeks away from turning fourteen now, and she knew her own mind right enough.

She hoped Mr Mitchell had got his bike back and didn't think badly of her leaving without saying goodbye. She'd jotted this concern down in her worry book.

Now, she turned onto Edge Lane with her head held high the way she always did when she wore her guiding uniform. So, what if it couldn't be seen beneath her coat? The wide-brimmed hat gave the game away, and she'd her Promise badge pinned to her coat collar. She'd attach it to her tie when she got to the hall. The uniform gave her a sense of pride. Even more so now, their hard-earned skills were being put to use for the war effort.

She'd taken the vow at the age of ten when she'd graduated from Brownies to Guides. Lily took her pledge to do her duty to God and the King, help other people at all times, and obey the Guide law very seriously.

The thrill of receiving a new badge was as fresh now as it had been when she'd got her first badge for Handwork and raced home eager to tell her mam and dad. She'd a slew of them carefully stitched onto the arms of her blue dress these days and was at present working towards her telegraphist badge.

It wasn't going to be easy, but she was determined. First, she'd have to construct her own wireless receiver and be able to send messages in morse code at a speed of thirty words a minute! She'd high hopes that Mrs Ardern might consider her for the role of patrol leader of the Edge Hill troop once she achieved this. She had it on good authority Juliet Rendell, their current leader, would be moving up to Rangers now she'd done four years with the guides.

Mrs Ardern, their group leader, was keen for their troop to pull together for the war effort. The guides were doing good work, she'd told them, and indeed, they'd spent their first weekend back in operation white-washing kerbs so people could find their way in the dark during a blackout. On Saturday just been, they'd been out, despite the diabolical weather, collecting funds for the ambulances. Tonight was a session on first aid, and Lily was eager to learn this new skill. She might need it one day.

This was why she didn't mind venturing out into the cold this evening, even though with each footstep, her shoes plunged through wet, dirty snow to the icy pavement below. Her toes would be numb by the time she reached the hall.

The sandbags outside the shops, churches and community buildings she passed each day had become commonplace now. What she still couldn't get used to, however, she thought, glancing to the pillar box on her right, was the sight of them painted yellow. Of course, a pillar box should be red, and that was all there was to it. The yellow paint was special, though, because it would protect the boxes from gas.

They had to take their gas masks everywhere these days, and hers clunked against her side with each step. This was something they'd learned the hard way when Edith had been turned away from the cinema, having left hers at home. It had been disappointing but not as frustrating as it had been for Elsie. She'd howled on account of having dropped her sweet coupon on the way to the cinema.

Mam had told her, too, there was a wedding boom going on as couples hurried to be wed before their fellas were called up. She'd got a faraway look on her face then and said she was glad Dad wasn't here because she didn't think he'd survive a second war. The first had knocked the stuffing out of him and so many others.

Lily's teeth chattered as she was hit by a gust of Arctic wind. The light was eery thanks to the snow, and the sky above her was a heavy, blanketing expanse. She couldn't help but wonder what it would be like when it was full of fighter planes. The thought made her even colder, and she hurried on.

The church hall was already noisy with laughter and conversation when she barrelled in even though she wasn't late. Groups of girls in matching blue uniforms with belted waists milled about waiting for Mrs Ardern to clap her hands and call them all to order. Coats had been discarded to be hung on the back of the chairs lining the edges of the hall.

Lily bravely shrugged out of her own and draped it over the back of one of the chairs, leaving her hat on as she made her way over to Sarah, who was standing a little ways off from Edith. She could see why. Ruth was bending Edith's ear, and Lily wondered what was being said because Edith had become animated. They both looked up, and Lily caught the sly expression that had crept over Ruth's face as she watched her approach.

'Lily!' Edith cried, her blue eyes dancing as she rounded on her. 'Give your hat a shake; you've snow on it.'

Lily did so, waiting to hear what had Edith so excited.

'Listen, you'll never guess who Ruth saw this afternoon?'

It irked Lily to give Ruth the satisfaction of asking who it was had them both jigging about like so, but curiosity won out. 'Who?' she asked the other girl.

'Max!' Ruth declared. 'Remember the boy from Skem you brought along to the community centre that evening? Sarah, you want to see him. He's a dreamboat.' Ruth pretended to swoon. 'I'm sure I went bright red when he said hello to me. He's living with his brother and his wife not far from here now.'

In Toxteth, Lily thought, and of course, she remembered him. A hot flush washed over her despite the chilly air.

'I've never seen eyes that blue before. He looks like Gary Cooper, don't you think?' Edith added dreamily.

'You've never even been to a Gary Cooper film,' Lily snapped, unable to help herself. Max was her friend. It was her he'd saved, and these two had no place carrying on as though they knew him well.

'I've seen photographs, haven't I?' Edith was equally snippy back, unsure as to why Lily was being terse with her.

Sarah watched the exchange, knowing why Lily had been offhand. She stayed silent, though.

Ruth was nodding emphatically, clearly enjoying the wedge she was driving between the two friends. 'I think you're right, Edith,' she said. 'He does have a look of Gary Cooper, and he remembered you alright. His face lit up when I said you were back in Edge Hill!'

Lily was positively burning now, wanting to know whether Ruth had said anything about her to him. If so, what had his reaction been?

Infuriatingly, Ruth didn't say anymore, and Lily couldn't help blurting, 'What else did he say?'

Sarah moved closer and took her arm. She gave it a supportive squeeze.

Edith and Ruth exchanged a glance weighing up whether Lily deserved to know the rest of the information Ruth had gleaned given her snotty attitude.

Edith was the decider. 'G'won tell her.'

Disappointment flickered over Ruth's face, but she didn't want to cross Edith. 'He's working in Ogdens, the tobacco factory over there in Everton, but he said as soon as his eighteenth birthday rolls around, he's enlisting.'

'Well, he's a few years to wait.' Lily's voice was clipped, but inside she was alive with excitement. Max was working at Ogdens! She'd go see him, she resolved. Thank him properly for what he'd done for her.

She wanted to tell Sarah her plan without Edith and Ruth earwigging, and her fingers itched to write in her worry book, *Will Max choose Edith*? Her friend was making it obvious she'd set her sights on him, and Lily knew how determined Edith could be. So mentally, she wrote, *How will we remain, friends, if she steals the boy I'm going to marry one day*?

At least she'd still have Sarah, she thought, her friend loyal by her side.

As it happened, Lily would soon have far more to worry about.

Chapter Eighteen

Liverpool, Spring 1982

Sabrina

Everton Brow was Sabrina and Adam's special place. Or at least it was so far as Sabrina was concerned because it was here on the grassy verge of the park where they'd exchanged their first kiss. There'd been lots more kissing since then, and they'd snuggled into one another on the bench where they'd sat down now to watch the seasons change from autumn to winter and now spring.

She smiled to herself, watching Adam unwrap the newspaper parcel they'd picked up from Clive's Chippy on their way there. But, unfortunately, he was more intent on getting his dinner down him than remembering romantic moments. Typical fella, she thought as her tummy rumbled at the whiff of the deep-fried, battered cod they'd ordered.

Adam offered her the first chip, and she helped herself. Biting into the crisp exterior to release a little puff of steam before juggling the hot potato middle from cheek to cheek.

Her mind was full of the story Mystic Lou had imparted to her the night before. She'd thought about nothing else all day, and she needed to share it with Adam.

First things first, though, dinner! So she picked up another chip.

Everything was a rich green, she thought as she ate. The sun that had shone all day brightly, causing customers to comment as they breezed in the door fanning themselves, that summer was around the corner, dipped low. Its dying rays had cast the hillside in vibrant warm light. Adam looked like a Greek God bathed in gold, she thought poetically before picking up her piece of fish and blowing on it.

'Penny for them?' Adam asked, feeling her eyes on him.

'I was thinking this fish looks bloody gorgeous.'

Adam laughed. 'Fibber.'

Sabrina grinned. 'Don't go getting a big head, but I was thinking you remind me of Adonis in this light.'

'That Greek God fella?'

Sabrina giggled and nodded.

'You can have another chip for that.'

The orb on the horizon sank lower.

'Five, four, three, two,' Adam counted, and as he reached 'one', it vanished altogether. The sky was washed with orange and yellow for a brief moment before it turned a more profound, dusky blue.

Sabrina licked greasy, salty fingers and was about to tell him about her encounter with Mystic Lou when Adam began talking. Instead, she listened as he told her about his day, which had involved an altercation with the owner of a business in one of the buildings Taylor Holdings leased out.

'He's driving around in a flash Merc and wearing natty suits, but he can't pay the rent.' Adam shook his head. It wasn't his favourite part of the job; he was all for an easy life. In that respect, he wasn't cut from the same cloth as his father, who took no prisoners when it came too late rent payments.

Taylor Holdings were in the property business, he'd explained to Sabrina not long after they'd first met. This entailed the buying of commercial properties and leasing them out. His father had started the business as a young man. He'd seized an opportunity that had come his way thanks to his time in the Lime Street Boys. The gang had been notorious in Liverpool back in the day.

Sabrina couldn't for the life of her visualise Ray Taylor as a fast-talking member of gangland Liverpool. But, according to Aunt Evie, he'd strutted about the city streets as if he owned them back in the day.

She eyed the last few chips and felt the waistband of her Calvin's digging in. She really shouldn't. Then again, hadn't she gone for a run the other night and suffered through a photoshoot while clutching a can of Weight Watcher beans? Well earned, she told herself, chomping down another handful and enjoying the tang of vinegar as it hit the back of her throat.

'That's Vega, that is,' Adam said a little while later after he'd binned the grease-soaked newspaper and sat back down to hold Sabrina's hand. He pointed to the bright star that had, like the flick of a switch, lit up the sky. 'We'll be able to see the summer triangle soon.'

'Since when did you know so much about consonants?'

Adam laughed, and Sabrina watched in fascination as his Adam's apple bobbed up and down. 'Consonants are letters that aren't vowels. You mean constellations, and it's not one of them. It's an asterism.'

'That still sounds like something my English teacher tried to drum into me,' Sabrina said. English hadn't been her strong suit. Instead of analysing Wuthering Heights, she'd been staring at the cover. Thinking the long-puffed sleeves of the Victorian era dress Cathy was wearing would work a treat on the wedding gown she was doodling on the back page of her exercise book.

Adam carried on, caught up in the star overhead. 'The summer triangle's made up of Vega, Deneb and Altair.'

Sabrina looked up at the star and then back at Adam's profile. He was constantly surprising her.

'They shine so bright come summer you can see them even when there's light pollution. Each of them is in a different constellation. Lyra the harp, Cygna the swan and Aquila the eagle.'

'Beautiful,' Sabrina breathed. She was seeing the night sky through new eyes. 'And how do you know all this?'

'I went up the Pex Hill observatory on a school trip when I was a kid, and Mam said I talked about it non-stop for weeks. She bought me a book on the stars that year for Christmas, and I read it cover to cover at least five times. I wanted to be an astronomer after that trip.'

'I never wanted to do anything other than make wedding dresses.'

'You're lucky. By the time I was set to leave school, I'd moved from astronomy to wanting to be a mechanic like Tim. It wor me arl fella who wanted me to go into the family business.'

Sabrina was unsure what to say, so she said nothing, squeezing his hand instead as she decided it was time to tell him about her visit with Mystic Lou.

'Adam, Flo and I went to see the psychic I told you about last night, Mystic Lou. Remember?'

Adam dragged his eyes away from where a carpet of twinkling stars was now appearing as the sky darkened. He turned to look at Sabrina, a question in his coal eyes. 'I remember.'

Sabrina nodded. 'Well, you won't believe what she said.' She stepped back into that dimly lit chamber once more as she elaborated.

***

The space where Mystic Lou dished out her prophecies was too exotic to be merely a room, and so Sabrina had settled on the word chamber. The psychic had called her in as she'd only see one client for a reading at a time, insisting the messages that came through to her could get muddled otherwise.

It was comforting for Sabrina to know Flo was sitting outside in the waiting room. Her friend was engrossed in the article in her latest copy of Cosmo titled, 'Ten signs he's into you.' She'd left her taking notes.

Mystic Lou was seated at the table covered with a red cloth upon which her pièce de résistance, a crystal ball, sat. The curtains were drawn despite it not being dark outside yet. The shadows of the flickering tealight candles danced eerily on the walls. Music was playing softly, and Sabrina fancied the strangely hypnotic sounds might have been the Cocteau Twins.

The poster she'd been transfixed by the last time she'd been here caught her eye briefly. The hands clasped around a crystal ball alive with lightning bolt energy was as startling this time around, she thought, turning her attention to the psychic herself.

If you were to have asked Sabrina to draw a picture of what she thought a fortune teller should look like, she'd have drawn Mystic Lou. Black hair hung straight down her back from beneath the red scarf knotted about her head. Gold hoop earrings dangled heavily from her ears, and she was wearing an Esmerelda-esque robe with an amber gemstone brooch fastening it.

Sabrina had none of the nerves she'd had fluttering about on her first visit. Instead, she clasped her hands in front of her on the table, leaning towards the psychic. Eager to get to the crux of the matter. 'I'm hoping you can tell me about a journey I'm to go on with my boyfriend, Mystic Lou.'

Mystic Lou, otherwise known as Louise Doyle, wearer of cardigans and slacks and possessor of a strong Scouse accent when she wasn't playing the role of a Gypsy-Romany, stared intently at Sabrina. This girl had the most extraordinary of auras. 'You 'ave been through ze timeslips we talked about on your last visit.' It was a statement, not a question.

'I have, and you were right. I did fall in luv with a man with dark hair and eyes, my Adam. And, I did go on a journey all the way back to nineteen twenty-eight where I met Jane and Sidney.' She thought back on her adventure where she'd met Jane, the young maid on Allerton Road who'd fallen in love with her mistress's son, Sidney. They'd got their happy ever after. She'd been there to witness their autumn wedding.

'I also went back to nineteen sixty-two.' That had been every bit of an adventure as her first journey. She'd even seen John Lennon, and on that occasion, had helped her friend, Bernie, choose her gown for her winter wedding.

Louise nodded, unsurprised her prophecies had come true. She began polishing the crystal ball on its mounted stand until satisfied; she picked up a candle, lit it and wafted it back and forth over the top of the orb. She then sat back in her chair and stared into the ball, waiting for its mists to clear.

Sabrina was sure it was only a few seconds as she squirmed anxiously on her seat, but it felt like minutes until Mystic Lou spoke. Her nails were digging into her palms as she listened.

'I see a reunion in a different time.' She ran her palms over the orb. Her eyes focused on the crystal. 'You're caught up in a great celebration, and your boyfriend, the man with the dark hair and eyes, is with you. I'm glad,' she added softly, looking up as the veil came down and she could see no more.

Sabrina bit her bottom lip. It wasn't enough. 'Please, Mystic Lou, could you take another look and see if there's anything else?'

Louise closed her eyes. Her head always pounded after a reading.

Sabrina was uncertain whether she'd even heard her. Her lashes were spidery against her pale skin under the flickering candlelight.

'Mystic Lou?'

'I heard you.' Louise's eyes snapped open. 'It doesn't work like that. The ball will only show me what it wants me to see.'

'Please.' Sabrina's voice took on a begging note. 'Please, could you try? It's important.'

Louise rubbed her temples. She could sense Sabrina's desperation, and she was curious herself to see if anything further might be revealed. This session was by far and away more interesting than the one that had preceded it.

The woman who'd left five minutes before Sabrina arrived had reminded Louise of her neighbour's bulldog. She'd wanted to know whether her sister had taken their mam's, who'd recently passed over, engagement ring. The younger sister was claiming to have no idea where the ring might be. The crystal had shown Louise otherwise. She didn't fancy being in that woman's sister's shoes when she got hold of her! She'd left her rooms snapping and snarling.

'Ahright,' her accent slipped. 'I'll take another look.'

'Ta.' Sabrina, with all her muscles tensing in anticipation, didn't pick up on the slip.

Louise went through the same ritual as before; her eyes narrowed as she sought to see the secrets the crystal ball might still hold in its murky depths. Finally, after a moment or two, she spoke. 'There's a parade of some sort.' She peered closer, trying to understand. 'Excitement, because it's a momentous occasion and I see fire, flames dancing. Look for the woman you seek amidst the celebrations.' She blinked and held Sabrina's gaze. 'That's where you'll find her.'

Sabrina was speechless as fear and anticipation fought to take the lead. Finally, she would find her mam!

Mystic Lou wasn't finished, however. 'Be careful. You might not find what you expect.'

The warning fell on deaf ears.

***

Now, as the lights of Liverpool twinkled below them, Sabrina waited to hear what Adam would say to the news that going through the time slip once more would mean she'd find her mother.

'Well, that's it then, isn't it?' he said after an age. 'We've no choice but to go back.'

Chapter Nineteen

Liverpool, November 28 1940

Lily

Grey-faced people hurried past Lily as she huddled in her coat, waiting for the bus in the deepening gloom of evening. Her feet ached from standing on them all day, and the wind was stinging her face. Fingers of fog were beginning to slither around street corners, and the air she was breathing was damp and filled with the distant smell of smoke. She'd be glad to get home tonight, she thought, shivering.

It had been a strange day. She'd woken with a sense of dread as if having had a bad dream, but she couldn't recall what it had been about. She'd been unable to shake off the feeling something terrible was going to happen all day, and it lingered even now.

Knowing she was in of a Thursday night, Max would sometimes swing by for a cup of tea to warm himself up if he had a window of time. So she hoped he'd call in tonight. She'd like to see him even if it was only for a few minutes to put her mind at rest that he was alright.

He was kept busy most evenings running messages across the city delivering news of the injured to anxious families. He volunteered to keep watch up the fire tower too. It was a source of great consternation that he wasn't old enough to enlist, unlike his brother, who'd entrusted him with the care of his wife and their baby boy in his absence.

The last they'd heard, he was headed for France. Max was desperate to fight for his country.

It worried Lily how fearless he was when it came to the air raids, which had begun with a sudden ferocity on August 28 last. They'd kept on coming night after night ever since, or, at least, that's how it felt. She'd spent more nights in the air-raid shelter at the bottom of the garden than she had her own bed these last few months. The sound of the siren was commonplace, as was the drone of planes, followed shortly after by the whistling and whump of bombs.

Lily, too, did her bit. Her time in Skem had changed her. She was braver. She worried less. And of course, now she had Max to help her stay strong. She'd have liked to have joined the ATS and become a FANY, but her mam wouldn't sign the necessary papers given she was only fifteen. She'd not been swayed when Lily had pointed out she wasn't all that far off sixteen. So, like Max, she found another way to serve her country. She and Sarah had decided to put the first aid they'd learned in the Guides to good use by volunteering at the Royal Liverpool. This meant an evening in was a rare treat. She'd soon stopped being squeamish at the sight of blood too.

Lily no longer felt like a fifteen-year-old girl. She'd seen too many folks coming in on stretchers at the hospital at the same time as she tended to those who'd presented with minor injuries. It made her feel world-weary and sometimes sad that lives could be changed forever in a split second. She knew this first-hand, thanks to losing her dad. Her compassion was wasted in the world of parachute making one of the nurse's had said to her the other night. She should think about nursing. She had a vocation for it.

Lily further resolved to join the FANY's as soon as she turned eighteen.

As the bus belched to a stop and she clambered aboard, she wondered if Mr Peterson would be there for his tea again when she got home. She'd mixed feelings about Mr Peterson. Unlike her mam, who'd made her feelings quite clear.

He was a big man with a booming laugh that made Lily jump. His hair was thinning, and he'd red cheeks and a large nose. To Lily, he was reminiscent of a giant gnome not handsome like her dad had been, and for the life of her, she couldn't see what her mam saw in him.

Sarah said her mam was lonely, and Mr Peterson was lonely too. Lonely hearts gravitated to each other, she reckoned. Lily was sceptical about how Sarah knew so much about lonely hearts. She supposed her mam must be lonely too with Sarah's dad, who was a lovely man, away at sea.

She'd have liked to have asked Edith's opinion on the matter, but they were no longer friends, having fallen out when Lily began stepping out with Max.

She and Ruth had got about with their noses in the air and their arms linked. Until Ruth, having lied about her age, left to join the Land Army. Edith, meanwhile, was working in an office and had left guiding to join the Sea Rangers.

Lily had been on the same bus as her former friend one evening and had overheard Edith holding court to those seated around her. She'd flashed the special pass needed to enter the dock area and had been full of how she'd learned to ship oars and how choppy the waters were near Pier Head.

Edith giggled and told her audience that the port was full of Allied ships and sailors who'd wave to her and the other girls.

Lily had uncharitably wondered if this was Edith's primary motivation for joining the Sea Rangers.

At first, Lily had been heartbroken by the fallout, but then it had dawned on her that if Edith was any sort of a friend, she'd have been happy for her. Especially knowing the sadness, she'd suffered losing her dad. Edith was anything but happy where Lily and Max were concerned, though, because Edith was a girl who was used to getting her own way. She was spoiled in the way that beautiful girls sometimes are. Lily knew, even though she'd never come right out and said it, she couldn't understand why Max should prefer Lily with her red hair and freckles to her.

Thank goodness she still had Sarah.

Max had told her he couldn't be doing with a girl that talked as much as Edith did. Not that she'd passed this on to Edith, of course, but Sarah had laughed when Lily confided what he'd said. 'He's got a point,' she'd giggled. For her part, she didn't seem perturbed by the end of the friendship.

As for Mr Peterson, he'd come to their house for his dinner three times now. On the first occasion, she'd arrived home to find her mam's boss sitting at the table waiting for his tea. She'd been uncomfortable seeing another man so at ease where her father had once sat. She'd not had much appetite for the sausage roll served up alongside a plate of veg, and her mam had snapped at her that it was a criminal waste of food when she'd cleared her plate from the table. Nevertheless, the sausage roll had found its way into her lunchbox the next day.

When Mr Peterson had gone home that evening, her mam had announced, 'There's lots to be said for a man who makes you laugh, Lily.' She'd spoken to Lily as though she were confiding in a friend adding, that she was lonely.

Lily had replied, 'But we've got each other, mam.'

Her mam had looked at her sadly like she didn't understand anything at all.

Lily knew her mam was being talked about in the neighbourhood too. She'd overheard snippets between gossipy Mrs Dixon and plump Mrs White as they chatted over the fence. Lily had been sitting on the back doorstep out of their line of sight. She'd blanched hearing them tut that Sylvie Tubb's behaviour was disgraceful given poor Mrs Peterson was barely cold in her grave.

She didn't know about disgraceful, but she did know that it would no longer be just her and her mam one of these days. She didn't want to think about that, and if she got wind of any plans, her mam had to wed Mr Peterson, then she'd make her sign the papers allowing her to join the FANYs. She'd not live under the same roof as him.

The bus stuttered off, and she plucked her hand from her pocket, putting it over her mouth to stifle a yawn. She couldn't remember the last uninterrupted night's sleep she'd had. It was the same for everyone. She hadn't seen her guardian angel for a while either, she thought, stealing a side-glance at the woman sitting opposite her. She was clutching her purse on her lap and wearing a red Tam O'Shanter beret from under which brown curls peeked. Lily couldn't help but think that a jauntily placed bow on the hat would have elevated it from non-descript to knock-out.

She noticed hats all the time these days, having had a brief stint as a milliner's apprentice at Hats by Jacqueline on Great Charlotte Street not long after she'd left school. She'd never had any interest in hats before and had only got the job because her mam's cousin, Jeanne was great pals with Miss Jacqui, as she liked to be called. According to Jeanne, the milliner was looking for the right kind of girl as an apprentice.

To Lily's surprise, it turned out she was the right kind of girl.

As for Miss Jacqui herself, she was pencil thin and glamorous. She could make something beautiful from a flour sack if need be and was a dab hand at turning the fabric remnants she could get her hands on into works of art. She also ran hot and cold. Some days she'd been effusive in her praise of Lily's burgeoning hat-making skills, and other days, scathing. Lily had put it down to the fella she was seeing. He was home on leave at the time, and if she'd heard from him, she was happy. If not, she was a bite.

She'd had a good mind to seek him out herself and tell him to stop messing Miss Jacqui about because he was making her life miserable too! Before she could, though, she'd lost her job. As a thirty-two-year-old woman who was single for all intents and purposes, Miss Jacqui had shut up shop to join the WAAFs after conscription had begun. She'd opted for the airforce rather than the Land Army. She'd confided this was because she couldn't stand the thought of dirt under her fingernails.

Lily had been making mental tweaks to every hat she saw ever since. In her short time under Miss Jacqui, she'd learned that the slightest embellishment could make all the difference.

There was no glamour in her new job, but Lily didn't mind. At least it was useful. She worked at the warehouse Littlewoods had converted on Hanover Street and had been instructed along with the other girls by an expert in the cutting out, sewing, rigging and assembly of parachutes.

Once lit by yellow hissing lights, the streets were dark these days, and sometimes Lily could pinch herself at all that had happened in the space of a year. The sights and sounds she no longer blinked an eye at were ones she could have never dreamed of before the war began in earnest.

This morning, for instance, she'd seen little ones picking through the rubble as she'd made her way towards the factory. When she'd asked them what they were after, a little boy with a grubby face informed her there were sweets to be had. He'd held up a lemon sherbet jubilantly as proof of this. The rubble was the remains of a grocers and confectioners. Mercifully, not Petersons.

It was the norm, too, to see families with bedding tucked under their arms making their way to the larger shelters once six pm rolled around. As had the craters that would appear overnight, the debris-filled streets and the smoking skeletons of houses and buildings. The sky, once black at night, would turn red.

Lily was fortunate; she knew this. The war had yet to touch her or her mam personally. That wasn't to say they hadn't suffered, though, because they had. However, their suffering had come before the war started. Families were suffering everywhere now, and more grieving was to be done with each dropped bomb. There seemed to be no end in sight to it all.

Other things had changed too, being Max's girl for one.

It had been just before last Christmas when she'd decided to be bold and take herself off to the tobacco factory where he'd not long started work. She'd hung about outside that enormous, Victorian building waiting for him to finish for the day. It had given her a rebellious thrill to think how livid her mam would be if she were to find out what she was up to.

Her anxiety had increased as the minutes ticked by. What would Max think seeing her there? She resolved to tell him she'd come by to thank him for his help back in Skem. This was partially true. She did want to say to him how much she appreciated what he'd done for her. However, she also wanted to see him with a desperate, unfamiliar longing which she would not breathe a word of to him.

As the factory workers had begun to stream out from the building, her worry over what he'd think morphed into how on earth she'd spot him in the sea of men and women. He saw her before she saw him, and he'd made his way towards her smiling that slightly lopsided grin, his eyes a flash of colour at the end of a dull day. Her heart had soared.

They'd become firm friends over the ensuing months. Then one evening, as he walked her home having treated her to dinner in a café which had made her feel ever so grown up, he'd suddenly come to a halt. 'Lily, can I kiss you?' Later Max told her he'd felt if he didn't throw caution to the wind there and then, he never would.

'Erm, yes,' she'd replied, uncertain of what she should do and uncaring of the foot traffic stepping around them.

His soft lips had settled briefly on hers, and they broke apart giggling as an older woman tutted. She muttered that the war is no excuse for indecent behaviour.

Lily, once she'd stopped laughing, had gazed into Max's eyes and said, 'Max Waters, I'm going to marry you one day.'

He'd replied, 'I don't doubt it for a minute.'

He'd won her mam over when he'd presented her with a tin of broken biscuits. Goodness knew where he got them because they were gold dust since rationing had begun in earnest. But after that, he couldn't put a foot wrong. Of course, it had helped that when she'd opened the door to him, he'd asked if her sister was home!

Lily, lost in her thoughts, nearly missed her stop and had to call out to the bus driver. He slowed once more, allowing her to jump nimbly down and step onto the pavement. She pulled her coat around her and walked quickly down the foggy street. A man loomed up in front of her, and she nearly jumped out of her skin in fright.

'Lily Tubb, is that you?' a voice she recognised asked, and a torch was flashed in her face.

Lily, her hand still on her chest, blinked at the sudden light and then peered closer at the man. She could just make out he was wearing a steel helmet with a large 'W' on the front of it and, he'd an armband on too, signalling he was an ARP warden. It was Mr Green. She'd taught his daughter when she'd had a brief stint helping home-school some of the local children shortly before starting work for Miss Jacqui.

'It is, Mr Green.'

'The fog's going to be bad tonight, girl. A right pea-souper. You're not going out again, are you?'

'No, not tonight, Mr Green.'

'Get on home then, queen. Let's hope for a quiet night.'

She heard his footsteps echoing down the street as she did exactly that.

She opened the door to the smell of fried onions, and, divesting herself of her coat and hat, she hung them up.

'That you, Lily?'

'Yes, mam.'

She stood in the hall for a split second, listening out but couldn't hear voices which was a good sign. Then, ducking into the front room to check the fire, she saw it spluttering in the grate, so she poked it. Her mam had heaped slack on it to keep it banked, but once they'd had their dinner and moved through to here where they'd while away the rest of the evening, they'd get it roaring again until bedtime. Satisfied it wouldn't go out on her, she went in search of her mam.

She found her at the stove stirring a pot, and the knot between Lily's shoulders loosened, seeing there was no sign of Mr Peterson. She gave her mam a spontaneous hug causing her to nearly drop the spoon in the creamy, greyish coloured liquid.

'Lily, your hands are freezing!'

'Sorry.' She grinned. 'It's bitter out there tonight, Mam.'

Mrs Tubb put the spoon down on the breadboard and said, 'Give them to me.'

Lily held her hands out, and her mother rubbed them with her own warm ones until they'd thawed.

'Why didn't you have your gloves on?'

'I couldn't find them this morning.'

Mrs Tubb gave an exasperated sigh. It was a bone of contention that Lily left it until the last possible minute to get out of bed each morning. 'I don't know. G'won. Sit yourself down, luv. A bowl of soup will warm you up.'

'You can work wonders with a spud, Mam,' Lily declared, tucking in. The soup, despite its unappealing colour, was thick, hearty and hit the spot.

They fell into their usual routine whereby Lily washed up, and her mother got the fire blazing. Then they sat in companionable silence, warming their toes beside the flames listening to the wireless and knitting. Lily must have dozed off at some point because she opened her eyes to find her mam standing over her. 'Get off to bed, Lily.'

'What's the time?' She yawned widely. The warmth of the room had sent her off, she thought, unfolding herself and standing up.

'It's nearly eight.'

'Max might call.'

'Well, if he does, I'll wake you. So grab some sleep now while you can.'

She was too tired to argue. 'Night, Mam. I luv you.'

'I luv you too, sweetheart.'

Later, Lily would wonder why her mam had her coat on, but in her drowsy state, she took herself off up the stairs to bed. Perhaps tonight, the Germans would give them a reprieve.

***

The piercing siren woke her not long after she'd drifted into a deep sleep. Lily dragged herself up feeling woolly-headed as she shoved her shoes on her feet and shrugged into her dressing gown, belting it tightly.

'Mam,' she called out as she stepped onto the dark landing. 'C'mon, Mam.' She pushed her bedroom door open, but the bed was empty. Thinking she must still be downstairs, she trooped down the stairs wondering how bad tonight would be.

The fire had been banked. The living room was in darkness, but it was empty, apart from the glow of embers beneath the heaped slack.

Where was she, Lily wondered? Had she popped over to the neighbours, perhaps? There was no time for wondering because suddenly the house lit up and the windows shattered.

Lily acted without thinking and ran out the back door. She clambered inside the shelter seeing the sky lit orange as she pulled the door shut behind her. Her heart was thudding, and she sat there in the darkness, wondering where her mam was.

Chapter Twenty

Liverpool, Spring 1982

Sabrina

'Ahright there, Fred? If I'd known you were down here already, I'd have brought you a Horlicks,' Sabrina called out as she glanced down the street to the mound in the shop doorway. She pulled the door to the bridal shop shut.

'Sabrina, my love, is that you?' Fred sang back.

'Who's Fred?' Adam asked, scanning the pavement ahead and seeing nothing except a pile of blankets, or was it old coats, in a shop doorway.

'It's me ahright, Fred.' Sabrina fished her keys out from the pocket of her jeans and locked the door. She turned to Adam, who was waiting with his hands jammed in the pockets of his leather jacket. 'Fred's Bold's Street's nightly visitor. His favourite spot is the doorway of what used to be the Christian bookstore up there. I bring him down a bowl of porridge of a morning.'

'You're a soft touch, you are.' Adam shook his head.

'No need to worry about me, Sabrina, girl. I've man's best friend to keep me warm.' Fred's throaty voice floated towards them.

Adam nudged Sabrina. 'Has he gorra dog under those blankets then?'

Sabrina laughed. 'No. He's on about his whisky bottle. His one true love.'

Adam nodded; that made more sense. He glanced in the window of the darkened bridal shop as Sabrina pocketed the keys. Her aunt had been off with him tonight. He wasn't sure what he'd done to upset her. He was about to open his mouth to ask Sabrina what the problem was when Fred called out again.

'Who's that you've got with you on this fine evening, Sabrina?'

'Adam, Fred. You know the fella I told you about?'

'All good, I hope,' Adam's ebony eyes danced.

Sabrina tapped the side of her nose. 'That's for me to know.' She pulled Adam along in the direction of Fred's voice, and they both jumped as a pigeon feasting on the remnants of a discarded sandwich flew up in front of them.

'Bloody things,' Adam said, shooing it away with his hand. He'd gone off the entire pigeon species after one had taken aim and fired at his leather jacket.

'Come, come, don't be shy, young man. Introduce yourself. I must see for myself if you're worthy of the affections of the lovely Sabrina.'

'Jesus,' Adam muttered, side-eyeing Sabrina. 'What planet's he from?'

'He's a sweet old fella. I think he must have been on the stage at some point in his life. I'm fond of him.'

'Soft touch,' Adam repeated softly, knowing he wouldn't have her any other way.

They drew level with the blankets under which Adam could see a grizzly old man with whiskers and the red nose of a drinker. He'd a woolly hat pulled down low on his forehead, and grinning up at them, he revealed a missing front tooth.

Adam held out a hand which Fred genteelly shook with his fingerless mittened hand. 'I'm happy to make your acquaintance, young Aaron. Shall we drink to this salubrious occasion?'

'It's Adam and no, erm, cheers though.'

'Adam.' Fred stood corrected. 'Don't mind if I do.' He produced a bottle from beneath the blankets, and unscrewing the lid, he raised the molten liquid to his mouth and glugged at it as though it were a glass of milk. When he was done, he wiped his mouth with the back of his hand before giving a satisfied, 'Aaah. Elixir of the Gods that is.'

'It will kill you that stuff, you know, Fred,' Sabrina said.

Adam was wincing at the thought of the whisky burn in the old man's stomach.

'Sabrina, you aren't the first person to say that, and I doubt you'll be the last but tell me, my girl. Would you deprive a fellow of the one thing on this earth that gives him pleasure above all else?'

'Well, would you?' Adam echoed, amused.

Sabrina sighed; she knew she was wasting her time delivering a lecture on the perils of hard liquor. The God botherer, determined to get Fred off the sauce and into the church, had been trying forever. 'No, I wouldn't.'

'Glad to hear it, my girl, glad to hear it. Now then, where would you two Liver love birds be off to on this fine spring evening?'

Sabrina and Adam exchanged glances. They knew how it would sound if they were to tell him their plan.

'We're off for a walk, Fred. Fancied some fresh air,' Sabrina fibbed. The air was crisp with a springy bite to it. It was a good night for a stroll.

'A moonlit stroll.' Fred clapped his hands delightedly before tossing back more of the whisky. As though it had heard him, the moon chose that moment to come out from behind the clouds, and Fred promptly burst into song. His off-key version of Moon River garnered him strange looks from a couple wandering past with their arms linked. He raised the bottle to them. 'Cheers.' They hurried on their way, and he carried on with his song.

'We'll leave you to it then, Fred. Aunt Evie will bring you your porridge in the morning if I'm not about,' Sabrina said, signalling to Adam with her eyes that they should be on their way.

A window above them was wrenched open. 'Oi! Put a flamin' sock in it.'

Fred sang louder as he reached the chorus.

Adam and Sabrina looked at one another and laughed.

'Good night then, Fred,' Sabrina said as they turned away, and his not so dulcet tones wafted down the street after them.

'Want one?' She produced her Opal Fruits from her jacket pocket and waved the sweets at Adam, who helped himself to the top one.

'Strawberry.' He sounded pleased as he unwrapped the sweet.

Sabrina took the orange one beneath it. The street lights cast shadows on the pavement, and the shops were all in darkness as they made their way toward Hudson's. The traffic was sporadic now, rush hour was a memory, and only a few souls were wandering about.

Adam, his hands still in his pockets, remembered what he'd wanted to ask Sabrina earlier. 'Have I done something to upset your aunt?'

Sabrina popped the orange sweet in her mouth and chewed, using that to buy her a moment or two to think of an answer. She couldn't tell him her aunt referred to his dad as a 'wide boy'. Or, that she'd got it in her head, Adam and Sabrina's relationship would end in tears. Her reasoning based on who his father was. Nor was there anything to be gained in telling him her aunt and his dad had an odd relationship. One that she didn't understand.

Aunt Evie became animated and had a glow about her whenever Ray Taylor graced the shop. This was despite her protestations that she couldn't be doing with all his bluster and swagger. For his part, he knew things about her that an acquaintance from one's youth wouldn't. Like, for instance, what her favourite flowers were, and he never missed her birthday. There was no point mentioning this to Adam because he could be prickly where his father was concerned. Instead, she opted for half-truths.

'It's the timeslip, not you. The photograph with you and I in it unsettled her,' Sabrina said, knowing Aunt Evie wasn't silly. She'd have guessed something was up when Adam hadn't arrived on his motorbike this evening. Speaking of which, she'd forgotten all about the picture in her anxiousness over this evening. It was securely tucked away in the inside pocket of her bomber jacket.

She put her hand in there and pulled it out. 'Here, take a look. I can't believe I forgot I had this.' She handed the cardboard frame to Adam. He took it, holding it carefully by the corners as he moved under the street light to examine it while Sabrina explained how she'd come to have it.

'Alice Waters called back into the boutique today.' She might have thought the timeslip story was a lorra rubbish, but she'd given her a note to pass on to her nan, just in case. That, too, was tucked away in Sabrina's pocket.

'I asked her if I could borrow the photograph because we planned on trying to go back in time, and it would help me recognise her nan.' Sabrina had been glad Aunt Evie was out the back and not privy to their conversation as she'd tried to persuade the reluctant Alice. 'I promised her I'd guard it with my life.'

Adam was focused on the evidence he was holding in his hands. It was making him feel odd to see himself in another era.

'Adam?'

'Sorry, I was listening. It's just it's—'

'Weird. I know.'

'I told me, dad, I'm going away for a couple of nights with some of the lads. He weren't best pleased with the short notice, but he'll survive.' Adam handed the photograph back to Sabrina, and she put it safely away once more.

'I didn't tell Aunt Evie anything.' Sabrina would have liked to have shared Mystic Lou's prophecy with her that this time she'd find her mother, but the words wouldn't come. Her loyalties felt divided. 'She'd only try and stop us if I had told her, and she'd be wasting her breath.' Sabrina shrugged.

She felt terrible putting her aunt through this on each occasion she stepped back through the timeslip. Hopefully, this would be the last time she'd do so because she'd finally have the answers she needed.

Hudson's book shop came into sight. Adam's step faltered. 'So, what do we do now?'

'We walk back and forth. It doesn't always happen on my first attempt.' Sabrina thought back to those dark days of nineteen twenty-eight when she'd paced until her feet ached and nothing had changed. She'd been frightened she wouldn't get back to her own time. There was no rhyme or reason to it. The strange forces at work here on Bold Street decided of their own mysterious accord when she would step back or forward in time. 'It might not happen tonight,' she warned, taking hold of Adam's hand. She clasped it tightly because if it did happen, she didn't want them to be separated.

They began to pace.

Part Two

Chapter Twenty-one

Liverpool, April 1945

Lily pushed open the door of Brides of Bold Street with a heavy heart and stepped inside the shop. As the door closed, her eyes swept the space. How was it possible that less than a fortnight before, she'd been twirling in her mam's wedding dress before having it pinned by Evelyn Flooks?

They'd whiled away a lovely hour catching up on each other's lives, and now here she was, back for an entirely different reason.

She'd known Evelyn from their brief time at Littlewoods making parachutes. Evelyn had taken her under her wing upon hearing her mam had been killed in the Durning Road bombing. She'd been one of over one hundred and sixty others who'd lost their lives on that fateful night in November of nineteen forty. The tragedy had been so raw, it still was, and Evelyn's kindness to her gratefully received. She'd seen her as a mother figure of sorts. But when Littlewoods had been destroyed in the blitz, they'd gone their separate ways. There was no one else she'd trust to lay a finger on her mam's precious wedding gown.

The dress and wearing it on her own wedding day would make Lily feel like her mam was there with her. All she had left of her was the house, the headstone next to her dad's engraved with the name Sylvie Tubb, beloved wife and mother, and the dress.

It was all by the by now, though, and she wished she could talk to her and ask her to explain why she and dad had never told her the truth. But, instead, she felt cheated as though her whole life had been built on a lie.

Lily had found out later that the night her mam died, she'd been on her way to Mr Peterson's when the siren had sounded. She'd headed to the closest shelter beneath the Ernest Brown Junior Instruction College. She'd packed in there along with three hundred others and must have been hoping the raid would be over quickly so she could carry on her way. It wasn't to be, though, because the bombs had rained down for eight hours solid, and the college had been hit by a parachute with a landmine attached to it in the early hours of the twenty-ninth of November. The Germans aiming for the railway station had miscalculated, dropping their load on Durning Road instead.

The college furnaces had burst, and hot water and steam scorched many of those trapped inside. Others were killed by the falling debris, and all the while, fires had raged.

Lily couldn't bring herself to think about her mother's fate.

It was a terrible, terrible thing, and all of Edge Hill had been in shock for days, weeks, even months after. Everybody seemed to know somebody who'd been in that shelter. Life as their tight-knit community knew it had been picked up and spun around on its axis, and when it had stopped spinning, it was altered forever.

That period of Lily's life was all a blur. She'd known in her gut her mam was gone by first light when she still hadn't returned home, but she'd searched for her nevertheless.

There was a vague memory of gossipy Mrs Dixon making her a sweet cup of tea. She'd sat with her after delivering the news that her mam was one of the Durning Road casualties.

Winnie, as they called Winston Churchill, was saying it was the single, worst incident of the war.

For Lily, being orphaned when once she'd been so cherished was incomprehensible.

She'd been grateful for the support Sarah and her family had offered her along with Max's strong shoulder, which she'd leant heavily on in the immediate aftermath. He'd begun calling her his little Viking, knowing the story behind the name. It had stuck.

Sylvie Tubb's younger sister, whom she'd fallen out with years ago, had appeared out of the woodwork in the days following Sylvie's death. Lily had known her mam had a sister, but all she'd ever said about her was she'd been wild and had chosen her own path. She'd introduced herself to Lily as her Aunt Pat, insisting Lily come and live with her and her Uncle Gordon at their house in Vauxhall. She was too young to fend for herself, and it was the least she could do for poor Sylvie, she'd said.

Lily found it hard to imagine this woman with the smiley face, freckles across her nose and well-padded frame ever having been wild. It was also strange to think her mam had a younger sister she'd stopped talking to. A sister that hadn't lived far away from them but one whom Lily couldn't remember meeting. Whatever they'd fallen out about must have been significant to cause such a rift.

Despite being unable to recall ever having met her aunt, Lily immediately felt she knew her. She put this down to the similarity between her and her mam. She was a younger version of her with even redder hair than her own.

Lily had packed her bags, eager for someone else to take charge. It had been another wrench to leave Needham Road. Mrs Dixon saw her off with a tear in her eye. She promised to keep an eye on the house. It would stand empty until Lily was of an age to decide what to do with it.

She'd soon settled in with her Aunt Pat and Uncle Gordon, who'd made room for her in the tiny box room upstairs. At first, she'd worried their three boys, Donny twelve, Gerald ten and Charlie seven, who shared a bed in the room next door, would resent her presence. They'd taken their cousin's arrival in their stride, however, and treated her like a big sister. As for her aunt and uncle, they'd been kindness itself to her. So she slotted in, and she was grateful to them for having come for her.

Whatever bad blood had passed between her mam and her sister, Lily didn't care. It was nothing to do with her. She'd asked Aunt Pat about it, but all she'd say on the subject was how inconsequential it was in light of all the suffering the war had wrought. 'Families can be peculiar at times, Lily,' she'd smiled sadly.

For the longest time, things seemed to happen around her. Lily felt as though she were wading through her days. Without Max, she didn't know how she'd have survived her grief but survive it she had.

The war was all but over now, and Lily had been determined to embrace her future. She was training as a nurse at long last. Max, who'd enlisted as soon as he turned eighteen with the Liverpool Irish Battalion, had returned from active service a few short months later. He'd been discharged after suffering blast injuries which, thankfully, he was now mostly healed from, but the mental scars would stay with him a long time. Lily knew he dreamed of what he'd seen and done, but she hoped the nightmares would ease with time. He'd been stationed in Southampton before shipping out as part of the D-Day invasion.

Lily had missed him every single minute he was gone. At night she'd dig out her worry book to write in before getting down on her knees to pray he'd come back to her.

God had answered her prayers.

He'd been different when he returned, that devil may care attitude of his tempered by things seen and done, but he was still her Max. At least the stutter he'd mentioned to her the first time they'd met hadn't returned. He'd not been bothered by it since he'd left Skem, and upon coming home, he'd started back at Ogden's. He'd enrolled in night school, too, where he was studying technical drawing. Draughtsman would be needed, he said, and he owed it to the boys who didn't make it back to do something with his life.

Max popped the question a week after he came home as they jitterbugged enthusiastically on the crowded floor of the Grafton Rooms three months earlier. It was shortly after her eighteenth birthday. He'd shouted over the top of the lively beat, 'Lily will you marry me?' and she'd shouted back, 'I thought you'd never ask!'

At that moment, Lily felt free, lighter than she ever had before. With Max by her side, she could tuck her worry book away forever. Her beam lit up her face. It was unencumbered and reflected the joy inside her. She knew the nervous smile that had plagued her throughout her childhood wouldn't bother her again. Marrying Max meant she'd always be his little Viking, and Viking's were fearless.

A well-groomed airman with a parting straighter than a ruler who'd overheard the exchange nudged his pals, and the next thing, she and Max were airborne over the crowd as a cheer went up.

Aunt Pat and Uncle Gordon had hosted a small party to celebrate the good news.

She'd chosen a gold band with a pear-shaped emerald surrounded by a floral, platinum halo for her engagement ring. And each time the light caught the precious, stone Max had said brought out the green in her eyes, she'd feel the sorrow of the last few years dissolve a little more.

She'd felt her mam's absence keenly, but she was up there in heaven with her dad and one day soon, Lily hoped she and Max would have a family of their own.

Now, here she was, standing on the shop floor of Brides of Bold Street as afternoon sunlight pooled in through the front window, dead inside.

Her life had been built on a lie, and she'd no need of the dress now. She wouldn't be wearing it. Her reason for calling into the bridal shop was to pay Evelyn what she owed her. After that, she could do what she liked with the dress. She picked the bell up off the counter and rang it.

She would not wear her mam's dress. Not after the lie, she'd told.

Chapter Twenty-two

Liverpool, April 1945

Evelyn Flooks heard the tinkling bell signalling she had a customer out front in the shop and took her foot off the Singer's treadle. She left the cuff she was sewing on the doeskin, beige suit jacket sleeve, inspired by Lauren Bacall's lowkey wedding to Humphrey Bogart, where it was and stood up. Beige for a wedding? Whoever heard of such a thing? She gave the jacket sleeve a disparaging glance and yearned for the thirties' long sweeping lines and moulded shapes. This war had a lot to answer for.

She patted her hair, recently set in the latest side-sweep craze, then pushed her glasses which always slipped down her nose when she was at the machine, back up before smoothing her shop coat. The coat, like the beige fabric, was dull. The plain navy fabric was the only material she'd been able to spare. Oh, how she longed for the end of rationing. She'd vowed when there was no longer a shortage of material; she'd sew herself a shop coat in a different colour for each day of the week. She'd be a rainbow.

Her business since she'd reopened a few short months earlier had mainly involved repurposing previously worn old bridesmaids' dresses or heirloom wedding gowns.

Lily Tubb's poor Mam's dress was hanging on the rail, and she eyed it now. All it needed was a nip and tuck for Lily to make it her own. And speaking of the devil, she thought as she stepped into the shop and saw Lily herself at the counter.

Evelyn beamed, but her tone was questioning, 'Hello, Lily?' She was sure they'd organised for her to collect her dress next Thursday. These young brides could be so eager, but she'd yet to make the necessary alterations. As she moved behind the counter, she took stock of her. She was pasty, and her hip bones were jutting out of her skirt. By the looks of her, she'd have to re-pin the wedding dress, or it would hang off her. 'Is everything ahright, luv? You're looking peaky on it if you don't mind me saying, and you've lost weight.'

It was true she was, and she had, Lily thought in silent agreement. She'd barely eaten these last two weeks. The thought of food turned her stomach. Since stumbling across the slip of paper that had upended everything she thought she knew, she'd struggled to sleep. The concern in Evelyn's eyes tipped her over the edge, and she burst into sobs. Evelyn came out from behind the counter and steered her out the back.

'There, there, Lily sweetheart. It can't be as bad as all that. I'll put the kettle on, and you can tell me all about it.'

'It is as bad as all that,' Lily said before gratefully taking the handkerchief being pressed upon her. She blew her nose and sagged down on the chair Evelyn had dragged over for her.

As Evelyn disappeared upstairs, she dabbed her eyes in an attempt to pull her emotions into check, hoping nobody called into the shop in her absence. She'd frighten them off with her red nose and leaking eyes.

Once she'd got herself under control, Lily took stock of the workroom where she sat. The shelves were laden with jars filled with everything from buttons to pearls. There were rolls of lace, reams of ribbons, a measuring tape, a row of thimbles and a fat pincushion. On the work table was a pattern ready for cutting out, and she could see a half-finished jacket in beige being cobbled together over by the sewing machine.

The colour reminded her of the suit Lauren Bacall had worn for her wedding to Humphrey Bogart. The pictures had been in all the magazines, and she'd found it a little disappointing that a film star had opted for such an everyday outfit for her wedding. But, on the other hand, she'd felt a little smug thinking of her mam's beautiful dress she planned on having altered for her big day.

The shop remained empty, and Evelyn returned carrying a tray with their tea things on it. Lily watched as she set them out and nodded yes when she held up the milk jug. It did have therapeutic properties, she thought, sipping the hot, sweet liquid, feeling it calm her. She didn't usually have sugar, but Evelyn had dolloped a spoonful of the precious sweetener in her cup anyway. Her breath had steadied.

They drank in silence for a few minutes before Evelyn spoke up. 'Now then, Lily luv, why don't you tell me what's been going on?' She wondered if it had anything to do with that fiancé of hers.

She remembered having seen him waiting for Lily outside Littlewoods when they'd worked there. The devotion on his face at the sight of her had been plain to see. Heart-warming it had been. Perhaps they'd had a falling out. Emotions ran high around weddings, and Lily wouldn't be the first bride who'd announced the wedding was off in the heat of the moment. In Evelyn's experience, these things usually sorted themselves out in time for the couples' big day.

Lily raised her watery eyes, which were looking decidedly green now they were bloodshot. 'I can't wear my mam's dress, Evelyn. And I'm sorry to have troubled you with it and for the work you've done. I'll pay you, of course.' She sniffed loudly. 'I don't want it back. You could sell it in your shop if you like.'

Evelyn frowned. 'I don't understand, Lily. It's such a beautiful gown, and you'll be hard-pressed to find anything else as luvly with the rationing.'

'I've gorra suit I can wear. It will do.' She blew her nose again and made to get up. 'Thank you for the tea. I'm sorry to have carried on so.'

Evelyn flapped her hand, 'Nonsense, and sit back down. You're not going anywhere until you've told me what's happened.'

Lily did as she was told, and closing her eyes briefly; she took a deep breath as she found herself back in her childhood home once more.

***

She went back there, to the terraced house on Needham Road where she'd grown up, now and again. The visits were bittersweet because she felt closest to her parents there, but was achingly aware that neither of them would ever walk in through the front door again. She'd never again hear their voices filling the spaces she'd called home.

The windows had been boarded up initially, and Uncle Gordon had helped her sweep up all the broken glass. Everything inside was as it had been. It was as though her mam had merely stepped out, which, of course, was what she had done. Only, she'd never returned. The jumper she'd been knitting for the war orphans was still in the basket by her chair. Lily had vowed to finish it one day but had been unable to bring herself to pick it up. She'd take it back that night and give it to Aunt Pat. She was a skilled knitter who'd have it finished in no time.

Things were slowly changing inside the old place with the house getting ready for its new occupants.

That afternoon, once Lily had managed to disentangle herself from Mrs White, who'd wanted all the details of Lily and Max's upcoming nuptials, she'd smelled fresh paint as she stepped inside the front door. Uncle Gordon and Aunt Pat had worked miracles. The windowpanes had been replaced, a fresh coat of paint in the absence of wallpaper covered the walls, and Aunt Pat had managed to source fabric from goodness knows where which she'd made into curtains.

Lily stood there in the front room with her eyes flitting about. The old memories would linger, but the sadness would be chased away as she and Max put their stamp on the house and created happy new ones. For a moment, she imagined what it would be like when the sound of a child or children's laughter filled the room and felt a surge of happiness.

They'd move in straight after their wedding, and Lily couldn't wait. She wanted to be Max's wife in every way.

What would it be like to lie next to him each night in bed and to finally be able to give in to the desires they'd both kept at bay with increasing difficulty!

She hadn't come here today to daydream, though. She needed her birth certificate to take to the registry office. Her mam had kept a shoebox under the bed filled with important papers and the like. Lily had been told it was out of bounds.

'Mam, that doesn't count anymore now you're not here,' she said out loud as she took to the stairs and ventured into her parents' old room. This would soon be hers and Max's room, she thought, visualising the new quilt spread out on the bed. Aunt Pat was patching it together with the scraps of material she'd had tucked away. It would look lovely, she decided, venturing over to the bed and getting down on her hands and knees.

She sneezed as she lifted the bed skirt, disturbing the dust that had gathered under it and resolved to give upstairs a good going over after church on Sunday. The box had been pushed right under the bed, and she had to flatten herself out and stretch long to retrieve it. 'Mam, I'm going to be covered in dust,' she muttered, dragging it out and then sitting back on her haunches to open it.

She placed the lid to one side and sifted through the papers. There weren't many, and they were dry to the touch. Some were yellowed by age and plucking out an envelope, she turned it over to see who it was from. A solicitor's address on Bold Street was stamped on the back, and pulling the contents out, she saw it was her grandparents Will. She scanned the wordy text briefly and then gave up, putting it back where she'd found it.

Her fingers alighted on her parents' wedding certificate next, and hot tears stung her eyes. She blinked them away. They'd been luckier than most, her mam and dad. Their time together might have been cut short, but what they'd had, had been happy. She swallowed the lump that formed in her throat, and as she shifted an insurance policy to one side, she saw the plain white envelope with her name neatly handwritten on it.

'Ah-ha, there you are,' she said, unhooking the envelope flap and sliding what had to be her birth certificate out. She scanned the typed text and frowned. *Why was there no entry next to Father?* Something was wrong, she thought, reading the brief document slowly once more to ensure she hadn't made a mistake because next to 'Mother' was Patricia May Rigby's name.

Her name was there, Lily Jean. There was no mistake; it was her birth certificate and The truth was staring up at her plain as day.

Lily switched into automatic pilot as she scrambled to her feet and kicked the box back under the bed. She shoved the certificate back in its envelope and into the pocket of her dress, then fled the house. Mrs Dixon called out as to what her hurry was from her front doorstep. Lily ignored her. All she could think about was getting home to confront Aunt Pat with what she'd found. Adrenalin made her shake as she rode the bus, unaware of her surroundings as it carried her back to Vauxhall.

'Aunt Pat!' she yelled, bursting through the front door as though the hounds of the Baskervilles were snapping at her heels a short while later. She pushed the door shut behind her with unnecessary force.

'Good God, Lily, I'm not deaf! What's happened, girl?' Aunt Pat appeared in the kitchen doorway, wiping her hands on her pinny.

Lily stared at her, feeling as though the carpet had been wrenched from beneath her feet. How had she not seen it before? They were peas in a pod.

***

Lily blinked, coming back to the here and now in the bridal shop as she finished relaying her tale. Evelyn reached over and laid her warm hand on top of hers for a moment.

'It would have been a shock finding out like that.'

'It wor and I don't understand why they didn't tell me. I would have understood if mam and dad had told me the truth. Patricia was young; she wasn't married. My parents were desperate for a child but were unable to have a baby of their own.'

'Ah, Lily. Life's never black and white. People have reasons for doing what they do, but that doesn't mean they're always right. So don't be hard on them.'

'Me not be hard on them? Me mam wouldn't let Aunt Pat have anything to do with me. It was one of the conditions for her and Dad bringing me up. I was to be theirs.'

'We live in a narrowminded world, Lily. They loved you, and that's what you need to hold onto. Dwelling on the past doesn't do any good.' Evelyn knew this first hand because you had to keep moving forward to survive.

'Max said the same thing.' He'd tried to calm her down, wanting her to meet with her aunt and iron the past out, but Lily refused. Instead, she'd packed her bags the very afternoon she'd confronted Aunt Pat, who'd turned whiter than a ghost as the birth certificate was flapped in her face. The last words she'd said to her aunt were, 'You're a liar, me mam and dad were liars, and I don't want to see you ever again.'

'Well, I think that fella of yours sounds a sensible young man.'

Lily shook her head. She was too angry. What frightened her was what would happen when she stopped being angry, what then? She was scared of the hurt that lay beneath her bubbling rage.

She stood up once more. 'I've gorra go. Let me fix you what I owe.'

Evelyn shook her head. 'No. I've not done any work. I'll hold the dress for you, Lily. It will be here when you come to your senses.'

'Please, don't. I won't need it. Thank you for listening.' Lily remembered her manners as she made her way from the workroom, feeling Evelyn's eyes on her back.

She pushed the door of the shop open and nearly collided with a young couple. 'Oh, I beg your pardon,' she said, hurrying off up the street.

Chapter Twenty-three

Liverpool, 1945

Sabrina massaged her temples as she tried to get her bearings. Where it had been night a few minutes earlier now, it was daylight. *It had happened!* She and Adam had stepped back in time, but to when, she wasn't sure.

Adam, too, was disorientated, and his grip was so tight on her hand it almost hurt. His gaze swung about madly, trying to put the pieces as to what had happened together. They'd been pacing back and forth in front of Hudson's bookshop hand in hand. The novel North and South was visible in the shop window thanks to the street lights reflecting off the glass. He'd caught sight of the pair of them in it too and had begun to feel foolish. Nothing was happening, and he was worried the Bobby who'd passed by five minutes earlier might return and demand to know if they were casing the business.

Finally, he'd had enough and had been about to tell Sabrina that they should call it a night when the air had thickened about them.

It had made him feel strange as if he'd stepped off a plane into the tropics. The sounds around them faded as though someone had turned the volume down. He'd shut his eyes for a split second, and when he'd opened them, Hudson's wasn't there. In its place was Cripps, the Dressmakers. Even stranger was night, had suddenly turned to day like a light being switched on.

Bold Street was busy with people toing and froing about their business. There was nothing unusual in that, but the sights and sounds he took for granted were different. Where were the women in bright saris or groups of teens with teased hair? There were no punks with safety pins protruding from parts of their body, no safety pin should ever go, or young men like him with longish hair wearing jeans and leather jackets.

In their place were women in dresses and cardigans clutching handbags, with their hair styled in victory rolls, and men in suits with trilby hats. Clusters of young men no older than Adam and in military uniform ribbed one another and laughed as they strode past, flicking cigarette butts with careless abandon. The cars, too, were different. He recognised a 1939 Vauxhall 12 puttering up the Street along with a Hillman Minx, and while the pavements were as busy here on Bold Street as they always were, the road was decidedly quieter.

'We're here,' Sabrina whispered, pulling him out of the way of a woman with a shopping bag slung over her arm, hurrying past. Wherever here was.

Adam pinched his arm to make sure he hadn't dreamed up this whole business. Perhaps he'd wake up with a banging head and realise he'd overdone it on the ale the night before. That might be preferable to his current bewildered state.

'It's real, Adam,' Sabrina said. 'We've gone back.' What she wanted to know, though, was to when? The door to the dressmakers burst open, and two giggling women around Sabrina's age in smart belted jackets with slimline skirts wandered out with their arms linked through one another's. They were chattering on about the dresses they'd ordered.

'Excuse me,' Sabrina interrupted, stepping in front of them.

They stopped, and both eyed her strange gear suspiciously.

'Could you tell me what the date is, please?'

They exchanged a glance, and the shorter of the two gave a slight shrug. 'The seventh of May.' Her friend made to pull her away, keen to put distance between themselves and the odd duo.

'Ta very much, but what year is it?' Sabrina persisted.

The woman was unnerved at the intense look on Sabrina's face as she waited for an answer.

'Please, it's important.'

'Nineteen forty-five, of course.' The taller girl spoke up before they hurried away, heads bent together in conversation about the peculiar pair.

'We made it, Sabrina,' Adam said, shaking his head as though he'd water in his ears.

'It's the day before VE Day,' Sabrina murmured. Mystic Lou's words made sense now. She turned to Adam, who was watching the goings-on around him with his mouth slightly agape. 'Adam, did you hear me?'

'Sorry, what?'

'It's May the seventh, nineteen forty-five,' she said with an excited urgency. 'Tomorrow victory's declared for Europe, and the war is officially over. Mystic Lou mentioned a celebration when Flo and I went to see her. She said it was a momentous occasion, and she saw fire, dancing flames, she said. Don't you see? It must have been Victory Day, and the flames belong to the bonfires that were lit that night.' The blood thundered in Sabrina's ear at the thought of it. Finally, she was close to finding the answers she needed so badly.

Adam was still trying to wrap his head around it all. He attempted to put what Sabrina was saying into some sort of order. They had stepped back in time. It was nineteen forty-five, and the Second World War was about to be declared over in Europe at least. He rubbed his ears to try and get rid of the fogged-up feeling. It didn't help, and he mulled over what Sabrina had said, deciding not to mention that if there was going to be a massive celebration throughout Liverpool, how were they supposed to find her mam? A needle in a haystack sprang to mind.

Sabrina must have seen the doubt in his face because she said more firmly than was usual, 'I will find her this time, Adam. I have to.'

At that moment, given the look on her face, Adam believed she would. Right now, though, a stiff drink was in order or, failing that, a pint. What was the Swan Inn like in the forties, and how could he cadge a free pint because he doubted he'd get far with the small change rattling about in his pocket? He was about to suggest they pay a visit to the pub when Sabrina began to tug him by the hand.

'We should go and see Aunt Evie. We can't stand about here all day.'

After the chilly reception he'd been on the receiving end of a few short hours ago, a pint sounded much more appealing. But, then, a thought occurred to him. 'But your, Aunt Evie won't know who you are?'

'No, you're right. She won't. She'll think I'm mad but come nineteen eighty-two, she'll remember me calling in to see her in nineteen forty-five, and she'll remember me telling her not to worry about me. So, when I don't come home this evening or the night after, or for however long we're going to be here, she'll know I've gone back to another era again.'

'It is bloody madness,' Adam mumbled, following Sabrina's lead anyway.

People elbowed one another and nodded in their direction as they weaved up the Street towards the bridal shop.

'Adam,' Sabrina said eyeing him, 'Stop swivelling your head all over the place. You look demented.' He was wild-eyed, she thought, which wasn't helping. It was bad enough their clothes were so out of place.

'I can't help it,' he said, running his fingers through his hair, long by the other men's standards as they reached the shop. 'I feel like a fish out of water.'

So did she, Sabrina thought, her attention caught briefly by the shimmering satin and lace gown in the window of Brides of Bold Street. Her hand reached out for the door handle, but she snatched it away as the door was flung open.

They took a step back as a young woman with fierce red hair exited the shop. She mumbled an apology and hurried off up the Street.

Sabrina only caught a glimpse of her, but there was something familiar about her. The picture was black and white. It didn't offer any clue as to the vividness of her hair which had been up in it. She'd been wearing a wedding dress too, of course, but it was Lily. Sabrina was certain of it.

Her mouth formed an 'O'. She stared after her, catching a flash of red hair now and again bobbing between the sea of heads.

She couldn't believe their timing that Lily should be leaving the bridal shop as they were about to enter it, and she was losing sight of her! Sabrina blinked and told herself to snap to. There would be time to see Aunt Evie later.

'That's her, Adam! Look up there with the red hair, see? It's Lily from the photograph I showed you. C'mon, we have to speak to her!' Sabrina hared off, desperate not to lose her with Adam hot on her heels.

'Sorry,' she apologised, pushing past a dawdling couple, her eyes trained on Lily's hair. She ducked and dived her way forward until she could reach out and tap the other girl on the shoulder.

Lily spun around, startled, affixing her hazel eyes on the sweating girl.

'Lily,' Sabrina panted, her face hot. 'I was worried I wouldn't catch up to you.'

Lily stared at the strange woman, sure she didn't know her or the man beside her, yet she knew her name. Moreover, she vaguely registered they were dressed in odd garb. 'Do I know you?' she asked, wondering what they wanted with her.

'No, well yes, sort of.'

Lily frowned. She'd a right one here, she thought, uncertain what to do. 'Sorry, but I'm in a hurry. I've gorra a bus to catch.' She made to move away, but Sabrina's hand reached out and took hold of her forearm. She wasn't about to let her slip away.

Lily stared at the girl's hand in alarm.

'Please, Lily, it's important.' Sabrina loosened her grip but didn't let go. Is there somewhere we could talk? I can explain then.'

Lily frowned and bit her lip as people sidestepped around them. She didn't know this woman or her fella, and she shook the woman's hand off her. 'Sorry, I've got to go,' she repeated, making to walk away and trying not to let on as to how unnerved she felt by the desperation she sensed coming off this strange girl.

Sabrina grasped for something to make her stop and listen. 'Please, Lily, I know Max,' she blurted after her.

Lily stopped and turned around once more. 'How do you know him?' she demanded. This was getting odder by the second.

'I've gorra a photograph. Look.' Sabrina pulled the picture from her pocket.

Against her better judgment, Lily took the cardboard frame from her, and as she realised what she was looking at, a frown settled between her eyebrows. She looked up and stared at Sabrina, not understanding. 'What is this? Some sort of trick?'

'I can explain if you'll let me,' Sabrina said.

Lily thought quickly. There was a tearoom around the corner. She'd be safe there if these two did turn out to be after money or something. Curiosity was overriding common sense because she had to know how this woman had come by a photograph of what appeared to be her and Max's wedding with these two strangers standing on the church steps behind her.

'There's a tearoom not far from here,' she said, her mind made. She began to walk, and Sabrina and Adam hurried after her.

Chapter Twenty-four

Liverpool, 1945

'Lily, we're brassic, erm I mean, we've no money,' Sabrina offered up lamely as the door to the bustling tearooms tinkled in response to Lily pushing it open. Adam had already produced his wallet, but Sabrina shook her head. The notes would be different, and the last thing they needed was to draw further attention to themselves.

Lily pursed her lips. Her suspicions that these two were after money and had targeted her for whatever reason deepened. Perhaps they'd heard she had a house and thought her rich. But, all that aside, she was gasping. She could spring for a pot of tea. The place was heaving, she saw, glancing around at the full tables. She'd be safe as houses here. 'I'll order for three if you get a table,' she said, having her made her mind up as she tagged on the end of the queue of people waiting to be served.

A young girl with a shock of black curls, wearing a full white apron, was clearing the table in the far corner of the room, and Sabrina and Adam made their way over to it. Adam wished he smoked as he sat down at it. He was fidgety and didn't know what to do with all the energy he had coursing through him.

'Sabrina,' he said, fiddling with the sugar pot, 'what are we going to do? We've got no money we can use and nowhere to stay?'

Sabrina shrugged. She'd been in this position twice before, and it wasn't anywhere near as frightening this time because she was with Adam. 'I don't know. We'll find something. It will work out, you'll see. It always has before.'

'Yeah, but that was when it was just you. People are bound to be more accommodating to a woman by herself than when she's got a fella with her who looks like—'

'He's landed from another time,' Sabrina finished for him.

He nodded. 'I want to get a haircut, for starters.' He ran his fingers through it, looking about the café at the men with tidy short back and sides.

Sabrina nodded, a haircut would help him fit in, and as for her, a dress would be more suitable than her Calvin's and bomber jacket. First, though, she needed to convince Lily they were from the future because she sensed their stories were intertwined. The photograph was evidence of that.

Lily took advantage of the few moments to weigh up the couple as she waited to order. They didn't look like con artists but then what did she know? A con artist wouldn't get about looking like one. And, there was that photograph. There was no time to dwell further as she reached the front line and placed her order. Then, deciding it was better to be safe than sorry, she put her purse away, being sure to tuck it right down the bottom of her bag before closing it.

She made her way over to the table and sat down across from the couple. Her knuckles were white, so tight was the grip she had on her handbag. There was no point in dancing around why she was here with them, she decided, launching straight in. 'How did you come by that photograph?' She watched as Sabrina tucked her hair behind her ears and licked her bottom lip. There was something about this girl. Had they met before?

Sabrina could feel Adam's thigh resting against hers under the table, and she found it comforting. She drew strength from his nearness as she began to speak, 'Listen, Lily, this is going to sound farfetched, but I promise you every word I'm about to tell you is true.' Sabrina wished the tea would hurry up because her mouth was suddenly dry.

Lily cast an annoyed glance at the table on her right as a teacup clattered down in its saucer. It was followed by the scrape of a knife and fork, both of which sounded unbearably loud. She leaned forward in her seat, wanting to be sure to hear every word this girl was about to say.

Sabrina thought she'd best start by introducing herself and Adam. 'My name's Sabrina, and this is Adam. Erm, the thing is, Lily, we're from the future. Nineteen eighty-two to be precise, and I've met your granddaughter, Alice.'

Lily's head flicked back as though she'd been slapped. She'd not expected that. It was ridiculous, she thought. This girl was certifiable, and the lad nodding along with her, he was no better. She pushed her seat back, nearly colliding with the waitress carrying the tray with their tea things on it. She was too flustered to apologise, and as the waitress, oblivious to the drama, set the cups and saucers, teapot and milk jug down on the table, she stood up. 'I've gorra go.' She wanted to put distance between herself and the pair. The photograph must have been doctored. There was no other explanation.

Sabrina fast-fired across the table at her. 'You've gorra an engagement ring, Lily. It's a pear-shaped emerald set in platinum. I don't know why you're not wearing it.' A long shot because, for all she knew, Lily and Max might not have chosen the ring yet, but she had to try.

Lily stood stock still and glanced down at her ring finger. It felt naked. She'd lost weight these last few weeks and had been frightened she'd lose her precious ring. She'd taken it back to the jewellers where she and Max had bought it to get it resized yesterday, but how could this Sabrina have known she'd chosen a pear-shaped emerald? She waited until the waitress hurried off to serve another diner.

'It's true what I said, Lily.' Sabrina's voice was soft.

Trancelike, Lily sat back down. She needed a cup of tea, but first, she wanted to see the photograph again.

As if she'd read her mind, Sabrina got the picture out once more and slid it across the table to her.

Lily stared down at it. There she and Max were plain as day. Sarah was next to her in the dress she was also having altered, and her aunt, she couldn't bring herself to call her mam, and uncle were standing on her left. They both looked proud as punch. Her stomach tightened as she tried to make sense of it. She'd only just called into Brides of Bold Street to tell Evelyn she wouldn't be wearing the dress after all, and yet, here in front of her was a picture that told a different story.

Sabrina set about pouring the tea, putting milk and sugar in each of them. 'Here drink that,' she said to Lily, who usually took her tea black, a habit she'd fallen into with rationing. Today, however, Lily needed the milky, sweet drink, and she didn't look at either of them as she sipped away at it.

'Tell me more,' she said.

By the time they'd drained the pot of tea, Lily had heard a fantastical story about time travel, an abandoned child and a missing mam. It was so farfetched it couldn't possibly be true, could it? And yet, there was a sincerity to the pair that had grabbed hold of her. It was why she'd stayed and listened to what Sabrina had to say.

She'd also been informed that she was connected with this mysterious Sabrina through her mam's wedding dress. The same dress she'd left a little over an hour ago at Brides of Bold Street with instructions for it to be given away or sold.

Sabrina had told her from the age of three she'd been raised by Evelyn, whom she called Aunt Evie and that she'd gone into the bridal business alongside her. She was altering the same dress for Lily's granddaughter to wear in nineteen eighty-two. A dress Lily was, right at this moment in time, determined not to wear on her wedding day.

It was all too much; her head was throbbing as she processed everything she'd been told, and the photograph taunted her.

'It's a lot to take in, I know,' Sabrina said gently.

'You say the dress connects us?'

Sabrina nodded.

'Well, I'm not going to wear it.' Lily's tone was clipped.

'But why? You're still getting married, aren't you?'

Lily nodded and then hesitated. She didn't know these two. Was it wise to share her family secrets? She wrestled with herself for a moment before deciding she'd nothing to lose.

'Me mam and dad have both passed on now.'

Sabrina looked stricken. 'I'm sorry to hear that.'

Adam followed up the same sentiment. 'I lost me mam a couple of years back. It's hard.'

Lily dipped her head, not wanting them to see the tears that sprang to her eyes despite her festering anger. She blinked hard before looking up once more. 'The thing is, I found out recently me mam and dad weren't me parents.'

Sabrina reached over the table. She lay her hand on top of Lily's briefly. 'I understand that must have been a shock.'

'Me mam's younger sister is me, mother and you can't understand.'

'Lily, I told you I wasn't raised by me mother either, but it doesn't make Aunt Evie any less me mam.' It was true. 'Same as your mam's still your mam. The circumstances of your birth don't change that.'

Lily's mouth set in a stubborn line.

Sabrina didn't push further. Instead, she remembered the envelope Alice had pressed into her hand and retrieved it from her jacket. 'Your granddaughter gave me this.' The irony of saying this to the young woman seated opposite didn't escape her. She slid the envelope upon which the words *for my nan, Lily Waters*, were neatly written across the table. 'I don't know what it says,' she added.

Lily picked it up. It was odd seeing Waters and not Tubb was written as her surname, but she'd get used to it soon enough. She tapped the envelope against her hand for a moment, reluctant to open it. She'd heard enough for one day, and she waged a silent war with herself. Then, finally, her natural-born curiosity won out, and she slid the piece of paper contained inside it out, but there was something else in the envelope. Another photograph.

The colours grabbed her first; the picture looked so real. A young man and woman, arms wrapped around each other, stared back at her. She bit her lip. The woman had red hair the same hue as her own and could have been her sister. The hair, the clothes, they were bizarre, though. She bit her lip and stared at it a few moments longer before sliding it back into the envelope and turning her attention to the letter.

Sabrina and Adam watched as she unfolded the paper and held it up to read, both curious about what it said, but Lily's face gave nothing away.

Lily scanned the few paragraphs realising this Alice, who the letter was from, looped her g's the same way she did. No matter how many times her teacher had tried to correct Lily on this, she'd persisted in her own overtly flamboyant loop as Alice had. So she re-read it, slower this time to absorb the message.

10th April 1982

Dear Nan,

How strange it is even to be writing this letter. I expect if you're reading this, you're thinking the story Sabrina's told you is ridiculous, just as I did.

If you are reading it, though, then you'll know it is true. Sabrina and Adam have travelled back in time from nineteen eighty-two to nineteen forty-five when you married Grandad.

I'm going to pretend for a moment that you will get this letter, and I'm not going to think long and hard about what

I'm going to write, Nan. This is because I don't know if I believe Sabrina, and I don't want to tie myself up in knots thinking about what I should say if you're never going to read it. It's also because I believe a letter is always better written straight from the heart.

I don't want to reveal too many things because you've still got your life to live, but I want you to know I'm happy. I'm training to be a chef. Food's my passion, and one day I'd like to open a restaurant. In under two weeks, I'm marrying a man who makes me laugh and feel like the only woman in the world, and I can't wait to be his wife. His name's Mark Edwards, and he's in the army like Grandad was.

The day he asked me to marry him was the happiest of my life because I knew the moment I met him I wanted to be his wife one day. Grandad told me that you always said you knew the first time you saw him that he was the one for you even though you were only kids.

I wear your engagement ring as my own now because I know how happy you and Grandad were. I'm also going to wear the wedding dress you and your mam wore on my day, and one day I'll pass it on to my daughter if I'm blessed with one.

It's the dress that's brought this letter to you. I took it into Brides of Bold Street just as you did to have it altered and met Evelyn Flooks and Sabrina. Who knows, Nan, perhaps it was fate?

I do know, though, I love you, and I especially want you to know that.

Your Alice

PS: Grandad called you his little Viking. That's something only I would know.

Lily blinked. Was it true? It was too much to comprehend. How was she supposed to believe she was holding a letter from her future granddaughter? She folded it up and placed it back in the envelope with the picture before tucking it away in her handbag.

She could feel Sabrina and Adam looking at her expectantly.

'Where are you staying?' she asked after a beat.

'We've nowhere to go,' Sabrina stated simply.

Lily met Sabrina's umber eyed gaze across the table. There was something about her, it was there on the periphery of her mind, but she couldn't grab hold of it. It was like trying to remember a name. You knew it, but it wouldn't come.

She didn't understand any of this, but she did know what it was like to be alone. The scars left mentally by Mrs Cox still tingled from time to time, and the wound of the woman she'd called her mam's death throbbed despite what she'd since learned.

Max wouldn't believe them. He'd convince himself the letter and photograph were trickery being far too practical to take any of what she'd listened to this afternoon on board. Of course, he'd be angry she'd heard them out in the first place, but he didn't need to know, did he?

Her mind raced ahead. She could hardly believe she was entertaining taking them in, but she couldn't have them sleeping rough on her conscience. She didn't want to lie to Max either. She could tell him a half-truth. Something along the lines of how she'd met Sabrina and Adam in a tearoom today and got chatting. They'd lost their home, she could say vaguely. She warmed to her theme, and she'd asked them to stay because, well, because it was the charitable thing to do.

'C'mon,' Lily said, getting up from her seat before she could change her mind. 'You can come home with me.'

Gratitude flashed across their faces as they followed her from the tearoom.

Sabrina cast a wistful gaze over her shoulder as they left Bold Street behind. Aunt Evie would have to wait for another day.

Lily, now she'd made her mind up that Sabrina and Adam could stay, chattered on as they made their way to the bus stop. 'Me neighbour, Mrs Dixon, she'll cut your hair for you, Adam,' she said after he'd muttered he was feeling conspicuous as heads turned at his too-long hair and antwacky apparel. 'I'll sort you something of Max's to wear, and I've gorra a dress you can borrow, Sabrina. You two will fit right in by the time I'm finished; mark me words.'

The bus whined to a halt a few minutes after they'd reached the stop, and clambering aboard; Lily paid their fares. Sabrina squeezed in by the window, and Adam slid in next to her. The bus wasn't full, and Lily sat in front of them, twisting in her seat. 'Will you promise me something?'

Sabrina and Adam waited to hear what she was going to ask them.

'Don't breathe a word of what you told me to my Max.' She was worried he'd think she'd invited two lunatics into her home and would turf them out. 'He wouldn't believe any of it anyway. So I think it's best to tell him you're homeless, which isn't exactly a lie. I'll say we got talking at the tearoom, and given there's a spare room at mine, I invited you to stay. He doesn't need to know all the rest.'

'We won't say a thing,' Sabrina assured her, and Adam nodded his agreement. He was relieved they'd somewhere to sleep. 'But won't he want to know why we're homeless?'

Lily shook her head. 'Max takes things at face value. He won't pry. It's not his way.' He knew some stories were too painful to share and had never mentioned his childhood, not since the day he'd left it behind in Skelmersdale.

The trio lapsed into silence, and Sabrina, her nose pressed to the window, stared out in disbelief as the bus took them down streets where buildings were blown out and left standing like empty carcasses. Rubble was piled high on the pavement, so pedestrians had to step out onto the road to walk around it. She felt Adam's breath on her neck as he too leaned over to look, not recognising the streets they were rattling down, vanished landmarks transforming the cityscape.

These sights were the norm for Lily and the rest of Liverpool, Sabrina thought, her throat tightening at the destruction the blitz had caused. She'd seen photographs, of course, but they were nothing compared to seeing it with her own eyes.

'I lost me, mam, in the blitz,' Lily said.

Sabrina didn't know what to say, so she said the first thing that came to mind. 'It won't always be like this, Lily. Liverpool will be rebuilt.' She knew it was trite, especially for people like Lily who'd lost their nearest and dearest.

Buildings could be fixed, but people couldn't be replaced, she thought, chewing her bottom lip to stop herself from crying.

Chapter Twenty-five

Liverpool, 1945

'Lily! The Nazis have surrendered. Turn the wireless on. Winnie's going to speak at some point. We don't want to miss his speech.' Max burst through the door of the house on Needham Road. He'd been breathless to get there with the breaking news and had left his half-eaten dinner on the table at the flat he still shared with his brother's family. A third baby was on the way, and while the family would miss Max's lodgings money when he moved out after his wedding, the extra space would be welcomed. So it was good timing in that respect.

Lily shot out of the armchair where once her mam had sat of an evening knitting, hearing the springs protest as she did so. *The Nazis had surrendered!* This news swept away the strangeness of the afternoon. She shoved the envelope Sabrina had given her earlier in her pocket and, before she could reach the wireless, found herself being swung in the air by a jubilant Max.

'Can you believe it? It's over me, little Viking. We beat the bastards!' He was grinning from ear to ear.

She giggled with a mix of surprise and excitement at the news and at being picked up like so. Of course, the whole country had known it was coming, but it was a different matter altogether for it to be made official!

He kissed both her cheeks, his lips making loud smacking sounds in the quiet room where she'd been sitting reading through this girl, Alice's letter for the third or was it the fourth time? She'd held the creased paper to her nose to see if she could catch the essence of her. She was a stranger to her yet familiar all at once. Lily had spent the longest time studying the photograph while mulling over everything Sabrina and Adam had told her that afternoon too.

It didn't make any more sense to her now than it had when she'd first heard it, and in the end, she'd made her mind up not to ponder it too deeply. There would always be things in this world that weren't understood. Nor, she decided, would she ever share the letter or photograph with Max. If there was truth in any of this, then there was no need for him to know what lay ahead for them. Life should be a surprise. She hoped that their life together would be full of good ones.

She'd dwelled on Sabrina's desperation to find answers as to what happened the day she was separated from her mother too. She'd seen the need painted on her face as she spoke about it, and as the carriage clock ticked loudly on the mantle, it occurred to her that she was more fortunate than Sabrina. The answers she wanted surrounding her birth were within reach. All she had to do was ride a bus to her aunt and uncle's house and knock on their front door to hear them. Yet Sabrina, if all she said were the gospel truth, had had to travel through time.

It was inconceivable.

A hard kernel had settled inside her where her mam and aunt were concerned. It softened the more she'd pondered this. All the pain and anger consuming her at what should be a joyous time was no good. She was going to marry the man she loved, after all. There should be no clouds hanging over her.

It had occurred to her then that she couldn't change the past, but perhaps she could understand it a little better.

Sabrina and Adam were upstairs in her old room, worn out from their day. It had been a busy afternoon sorting out clothes for them. Not to mention fending off Mrs White's questions as she buzz cut Adam's hair in her kitchen, which smelled of the onions she'd been chopping when they'd knocked on her door. Dark hair floated down, landing on the sheet on the floor beneath the chair where she'd sat him down. His too-long hair and the reasons for him and his wife staying with young Lily was something to be investigated, the plump woman had decided.

Adam had held fast to the suitably vague story Lily had told her about how she'd met the couple who were married in a tearoom off Bold Street and had got chatting. They needed a place to stay for the short term. She'd not elaborated why. For the sake of decency, it had been decided Adam and Sabrina should pretend to be married if they were both staying under one roof.

At the mention of being Adam's wife, Sabrina's face had gone pink and her insides like a marshmallow. *Adam's wife, Mrs Taylor, Mrs Sabrina Taylor*. She hastily stomped on the vision of herself floating down the aisle in a dress she'd altered in her mind's eye so many times over the years as her tastes had changed with age. You couldn't design and create wedding gowns without dreaming of your own after all, but now wasn't the time and place for daydreaming. She'd tuned back into what Lily was saying to her neighbour.

'We've to help those less fortunate than ourselves, haven't we, Mrs White?' Lily had said wide-eyed with innocence.

'Yes, that's true, Lily, but where did you say yours and Sabrina's people were from, Adam?' Mrs White had been quick to ask in response.

'Ah, we don't have any in this part of the world,' Adam replied airily.

Mrs White had frowned so hard at this unsatisfactory answer she'd nicked the top of his ear. The question slipped from her mind as she fussed about sticking a piece of paper over the cut to stem the blood, full of apologies for her clumsiness.

She was like a chubby Miss Marple, Lily had thought, watching on amused. Her mam had been a fan of the Agatha Christie mystery novels, and it had been a relief when the haircut was finished.

Now, as Max twirled her again, she laughed, feeling giddy. 'Put me down; you're making me dizzy!' She wanted to hear the news with her own ears, and once her feet were back on the ground, she caught her breath and switched the radio on. The droll BBC announcer's voice filled the room, informing them that the Nazis had indeed surrendered.

Lily flopped back down in her seat. She couldn't stop smiling. 'There'll be a holiday tomorrow for sure.' It occurred to her then that as momentous as the news was, babies would still be born, people would still pass away, and the tide of the Mersey would ebb and flow. Life, as it had during the war, would go on.

Max shrugged, 'I heard talk the dockworkers might even get two days off after the official announcement's made. We won't know, though, until Winnie's said his piece. But, of course, no one knows when that will be.'

Lily wasn't a drinker, and neither of her parents had been either. A sherry decanter three-quarters full of the rich golden liquid was tucked away in the cabinet upon which the wireless sat, though. It was brought out for celebratory moments like birthdays and Christmas. This was definitely an occasion worthy of a tot! She retrieved two glasses, wiping the dust from them with the hem of her skirt before setting them down on the sideboard. The decanter's stopper was sticky, and she jiggled it, breathing in the foreign, spicy, almost woody aroma once she'd released it. Two small measures were poured before she handed a glass to Max.

'It's got to be a good omen for us,' she said as he clinked his glass with hers. 'Not starting married life under the shadow of war.'

Max nodded, and as Lily raised the glass to her lips, he said, 'I think I should make a toast.'

Lily paused and studied his face from under her lashes, unable to read his expression.

He stared at the amber liquid contents of his schooner for a moment and then looked up, raising his glass once more to Lily's. 'To absent friends and family. May God be with them.'

'May God be with them,' Lily repeated. She understood as she knocked her glass against his that while they were right to be triumphant, others were mourning loved ones whose futures had been cut short. Europe's victory over the Germans was bittersweet.

They drank the sweet alcohol down, and Max, hearing a creak followed by footfall on the stairs, raised a questioning eyebrow at Lily. 'Is someone else here?'

His cheeks had reddened from the shot of alcohol, and he turned expectantly to the door to see who it was. He instantly bristled at the sight of Adam, unsure why a strange man was in his fiancée's house. And not just that either, a strange man who'd come downstairs. There were only the bedrooms and the bathroom up there. Perhaps he was a plumber? He hadn't given Lily a chance to mention a leak or any other problems.

The rigidity of his shoulders softened as he realised the man wasn't alone; a young woman was following behind him. Still, it didn't make their reason for being there any clearer. He turned back to Lily, a question in his ice-blue eyes.

Lily smiled reassuringly. 'Max, this is Adam and Sabrina. Max is my fiancé.' Then, to Max, she said, 'I met them today.'

Sabrina peering around Adam recognised Max instantly from the photograph as the man Lily would marry. Alice's grandfather.

Adam thrust a hand out towards Max, who stared at it for a moment before deciding to give him the benefit of the doubt. He shook it a tad harder than was necessary to assert himself before releasing his grip and looking past him to where Sabrina stood. His smile was curious. He was still unsure as to what was going on. The girl looked familiar, but he was sure he'd never met a Sabrina before. She'd the most unusual coloured eyes too. They were similar in colour to the sherry. 'Have we met somewhere?' he asked, finishing his appraisal.

Sabrina shook her head. 'I don't think that's likely.'

He focussed on Lily, waiting for her to elaborate on what these strangers had been doing upstairs.

'We got chatting in a tearoom today,' she supplied, her eyes bright from the unaccustomed alcohol. 'I'd gone to see Evelyn at Brides of Bold Street to tell her I no longer need my dress.' She looked down at the swirls of patterned carpet, bracing for Max's reaction.

'Ah, Lily, why'd you do that?'

She wouldn't meet his gaze. 'You know why.'

'It doesn't mean I have to agree with it. You'll regret making decisions in anger. I don't want you to look back on our wedding day with any regrets whatsoever.'

They never fought, but they'd argued over her refusal to go and see her aunt and hear her out. Admitting she might have been wrong wasn't something that came easily to Lily, and she wasn't quite ready to do so yet.

'There's been too much loss, as is.'

'Don't, Max, not tonight.'

He sighed. She was right. It wasn't something they should be hashing over in front of a couple they barely knew. 'G'won then, you all met in a tearoom.'

Lily was relieved he wasn't going to pursue the conversation, and she carried on. 'Yes, and it was standing room only. We wound up almost elbow to elbow around a table together, which led to us passing the time. They're not from around here.'

Adam nodded confirmation of this. 'We needed somewhere to stay for a few nights, and your fiancée, Lily, kindly invited us to kip down here. We're very grateful.'

'We are,' Sabrina murmured.

'I couldn't have them wasting their money on a hotel, not when I've a spare room standing empty. It wouldn't be right.'

'What brings you here then?' They sounded local enough to his ears, Max thought.

'We're looking for Sabrina's mam. They were erm, separated a while back, and we heard there was a chance she might be in Edge Hill.'

'Does she look like you, yer mam? Maybe that's why you look familiar. Maybe I've seen her about the place.'

Sabrina was unsure how to answer. She didn't know if she did or she didn't. Her memories were fleeting and vague, with the only clear clue being her eyes. She remembered them being the same whisky colour as her own. 'We've the same coloured eyes, so yes, we look alike,' sprung forth.

Max nodded. That must be it. He glanced at Lily; her heart was too big for her own good, offering the use of her house up to people she barely knew. Still, it was one of the many reasons he loved her. He sized the couple up, giving them a slow once over. She was a good judge of character was Lily. If she thought they were sound, then he'd be hospitable to them, he decided, finishing his top, to toe appraisal. He showed them his glass. 'We were toasting the good news.'

'The Nazi's have surrendered,' Lily supplied. 'It's wonderful, isn't it? Would you like a sherry?'

Sabrina and Adam couldn't help but nod enthusiastically at this news. They'd seen the terrible destruction of their city for themselves that afternoon.

Adam was parched and would have preferred a pint. He wasn't much of a sherry man, but right now, after all, that had happened in the hours since they'd left their own time, he'd murder a glass, and he'd replied with a ta very much.

'Luvly,' Sabrina murmured.

'Why's he in my shirt and trousers?' Max asked Lily as if Sabrina and Adam weren't even in the room. It had dawned on him Adam was decked out in his best shirt and trousers and, he took stock of Sabrina now she'd stepped into the room properly. 'That's your dress, isn't it?'

Lily, who'd picked the decanter up, thought on her feet. 'Erm, their bag was stolen at the station. So they only had the clothes they were stood in, and they needed a wash.' She shrugged.

Max wasn't silly; he'd seen something in Lily's eyes then and a slight shift in the couple's stance. There was more going on here than met the eye.

Chapter Twenty-six

Liverpool, 1945

May the eighth dawned with no broadcast from Winston Churchill having been made as yet, but this had done nothing to dampen the sense of anticipation of the day that lay ahead. Nor did the gun-metal sky blanketing Liverpool flatten its residents' spirits because the streets were soon brightened with the colourful bunting being strewn across them.

Children ran about excitedly outside while mams busied themselves in the kitchen for the street parties that would surely follow. It was only a matter of time now until the ceasefire was officially declared. Dads whistled away outside as they painted the bomb shelters with colourful union jacks. The wirelesses were tuned to the BBC. Harry Leader and his band were broadcast into homes across the country before moving into the daily service.

On Needham Street, Sabrina watched the goings-on outside from the front room's window. She'd barely slept, but adrenalin at the thought of what today might bring prevented her from feeling tired. Adam, too was fidgety and had gone outside after breakfast to help fasten the bunting and hang the flags.

Lily had tucked the letter and photograph away in an old coat pocket in her wardrobe. She'd resolved not to dwell on it further. Not today, at any rate. She wasn't rostered at the hospital, but she knew her fellow nurses would be celebrating, and she didn't want to miss out. She was desperate to see Sarah and share the day with her too. She'd meet Max later, knowing he'd already be in his khaki uniform out on the streets with the other lads who'd served and made it home. She hoped today would be the last day he ever had to wear it.

'I'm going to head to the Royal. You and Adam should go to the town hall,' she declared, drying her hands on a tea towel as she ventured into the front room. She'd refused to let Sabrina help with the dishes. 'The mayor's going to announce the ceasefire from there. It's as good a place as any to start your search.'

The couple had made themselves scarce the night before after their tot of sherry, not wanting to fend off awkward questions from Max. They'd excused themselves by saying they were exhausted. It was true.

Breakfast had been a welcome sight indeed that morning, given they'd foregone dinner.

Sabrina nodded and let the curtain fall. That sounded much more preferable to sitting here doing nothing but wonder where her mother was and what she was doing at this present moment. She was so close she could almost feel her.

Lily fetched her purse from her handbag and held out some coins. 'Here, you'll need this to get about with.'

Sabrina hesitated.

'G'won take it. It's not much.'

'But you're already doing so much by letting us stay.'

Lily waved this away as though it were nothing, and taking hold of Sabrina's hand, she pressed the money into her palm. 'You'll need it, Sabrina. I can spare it.'

Sabrina smiled, her gratitude still feeling strange about taking the money but knowing she'd no alternative but to do so.

'Good luck today. I hope you find her, your mother.' Whether she believed Sabrina's story or not, it didn't take away from the fact that Sabrina clearly did.

'Ta, but you know, Lily, now I'm so close to finding answers, I'm frightened.'

'Of what you might find?'

Sabrina nodded. 'I've never thought further than finding her. It's what's spurred me on. Of course, I assumed she wanted to be found, but what if she doesn't?'

Lily gave her a spontaneous hug. 'Then at least you'll know. I think it must be the not knowing that's the hardest.' The same could be said of her own circumstances, she thought. Not knowing why her mam had chosen to keep the circumstances of her birth secret was eating away at her. She had to know.

Sabrina squeezed her back. She hoped she'd get the chance to tell Lily's granddaughter Alice that her grandmother had been a generous, trusting and warm-hearted woman.

Lily released Sabrina; today wasn't a day for uncertainties, today was a day for celebration, and with that in mind, she raced upstairs to change into her uniform.

Adam moseyed back inside, shaking his head and looking at him; Sabrina wondered when she'd stop getting a surprise upon seeing his short back and sides haircut.

'It's the weirdest thing,' he said, scratching the near bald side of his head.

'What is?'

'This,' he gestured around him. 'Being here in nineteen forty-five. Talking to people who don't know what happens over the next thirty-seven years. I mean there're cold wars, assassinations, Aids, Thatcher—'

'I get the idea.'

'It's weird though, int it? I mean right now, today, them out there don't even know about the atomic bombs on Japan.'

Sabrina wasn't arguing with him. It was weird. 'There are good things, too, though.'

'Yeah.'

Sabrina was suddenly desperate to find the good things. 'Like, man walking on the moon, the Concorde and, and,' she thought hard. 'And Woodstock.'

'Woodstock? Where'd you pull that from?' Adam stared at her, and the look on his face made her giggle. Then, he began to laugh too. 'If anyone could hear our conversation—' he began.

'They'd think we were raving lunatics.'

'Barmy,' he agreed, pulling her to him, and she rested her head on his chest, feeling his heart beating beneath the borrowed shirt.

'I'm glad I'm here with you,' he said softly, his breath ruffling her hair.

'I'm glad you are too.'

Lily bowled back into the room then, and they sprang apart.

'Lily, I wouldn't have recognised you,' Sabrina exclaimed. She was transformed into a nurse. Lily grinned. 'The hair would have given it away.'

It was true, Sabrina thought, seeing the red tendrils escaping from beneath her nurse's cap. 'Did Sabrina tell you I suggested you should head to the town hall? There'll be loads of people gathering there to hear the Lord Mayor's speech.' Lily directed her question to Adam.

He, in turn, looked to Sabrina, who repeated Lily's earlier sentiment. 'It's as good a place as any to start.'

***

The heavens had opened by the time the trio left Needham Road, but nobody cared. They wouldn't melt. Tables were being dragged out onto the street. A hint of the parties to come regardless of what the weather decided to do. Adam and Sabrina waved Lily off in the direction of the Royal Liverpool. They joined the wet-bedraggled throng bunched up on a tram to rattle through streets where parades of people were already singing and dancing, undeterred by a spot of rain.

The noise was stupendous, with the bells peeling out from churches and municipal buildings across the city to mingle in with laughter and shouts from the celebrating thousands.

Adam nudged Sabrina. They grinned at the sight of a woman banging a petrol drum she'd slung around her neck with sticks as she led an enthusiastic crowd in It's a Long Way from Tipperary.

This would be a day no one here experiencing it would ever forget.

Sabrina felt a tap on her shoulder and twisting around was informed by the young woman squeezed in behind her that she'd paper stuck to her shoe. A glance down revealed some sort of flyer caught under her heel and retrieving it, she gave it a cursory glance.

It was a bright and bawdy advertisement for a performance of Lady Here's A Laugh. The text boldly stated there'd be glamourous dresses and beautiful scenery and two performances at the Shakespeare Theatre on Fraser Street that very day. The picture of the cast held her attention, though. The fellow peering around the lead actors had a twinkle in his eyes she recognised. She scanned the names of the performers, and her heart began to thump.

Fred Markham. It was him! Her Fred. She'd been right. He had been on the stage. She hoped she had time to see the play and to speak to him. She'd dearly love to know his story. She wanted to call in on Aunt Evie too today, though she had to find her mother first. Her eyes darted everywhere, scanning faces as she searched for something familiar in the strangers surrounding her features.

They jumped off the tram and joined in with the sea of bodies flooding onto Castle Street; they were all gathering to hear the Lord Mayor of Liverpool's ceasefire speech. The sight of so many people was disheartening, but Sabrina swallowed this down. They'd come this far. Fate would lead her to her mam somehow. Mystic Lou had prophesied it would happen, and this is what she had to hold onto. But, as they were jostled along, she decided that her priority needed to be holding onto Adam for now. She was terrified of losing him in the melee.

The rain was short-lived, and the clouds had been swept away to make way for sunshine by the time Lord Sefton stepped out onto the town hall balcony. From there, overlooking Castle Street, he announced to the waiting crowd the cessation of hostilities. Patriotic music blared, and the crowd erupted with hats being thrown into the air and strangers turning to hug strangers. The city was united in shared joy.

The music eventually quietened, and a hush descended over the revelry. Then, shortly after three pm, Winston Churchill's speech was broadcast through loudspeakers. He reminded the British people that while they could allow themselves a brief period of rejoicing, they must not forget for a moment the toils and efforts that lay ahead. He spoke too of Japan as yet being undefeated. And Sabrina and Adam clutched each other a little tighter. But, for now, though, celebrating was the only thing on the British people's minds. The victory bells began to ring out as their prime minister's speech drew to a close, and a cheer went up over the city, the likes of which had never been heard before or since.

On the Mersey, a ship's hooter rang out.

It was official the war was over.

Chapter Twenty-seven

Liverpool, 1945

Sabrina and Adam had skimmed over faces in the crowds around the town hall for hours to no avail. So finally, as the noise and volume of people began to take their toll, they decided to make their way back to Lily's house. A group of young lads already three sheets to the wind struggled to stay upright on the tram. They clutched on to one another, slurring, laughing and not giving a toss as to the spectacle they were making of themselves. A woman tutted under her breath as to what the powers were thinking of allowing the pubs to be opened an extra hour, VE Day or no VE Day.

'I wonder what the scene's like in the Swan,' Adam said to Sabrina as their stop approached.

'Probably full of lads like that.' She grinned over her shoulder before jumping nimbly down onto the pavement.

They arrived back at Needham Road to a busy tableau. Tables now lined the best part of the road. Sheets were draped over them, serving as tablecloths, and plates upon plates of food had been ferried out from the houses either side. Children wearing rosettes pinned to their chests and party hats on their heads enjoyed the treats on offer. They made the most of being allowed to help themselves. At the same time, parents dressed in their finery milled about beaming and keeping a loose eye on proceedings.

A woman with dark curls wearing a string of creamy pearls and a slash of red lippy along with a pinny over her dress approached them as they drew nearer to Lily's house. 'You're young Lily Tubb's guests, aren't you?'

'Yes, we are,' Sabrina affirmed.

'Well, here you are then.' She retrieved two plates from a pile on the table and said, 'Don't be shy. Fill your boots. There's enough food there to feed an army.' She surveyed her community's effort with pride.

'Ta.' Adam didn't need to be asked twice, and he reached over to pluck a sandwich from a plate, quickly moving on to the sponge cake. Sabrina realised she was starving too. They hadn't eaten since breakfast, and it wasn't long before they'd taken the woman at her word. The plates they were carrying in the direction of Lily's house were piled high.

They perched down on the front steps and ate lustily while watching the celebrations on the busy road. Adam had nearly cleaned up his lot when he mumbled through a mouthful, 'Here's Lily now.' He pointed her out, making her way down the road through the neighbourhood mass unmissable in her nurse's uniform. Her arm was linked through that of another nurse.

Sabrina waved out and received one by return as Lily hurried over to introduce her companion.

'Sabrina and Adam, this is my dearest friend, Sarah.'

Sarah smiled from one to the other, not in the least bit perturbed to see two strangers perched on her friend's doorstep.

She was familiar, Sabrina thought. Lily's bridesmaid! That's was it. She recognised her from the photograph.

If she were sick in hospital, Sarah had the sort of face she'd want to see administering her medicine to her. This was because her eyes, the colour of sable, were kind. The hair visible beneath her cap was almost inky too. A smattering of dark freckles decorated an upturned nose, and her wide mouth had a naturally upward tilt at the corners. Sabrina liked her on the spot.

Greetings were exchanged, and Lily offered the same explanation she'd handed Max about Sabrina and Adam's reasons for staying with her. 'How did you get on today?' she asked, a question burning in her eyes.

Sabrina just shook her head.

'The day's not over yet.' A reassuring smile framed Lily's face.

Sarah, who was as much of a soft touch as Lily, took her friend's explanation as to her new friends in her stride. She smiled broadly at them. 'Have you seen the size of the bonfire they're busy building on the Green at the end of the road?'

'No, but I did see some kids carting a load of stuff down the road earlier. So that's what it would have been for,' Adam said, half to himself.

'You probably saw our Alfie, me younger brother then, he's in the thick of it. A proper firebug, that one. They'll be lighting it once it's dark. We should go down and watch.' Sarah suggested.

Lily was nodding her agreement.

Sabrina was instantly on high alert, and any weariness from the hecticness of the day was banished. Mystic Lou's words, dancing flames, galvanised her.

An excited shout went up as the street lights flickered on for the first time in what felt like a very long while.

***

The flames were leaping high, consuming the effigy on top of the pyre. Young lads fed the fire with glee while mothers did their best to keep their little ones away from the showering sparks. The faces of the people gathered to celebrate glowed orange.

'There's me mam and our Alfie over there. The lad poking at the fire with that big stick. I told you he's a firebug.' Sarah laughed. 'Dad's in France still; he's hoping to be demobbed and back home soon. I wish he were here to see all of this.' Her voice trailed off wistfully.

Sabrina saw her squeeze Lily's arms and remembered she'd lost both her parents. There was no time to think about the pain she'd gone through, though, because Sarah was off weaving her way over to the woman she'd gestured to.

She tugged on her mother's sleeve and shouted the introductions over the din of squeals and laughter. 'This is me, mam, Mrs Carter.' She grinned, her teeth white against the night. 'Mam, this is Sabrina and Adam. They're staying with Lily for a few nights.'

The woman turned, illuminated by the flames, to greet Lily and meet her new friends.

Sabrina found herself gazing upon a face so, like her own, she knew instantly; she'd found her mother.

Chapter Twenty-eight

Liverpool, 1945

'Mam!' Sarah exclaimed as her mother swooned.

Lily was swift to take hold of Mrs Carter's elbow. 'Steady on there.'

All the while, Sabrina stared at her, unable to do anything else.

The older woman gathered herself and mustered a reassuring smile for her daughter and Lily. 'I think it must have been the heat from the fire and excitement of the day that made me feel faint there. I'm right as rain now.' Her gaze didn't flicker toward Sabrina.

The two girls seemed happy with the explanation, and Lily's hand dropped from Mrs Carter's elbow.

Max arrived at that instant, and Sabrina was vaguely aware of him holding a finger to his lips as he crept up behind Lily. She shrieked with fright and then laughed as he wrapped her in a bear hug before nodding his greeting to the small group.

Why weren't the others seeing what was right in front of them? Sabrina wondered as her eyes drilled into this woman, her mother, willing her to look at her.

In the background, Sarah and Adam were laughing over the day's revelry with Lily and Max.

Sabrina felt locked in the moment. She held her breath, waiting and watching.

Mrs Carter's hands fluttered lost at her sides before she clasped them in front of her.

The blood was beginning to rush to Sabrina's head when her mother slowly raised her head. Their eyes, identical whisky coloured pools, locked, and the sights and sounds surrounding them were muted as a current surged between the two women.

This was real, Sabrina thought exhaling. It was happening, but then Sarah leaned toward her mother to shout something in her ear, and the connection which had coursed vibrantly snapped.

Finally picking up on the change in Sabrina's demeanour, Adam pulled her off to one side. 'What's the matter? You look dead strange.'

'It's her.'

'Who is?'

'Mrs Carter, look for yourself and tell me it's not.'

'What do you mean?'

'Adam, it's me, mam,' Sabrina all but hissed, 'just look.'

'Alright, I'll look.' The nervous tension was coming off Sabrina in waves. He studied the woman as best he could in the firelight and tried to visualise her with hair hanging straight like Sabrina's instead of styled into the popular forties roll. The profiles were similar with the same slightly upturned nose. There was something about the way they both stood too, she'd one hip raised a little higher than the other like Sabrina was apt to do. 'Jesus, you could be right.' He turned back to Sabrina, unsure what to do next.

'I have to speak to her. I have to know.' Sabrina's voice came out in a strangled rasp.

'You can't say anything in front of Sarah.' Adam cast about and spied her little brother skipping around to the far side of the bonfire. 'I'll distract her for you.'

Sabrina licked her lips, trying to slow her heartbeats with her breath as she attempted to formulate what she would say when her chance came. In her head, she'd rehearsed this moment thousands of times, but now it was a reality her mind was blank.

Adam leaned towards Sarah. 'I think your Alfie's gone around the far side of the bonfire, Sarah. He was getting awful close to the flames before.'

'I'd better check on the little bugger.' She moved off.

With no one in earshot of them except Adam, Sabrina stepped closer to Mrs Carter and, before she knew what was what, 'It's you, isn't it? You're me, mother,' tumbled forth.

Mrs Carter jolted as though being startled out of a dream. She shook her head. 'I don't believe this is happening.' There was a thundering in her ears as she tried to correlate this grown-up stranger with the child who'd remained forever three in her mind. There was no one to see as her hand snaked out unbidden to touch Sabrina's cheek. Her fingers were fleeting as they made contact with her skin before falling away.

It was as though she was checking she was flesh and blood, Sabrina thought. Not some sort of spectre. There was an urge to reach out and grab hold of her hand. To clasp it tightly to ensure this moment wasn't a figment of her imagination because she, too, couldn't believe it was happening.

'I tried to find you. I tried so hard.' Her mother's voice gave way to a choked sob, and she stepped forward as if to embrace her. But, then, jumped back like she'd been scalded. Her face was pinched with panic, her eyes deep hollows in her face as she scoured the area around the fire for her children. 'Sarah and Alfie don't know,' she whispered.

'Please, can we talk? I've so many things to ask you.' Sabrina was suddenly desperate to be away from the bonfire. To get this woman, her mother on her own.

'Not here.' Her tone was vehement. 'Listen—'

And so they told Lily, who was obliviously wrapped around Max, they were going to head back to the house. At the same time, Mrs Carter, also declaring herself done in, left instructions for Sarah to watch her brother like a hawk. 'Bring him home when the fire dies down, Sarah luv. I don't fancy me chances of dragging him home while the other children are still running about.'

'Are you sure, Mam? It will be hours yet?'

'It's not every day the war's declared over I'll let him have a lie-in tomorrow.'

Sarah was happy enough to oblige, and she waved her mother on her way. She didn't want to risk her fainting because she'd looked close to it earlier and thought bed was the best place for her.

The trio walked away from the festivities in silence.

Chapter Twenty-nine

Liverpool, 1945

The Carters' home was a carbon copy of Lily's terrace house. It was only a short walk from where the bonfire they'd not long left was still burning bright, a beacon against the night sky.

Mrs Carter let them in and fumbled about for lights in the entrance before opening the door to the front room on her left. 'Make yourselves at home, and I'll put the kettle on.' She hurried off up the hall before Sabrina had a chance to see her face clearly. She was obviously desperate for a moment alone to compose herself. Sabrina felt the same way and was glad of a few minutes to soak in her surroundings as she stepped into the sitting room, Adam a sturdy presence behind her.

It was a cosy, family room with a painting depicting a farmer in a field of haystacks hanging a little crookedly against the striped wallpaper. The carpet was busy and beginning to wear thin in places, and the furnishings looked lived in. It was the art deco sideboard that immediately drew Sabrina over, though. A wireless along with some china knick-knacks and a trio of silver-framed photographs were arranged on it.

Sabrina picked up one of the frames. Her eye grazed over the handsome man in uniform staring out at her. Mr Carter. Sarah had said her dad was still away and was hoping to be demobbed soon. It was from him that Sarah and Alfie got their dark good looks, she surmised, peering intently into unreadable eyes. What was he was like? Kind, she hoped.

She put the frame down carefully, feeling Adam move behind her to look over her shoulder, equally curious. She picked up another. It was of the family clustered out the front of the house here, behind them, the gate through which she and Adam had not long since entered. Sarah was younger, with her hair clipped back from her face and Alfie just a babe. She absorbed the image of their mother, *her* mother, young and pretty in a flowery dress with a shy smile for the camera. She looked to be in her later twenties. Her husband, in uniform, stood a head taller than her with his arm wrapped protectively around her shoulder.

'You're the spit of her, Sabrina,' Adam said gently.

He was right, she thought, rubbing her prickling arms. 'Sarah's my sister, and Alfie's my brother,' she murmured in wonder.

Adam put his arms around her waist, and she leaned against him. She was grateful he was there.

The last picture showed the Carters on their wedding day. The fashion was of the late twenties, and Sabrina wondered idly if she'd had her dress made at Brides of Bold Street. The couple had shied away from the stern-lipped fashion of the day and were smiling broadly at the camera. She made a beautiful bride, her dress exquisite, Sabrina thought. For an eery second, it was like seeing herself on her wedding day.

They heard the rattle of china approach, and she put the photographs down turning toward the door. Mrs Carter appeared with a tea tray. She set it down on a table with fold-down wings next to a, sunken armchair and set about pouring the drinks.

'Milk and sugar?' she asked, not making eye contact with either of them.

'Yes, please for both,' Adam answered.

It was all very formal, Sabrina thought, wishing she'd been offered something a little stronger. A shiver raced through her, only it wasn't from the cold.

She sat down at her mother's bidding on the sofa on the other side of the fire. Adam plonked down into the sagging seat next to her, his hand, unlike her own, steady as he took a sip of his tea. She didn't trust herself to hold a cup and saucer and placed hers down on the swept hearth before it spilt.

Mrs Carter fluttered about for a moment before perching opposite them in the armchair with a tapestry cushion behind her back.

She looked like she might take flight at any moment, Sabrina thought, noticing her pallor was ghostly. This was also her first chance to see her mother properly in the light. She took advantage of the moment, studying her blatantly.

There were the faintest of lines around her eyes and mouth, so at a guess, Sabrina thought she must be in her late thirties. Her hair, the same colour as her own, had barely noticeable streaks of grey at the temples and her face was bare of make-up apart from her crimson lips. However, the harder she looked, she saw that there were subtle differences between them. Her jaw was squarer than Sabrina's, and her forehead a little wider.

The hands holding the cup of tea perilously close to sloshing over the rim had fingernails bitten as short as

Sabrina's, a nervous habit she'd never been able to break. Aware of Sabrina's scrutiny, her mother put the drink down on the occasional table beside her. A clean ashtray also rested there. She fished in the pocket of her dress to produce a crumpled packet of Players and a box of matches. She offered the pack to Sabrina and Adam. 'Our Sarah batted her lashes at a soldier in the cinema queue. I'm eking them out.'

'No, ta,' Adam said while Sabrina shook her head.

She tapped one out, and Sabrina watched, fascinated as her mother's trembling hand placed one of the ciggies in her mouth before striking the match against the flint. Several attempts later, the flame flared, and she lit her cigarette inhaling deeply. Still, when she exhaled, none of the tension went out of her shoulders, and the hand holding the smouldering ciggy remained by the side of her face.

Sabrina had hoped desperately for this reunion, but she didn't know how her mother felt.

'I don't know where to begin,' Mrs Carter said, silver-grey smoke spiralling upwards to hover over them.

They all jumped at the sudden spluttering crack of fireworks. It was followed by raucous cheering.

Adam's tea slopped into his saucer, and he swore under his breath.

'Please, erm, Mrs Carter, just start at the beginning. I need to know it all.'

'Don't call me Mrs Carter,' she said abruptly and then hesitated. 'My name's Fern.'

'Fern.' Sabrina sounded the name. It was pretty and would roll off her tongue better than Mrs Carter. She couldn't bring herself to call her mother.

Fern sat smoking for a moment longer before speaking. 'I've thought long and hard about what I'd say to you if I ever saw you again, Sabrina, and now the moment's here, I don't know where to start apart from to say I don't expect you to call me mam. That's who I am, though, Sabrina. I'm your mother.' She fixed her gaze steadily on Sabrina's.

'I've thought about it too.' Sabrina leaned forward in her seat and urged once more, 'I spent most of my life thinking I'd been abandoned, so please, just start at the beginning. Tell me what happened.'

Fern dipped her head and flicked the ash from the end of the cigarette. 'I'd never have left you, but I lost you on a hot day in August nineteen eighty-three.'

Liverpool, 1983

It was a normal summer's day, albeit too hot. There'd been no hint of what was to come as Fern pushed Sabrina in the fold-out umbrella pram up Bold Street. At that moment in time, her main worry in life was her hair. She was worried the ridiculous heat would cause the hair she'd spent an age getting oomph into earlier that morning to flop. It wasn't even mid-day yet. The day was set to be a scorcher.

'Is he my daddy?' Sabrina demanded as she twisted in her seat, trying to see her mam behind her.

The plump, decidedly middle-class man, her daughter, was referencing shot Fern a panicked glance before hurrying on his way.

No chance, Fern thought as she leaned down towards Sabrina. 'I've told you, Sabby, your daddy, is away.' It was true, but she dreaded the day she'd have to tell Sabrina this was a permanent arrangement and not just a holiday.

Sabrina slumped back in her seat and shoved her thumb in her mouth.

Her hair was sticking to her forehead Fern noticed, relieved the heat meant she would be spared the usual tumble of demands to know more than just away. She blamed the animated woman at the storytime session she'd taken Sabrina to for having read, 'Are you my Mother?' to her toddler audience. Sabrina had replaced mother with daddy and had been questioning strange men ever since.

Pete, her dad, had buggered off when Sabrina was six weeks old. Fatherhood wasn't for him, apparently. *Moreover, it was negatively impacting his music vibes,* he'd said.

Fern hadn't known motherhood was for her either, but she'd not had a choice in the matter. There was no walking away from her daughter, nor had she wanted to once she was born. Fern loved her girl with a fierce might that had taken her by surprise. What had surprised her most, though, was the love she received in return. It was unconditional. She'd never experience a love like that before. Certainly not from her mam, who preferred the drugs to her. They'd killed her in the end.

As for Pete, unfortunately, he was more in love with himself than he was with her or Sabrina. He fancied himself Liverpool's answer to Phil Oakley from Human League. He'd even had his hair cut in the same lopsided fashion, and she'd had to hide her lipstick from him.

As he'd swung his duffle bag over his shoulder and headed out the door, Fern tossed after him that he couldn't play his stupid Yamaha synthesiser to save himself. His voice sounded like Marian Faithfull's, only *she* could hold a tune. Her parting shot had been a belter. 'You'd crack the tele screen if you ever make it on Top of the Pops!'

She'd met him on a night out with a lass from the hostel she'd moved into once she'd turned eighteen and was officially too old for the system. It was an interim fix until a flat could be found. She'd been in and out of foster care all her life. The arrangement becoming permanent when her mam overdosed. Fern had been eleven years old.

She'd thought Pete had a look of Adam Ant about him in his leather trousers and she quite fancied being a musician's girlfriend. Who knew? She might even make the pages of Teen Beat if he got one of the gigs he reckoned was in the bag.

So, she'd packed her bags and moved into his grotty little flat over a butchers one month later, glad to see the back of the hostel.

She'd enjoyed playing house even if the flat was small enough to be a doll's house. It was nice to have a place to call home.

However, Pete's habit of not putting his clean washing away when she left it in a pile on the bed for him had soon become irritating. Come to that, so had his aversion to doing dishes. Then there was the way he'd leave wet towels where they fell on the bathroom floor, so it smelled even damper in there. The gloss had worn off their living arrangement smartly. Worst of all, though, was how he flat out refused to air his leather trousers on the communal washing line out back for fear of someone nicking them. She'd fully expected them to get up and walk out of the door of their own accord.

Nobody's perfect, though and had he opted to stick around, she'd have been prepared to let his not so attractive traits go by the by.

Pete's leaving had meant two things. The first being she now had a deep and abiding dislike of the synthesiser as a musical instrument.

The second was that, like her, it was doubtful her daughter would ever know her father, which made her sad. Fern had wanted her daughter to have the sort of family she'd missed out on. The kind of family with a mam, dad and a little brother or sister. A proper family. Now Sabrina just had her, and she wasn't sure if she'd be enough. It was a lot to live up to being everything to someone.

As Fern carried on pushing the pram, she noticed Sabrina had undone the straps again.

'What have I told you, Sabby?' she huffed, veering out of the way of a woman in a pink sari with a hand-knitted sweater thrown overtop to ward off the awful wind whistling down the street.

'Don't like it, Mummy.' Sabrina wriggled to avoid buckling back in, but Fern was having none of it.

'Stop that right now, do you hear me? Or there'll be no chocolate bar when we get to the station.'

The wriggling stopped.

The shop beside them had a 'To Let' sign in the grimy window, and an empty lager can along with a collection of cigarette butts littered the doorway. Fern wrinkled her nose because she was sure she could smell wee.

She bent over the pushchair to click the strap back in, jumping as a piercing wolf whistle sounded. The culprit was a fella with longish hair leaning out the passenger window of a white van as it sailed past.

Pulling a face and pretending to be annoyed, she tugged the hem of her skirt down. Then, ignoring a group of lads with Mohicans in every shade of the rainbow, studded dog collars wrapped around their necks, and scrawny white arms protruding from Union Jack singlets, her eyes cut to the familiar striped awning framing Tabac across the street.

The café was a source of fascination because it was a great spot for celebrity spotting, and the food was good. Unfortunately, she was too skint to call in for coffee or a bite to eat, but she could veer past and see if anyone of note was dining in there today.

She waited for a break in the stream of cars. When it came, she bounced the pram across the road, coming to a halt under the awning to gawp in the window. But, unfortunately, there were no diners whose lunch was worth interrupting to ask for an autograph. So, with a disappointed sigh, she hurried on.

The sign for the wedding shop, tucked between two larger buildings a short distance ahead, caught her eye.

It was the boutique where one of the girls she'd been in care with had had her wedding, and bridesmaids' dresses made. Brides of Bold Street. She'd done alright for herself had Diane marrying a fella who worked for the bank. Her mouth tightened. She hadn't been asked to be a bridesmaid.

The irritation that still rankled at the snub disappeared, however, as she saw the newsagents where she'd called in to buy her monthly magazine treat just a week before had gone. In its place was a shop with posed mannequins in the antwacky gear she'd vague memories of her mam poncing about in. Retro was all the rage these days, she thought. Not that she'd be caught dead in clobber like that.

Her eyes swung out to the road. *How weird*. There were nowhere near as many cars as there'd been a moment ago. The ones tootling up the street were similar to the old banger her miserly grandad had refused to part with.

The air had changed too. It felt thick, almost as if Fern were wading through tepid soup. She came to a halt. The sensation wasn't dissimilar to the time she'd stood at the top of the Blackpool Tower, and her legs had threatened to give out on her.

'I'll just close my eyes for a second,' she mumbled, having decided she must be having a funny turn of sorts.

The whoosh of people carrying on about their business as they passed her by continued. Nobody seemed to find anything odd about her standing in the middle of the pavement with her eyes squeezed shut, clutching the pram for support.

She cautiously opened them once more and blinked rapidly to assure herself things were as they should be.

Only they weren't.

The blood turned to ice in her veins as she realised the pushchair was empty.

Chapter Thirty

Liverpool, 1945

'You were gone, Sabrina.' The cigarette was burning down between Fern's fingers. 'I tried to stay calm because you were forever running away and hiding. It was another of your games, and you'd done it to me before when we were out. So I told myself I'd find you giggling in one of the shops I wor stood out the front of. You'd get a smack on your bottom, and we'd go home and have bubble and squeak for our dinner. Only you weren't in any of the shops, and I knew deep down something wasn't right. That's when I began to panic. I remember I grabbed hold of this fella's arm and asked him to tell me what street I was on because even though it looked like Bold Street, the shops were different. He said what I already knew, I was still on Bold Street.'

Adam, whose hand was resting on Sabrina's knee, squeezed it gently. He wondered if Fern was about to relay the same story his uncle had so many times. Sabrina had to remember to breathe, and the room was so quiet as they waited for Fern to continue you could have heard a pin drop.

'I must have looked bewildered because he asked me if I was lost, and I told him no. Then I asked if he'd seen my daughter, and he looked at me like I were two pennies short of a shilling. He offered to buy me a cuppa so as I could have a bit of a sit-down.'

'It was my uncle you met. Uncle Eddie, back in nineteen sixty-three,' Adam interjected excitedly at having his uncle's favourite party piece confirmed.

Fern looked startled coming out of the almost trancelike state she'd gone into as she told her tale. She jumped as the glowing embers scorched her fingers and ground what was left of the cigarette out. 'But how?'

'Me uncle always talked about this strange encounter he'd had on Bold Street with a young woman who was looking for her child. He'd say she was adamant it was nineteen eighty-three, and how he'd put her right and told her it was nineteen sixty-three, but she was having none of it.'

'It was when Adam told me about his uncle and the woman he'd met that I began to wonder if I hadn't been abandoned after all. So I asked around about strange phenomena, and that's when I heard about the timeslip on Bold Street. I had to find out for myself if this was what happened.' Sabrina touched on her time spent in nineteen twenty-eight and nineteen-sixty-two. Then told Fern about Alice's photograph of her grandparents' wedding and where Lily fitted into the picture.'

'Me uncle said you ran off,' Adam said. 'He said you vanished, and it was like you disappeared into thin air right before his eyes.'

'I did run off to find Sabrina, but there was that shift in the air again, and then just like that, everything was as it had been before. The punks I'd seen earlier were hanging about outside a record shop; the woman in the sari had stopped to talk to another woman. It was all the same, but Sabrina was gone.'

Sabrina processed what she'd heard, thinking out loud as she unravelled the mystery of what had happened the day she'd been found outside Cripps by her aunt Evie all on her own. 'I must have got out of the pushchair and found my way down to Cripps *after* we went through the timeslip; it's where I was found. I stayed in nineteen sixty-three, but you went back through it to nineteen eighty-three.'

'Cripps?' Fern mumbled, dipping her head and rubbing her temples. When she looked up, Sabrina could see the anguish stamped in her eyes. 'I was pulled back to where we'd come from before I got that far. It was Hudson's bookshop when I went in there looking for you. I searched and searched that afternoon, but I knew I wasn't going to find you. I thought about going to the police, but if I told them what had happened, they'd have thought me barmy, and I was frightened they'd think I'd done something to you. A single mother, struggling. I know how they think. When you've grown up in the system like I did, you don't hold much faith in it.'

Sabrina felt a frisson of sadness for the girl her mother had once been.

'Who found you?'

'Evelyn Flooks, my aunt Evie. She's the proprietor of Brides of Bold Street—'

'I know it,' Fern interrupted.

'Did she make your dress?' Sabrina gestured to the sideboard where she'd seen the wedding photograph.

'No, I won't go near that part of town.' She rummage in her pocket once more.

Sabrina frowned, unsure what to make of this, but Fern had waited a long time to find out what happened to her oldest daughter and wanted to hear the rest of Sabrina's story.

She paused with an unlit cigarette halfway to her mouth, then thought better of it and put it back in the packet. 'And, what then? Did she take you to the police station?'

'No, she was going to, but she changed her mind.'

'Why?'

'Well, as I said, she found me outside Cripps.' Sabrina relayed how she'd tugged at Evelyn's skirt. 'I told her my name was Sabrina then asked her where my mam was. She enquired inside Cripps whether anyone's child had run off while they were in the shop. Then she spent an age stopping passers-by on the street to ask them if they'd seen a woman looking for her daughter. No one had. In the end, she took me back to Brides of Bold Street. She assumed you'd come barrelling in at some point, frantic, trying to find me. But, when that didn't happen, she decided there was nothing else for it but to take me to the police station.' Sabrina paused to draw breath and risk a sip of the tea. She reached down for it, managing not to slosh it on herself. It was tepid, but she drank it down swiftly.

'But you said she didn't go to the police?' Fern pressed.

'She got as far as the station, and when she saw there was no talk of a missing child, she decided she couldn't hand me over. Aunt Evie said there were whispers rife at that time as to what happened to children in care or those who were orphaned and the like. There was talk they were put on ships and sent to Canada and Australia never to be heard of again.'

Sabrina broke off, thinking about her friend Patty. Her brother had been sent to Australia, and she'd not set sight on him until she was an adult and had travelled to Australia to find him.

'Aunt Evie was worried about what would happen if you did turn up. For all, she knew you could've been in an accident and wound up in hospital. You could have lost your memory. If no one was looking for me, then I'd have been placed in care, and she couldn't risk me being shipped off to Australia.'

Fern stared down at her hands trembling in her lap.

'Days turned to weeks and then months with no word of a missing child, and eventually, it was like I'd always been with Aunt Evie. Nobody questioned the story that I was her niece and her me aunt.'

Fern raised her chin. 'Have you been happy?'

Sabrina nodded and looked at Adam, who gave her a smile, his hand still gently squeezing her leg. 'I've had a luvly life with Aunt Evie.'

Fern shut her eyes for a moment, and when she opened them, Sabrina saw the sadness marring her unusual iris's so like her own. 'I'm glad.'

Sabrina still had questions. 'Fern, what did you do once you realised I was gone? Properly gone, I mean.'

Tears welled in Fern's eyes, and Sabrina watched as a teardrop sat on her bottom lashes for a split second before spilling over to roll down her cheek. She swiped it away with her spare hand. 'I wanted to understand, to try and make some sense out of what was going on, and the only thing I could think of doing was going to the library.'

Sabrina screwed her face up without realising it. *The library. Her child had gone missing, and she went to the library?* Adam's grip had tightened, which told her he was wondering the same thing.

'It sounds mad,' she looked from Sabrina to Adam, who didn't say a word. 'But I thought maybe I wasn't the first person this had happened to, you see, and I was right. I asked the librarian if any newspaper stories were on file about anything odd happening on Bold Street. There was, of course, and I read about the timeslips; other people had been pulled back to another era and then wandered back out again. You hadn't been snatched. I knew what had happened then and that the only chance I had of getting you back was to try and make it happen again. The police, nobody could help me with that. I needed to step back to nineteen sixty-three if I was going to find you.' Fern's voice snagged with a sob.

Sabrina pushed Adam's hand away and got out of her seat. She knelt on the floor beside her mother and took Fern's hand in hers.

'I'm sorry!' she cried. 'I tried, Sabrina. I tried until my heels were rubbed raw with pounding up and down Bold Street, but nothing happened.'

'It's alright. I know how it is.' Sabrina tried to soothe her distress at reliving the events that had wrenched them apart.

Fern nodded, chewing her bottom lip. 'I went home that evening eventually, and by then, I could barely stand, let alone walk. I came back to Bold Street the next day and the day after that, and then it happened.'

'You went back,' Sabrina stated.

'I went back.' Fern confirmed, and something unreadable flickered across her face. 'To nineteen twenty-four.' Her shoulders gave a slight shrug. 'I don't understand how it works or why it happened to you and me, and it doesn't happen to others. None of it makes any sense, but this time I got stuck. No matter how many times I traipsed up and down Bold Street, nothing changed. I slept rough for the first few nights.' She winced at the memory of her nights in the open. They were obviously still raw.

Sabrina recalled her own evening spent huddled down an alleyway with rats for company. It was an experience she'd no wish to repeat.

'I was hungry and thirsty, and I stood out in my sweater and jeans, so I resorted to thieving. I stole an apple and a dress. I'm not proud of that.'

'You did what you had to do,' Adam said.

Fern nodded. 'Doesn't make it right, though.'

Sabrina pressed her hands around Fern's and received a wan smile.

'I can't believe it's you,' Fern half-whispered.

'It's me, alright.'

Fern freed her hand and reached out her hand to smooth Sabrina's hair back behind her ears. 'You're a sight for sore eyes you are.'

Both women were transfixed by one another, and Fern only picked up her story when Adam's shuffling in his seat reminded them he was also in the room.

'Kenneth saw me huddled in a doorway and took pity on me, offering to take me for something to eat. He wor so kind; I didn't want him thinking I wasn't right in the head, so I told him I'd come to Liverpool to find me, mam, only to learn she'd died. He accepted what I said and took me home to his mam. God rest Florrie Carter's soul. She wor a wonderful woman. The mother I never had. Kenneth's family became my family, and well, I fell in love with my Ken the moment he held his hand out to me on Bold Street. He felt the same way, and we were married after a few months. '

'And did you keep trying to go back?' Sabrina asked, surprised by how much whatever her mother was to say next mattered to her.

'I did—at first.' She twisted the wedding band on her finger. 'But then I fell pregnant with our Sarah and I realised something. Please don't judge me too harshly, Sabrina, but I was happy. Happiness wasn't something I'd had much of in my life apart from when you came along, of course. The thing was if I kept visiting Bold Street, there wor no guarantee I'd step back to nineteen sixty-three and find you. I'd have lost you, Kenneth and his family. They were the first proper family I'd known.'

Sabrina interrupted, 'But I was your family, too.'

'Try and understand, Sabrina. I was frightened.'

'So you chose to give up on me?' Sabrina's voice caught. 'I never gave up on you. Know that. I never gave up.'

'Sabrina, let Fern finish—' Adam cut in.

Sabrina wasn't listening, though. She'd risked everything for this woman who'd chosen a fresh start over her. She sprang to her feet, running from the room, not caring if she never saw Fern Carter again.

Chapter Thirty-one

Liverpool, 1945

Adam caught up to Sabrina, who'd pushed past the singing crowd of merrymakers winding their way home. He thought he heard Lily call out to them but couldn't be sure and didn't stop to see. The bonfire as they rounded the corner was beginning to burn down, and as he drew alongside her, he reached for her arm, pulling her to a stop.

'She didn't want me,' Sabrina sobbed out, trying to wriggle away; she wanted well away from Fern Carter and the hurt churning inside her. She didn't know what she'd hoped to find, but it wasn't what she'd heard this evening. She should have listened to Mystic Lou's warning.

'Ah, Sabrina, it wasn't like that.'

Adam's eyes glinted sympathetically under the street lights, and he tried to embrace her.

Sabrina stepped back. 'She chose them. You heard her!' She waved her hand up the street. 'I want to go to Bold Street now, Adam. I don't want to be here. I wish I'd never meddled with any of this.' If whatever it was at work on Bold Street didn't take them back where they both belonged, then she'd bloody well make it happen!

Adam shook his head. 'No. This might be your only chance to make your peace with your past, Sabrina. We're not going. Not yet.'

Sabrina's chin jutted out, and then her body slumped. The fight had gone out of her. She was spent, and this time she allowed him to hold her in his arms. He rocked her back and forth gently for a moment before saying. 'C'mon, we'll go back to Lily's for what's left of the night. We both need some sleep. It's been a big day. We can talk about this in the morning.'

Sabrina allowed herself to be led in the direction of Lily's house.

The house was empty when they ventured in through the unlocked front door. They were both grateful there'd be no need for polite conversation. It was all they could do to climb the stairs to their room.

Both were sound asleep despite the continued shrieks and odd bang of a rogue firecracker within minutes of collapsing onto the bed.

***

Sabrina woke to find the spot beside her where Adam had lain empty. It was still warm, she deduced, patting it. She lay there absorbing the sounds outside. The clink of bottles, the rumble of a car, a mother calling her child in. Downstairs she could hear people moving about. What she'd learned the night before came crowding back in on her, and she squeezed her eyes shut at the bolt of pain as her mother's face danced before her.

No more, she resolved, opening her eyes and shoving the covers aside. She'd wasted too much energy on Fern Carter. She'd not wanted her. Not enough, and that was all there was to it. She had Adam, Aunt Evie and Flo. She didn't need her.

Getting up, she stretched. Her limbs felt sluggish, and her head foggy with having slept too heavily, and she padded over to the dressing table to peer in the mirror. The dishevelled apparition reflected at her made her grimace. She'd fallen asleep in the dress borrowed from Lily, and it was crumpled. She did her best to smooth it before using the brush on the dresser to untangle her hair and, taking a step back, decided she'd have to do.

She could hear Adam and Lily talking as she went down the stairs. There was no point in lingering. Today, she and Adam would make for Bold Street. She hoped with all her heart that whatever mysterious forces were at work there would see their way to sending her and Adam back to their own time. She would never ever interfere with that which she didn't understand again, she vowed silently.

She found Adam seated at the table with Lily in the kitchen. It was flooded with sunshine, and she glanced at the wall clock to see it was nearly eleven am. She'd slept for hours!

'Why didn't you wake me?' she tossed at Adam.

He was already pouring her a tea. 'I'm not long up myself.' He slid the cup across the table to her as she sat down adding, 'I feel like I've been run over by a bus.'

'Well, at least you don't look like you have,' Sabrina said with a rueful glance down. 'I'm sorry about the state of your dress, Lily.'

Lily laughed, looking surprisingly bright for someone who'd been out the best part of the night. 'An airing will sort that out. But, I don't think either of you will be alone in feeling like that.'

'Where's Max?' Sabrina asked, looking over the top of her teacup.

'We said goodnight or good morning or worever it was around three o'clock. I don't think I'll be seeing Max until later. He'll be sound asleep about now.'

'How come you're up and about?' Sabrina asked.

'I can never sleep in. It's funny. I used to drive me mam potty lying in bed until the last minute, but I get up with the birds these days.' Her smile was wistful. 'Would you like a slice of toast?'

'No, ta.' Sabrina dug out a weak smile; she had no appetite.

'You should have something, Sabrina,' Adam urged.

She shook her head.

'Adam, I know you won't say no?' Lily got out of her seat. 'I'm starvin this morning.'

He flashed her a smile.

Lily began to saw two thick chunks of bread from the loaf on the worktop. 'Sabrina, Adam told me what happened.'

Sabrina raised her head and looked at Adam in surprise. Fern had said her family didn't know. She wondered what he'd said because Sarah was Lily's best friend. He'd trod on dangerous ground.

Adam elaborated. 'I told Lily we found your mam right enough, but she didn't tell you what you hoped to hear, that's all.' His eyes conveyed he'd not told her who Sabrina's mam was.

Sabrina exhaled slowly, relieved.

Lily popped the bread under the grill then turned to look at Sabrina. 'I understand how you must be feeling. My head's been all over the place since I found out me mam was me aunt and the woman I thought was me aunt, me mam. It's a tongue twister; just saying it.' She gave a wry laugh, but there was no mirth in her eyes. 'I realised something last night, though. It wor thinking about the lads who won't be coming home that did it. Life's short, Sabrina. It's too short for holding on to hurts. Talk to her before you go back to wherever it is you come from.' She couldn't bring herself to say the future. 'I'm going to see me aunt this morning.'

Sabrina stared at the dregs in her cup.

'I've something else to ask you both,' Lily carried on, her tone brighter. 'Max and I decided we've had enough waiting. We don't need a big do. We just want to be wed, so we've decided to get married as soon as we can get in at the registry office. Our plan's to head there this afternoon to see how the land lies. Oh, and I'll have to call in and see Evelyn as I think I'll be needing me mam's dress altered after all.'

Lily hoped after seeing her aunt she would be able to resolve things in her mind because she wanted her aunt, uncle and the boys there on her special day. It mattered to her too that this couple be there when their vows were exchanged. Even though she barely knew them. This was because Alice's words in the letter Sabrina had passed to her were haunting her. Every sensible bone in her body told her it couldn't possibly be from the granddaughter she'd one day have, but my little Viking had been Max's private name for her. If, and it was a big if, Sabrina and Adam were indeed from nineteen eighty-two, then she wanted them to take back to Alice the story of her wedding day.

'Please say you'll come?'

Adam spoke up, giving her a wry smile. 'Ta, Lily. We'd luv to. Besides, it's a foregone conclusion that we will be there,' he said, referring to the photograph.

As much as Sabrina wanted to put distance between herself and what had happened the night before, she knew he had a point. They wouldn't be going anywhere until Lily and Max were married. The past couldn't be undone.

Chapter Thirty-two

Liverpool, 1945

Sabrina volunteered to go to Brides of Bold Street on Lily's behalf that morning as she'd enough to do that day. 'I'll tell Aunt Evie you've changed your mind about the dress.' She was desperate to see her aunt, the one constant throughout her life. She wanted to stand in the boutique and feel like she was home. Even though she was years away.

It was odd hearing Evelyn referred to as Aunt Evie Lily thought, her brow creasing. 'Won't it be strange for you seeing her and her not knowing you, though?' She set her hat on her head, waiting for Sabrina's reply. 'What will you say to her?'

'It won't be the first time she hasn't known who I am, and I need to see her.' Sabrina shrugged. 'I've decided I won't say anything other than pass your message on. It will be enough just to see her.' She hoped this was true because it had to be enough.

Adam's thigh was resting against hers under the table, and she felt the warmth radiating from it. She'd be okay so long as she had him by her side.

Lily didn't understand, not really, but she nodded as though what Sabrina had said all made perfect sense. 'Have you enough money?'

'We'll be right, ta,' Adam said, and Sabrina murmured her agreement, thanking Lily for the funds she'd given them yesterday once more.

Lily waved the comment away. 'It's nothing and ta very much. One less job to do today would be a god send.' She struck a pose. 'Will I pass?'

'You look lovely. The hat's gorgeous.' Sabrina rallied.

'I made it myself during my brief time in the world of millinery.' Lily smiled, but it faltered as the nerves began to skitter at the thought of the reception she'd receive from her aunt. She hoped she wanted to see her after the hateful words she'd flung at her. 'Right-ho, I best be off.' She picked up her handbag from the hall table on her way out.

'Good luck today, with everything, Lily; I hope it goes well for you with your aunt,' Sabrina called after her as she headed towards the door. She hoped she, at least, got what it was she needed from being brave enough to face the woman who was, in fact, her mother.

'If we're going to see Evelyn, I better get this lot done,' Adam said, having got to his feet. He'd told Lily he'd see to the breakfast things, and he began rolling his sleeves up. 'Last chance for toast,' he directed at Sabrina.

'No, ta.' She pulled a face. 'It would be like trying to eat cardboard.'

Adam shook his head, but he'd already said his piece on the subject and didn't see the point in repeating himself.

A knock sounded and, given Adam had begun to fill the sink, it was Sabrina who got up from the table to answer the door. She padded down the hall, too foggy-headed to wonder who had come calling.

It was her mother standing on the front doorstep. There were dark circles under her eyes. The grooves on either side of her mouth added to her gaunt appearance in the light of day.

Sabrina, on the back foot, was uncertain what to do. She didn't want a confrontation, but she didn't want to see Fern either.

'Sabrina,' Fern spoke up assertively, 'you need to hear what I've got to say to you.'

No, I don't formed on Sabrina's lips. Still, she remained warily silent, torn between closing the door in her mother's face and bursting into tears. She did neither, though.

Fern glanced to her right, where the woman next door was sweeping her front step and eyeing her with blatant curiosity. 'Can I come in?' But, of course, she'd no wish to be the talk of the neighbourhood.

Spying Mrs White and Mrs Dixon peering over, Sabrina gave them a quick wave before stepping aside to let Fern pass, not wanting to engage with the amateur detectives. She closed the door firmly behind her. 'We're down there,' she tossed at Fern, who was standing awkwardly in the hall, before retracing her steps to the kitchen.

'Morning, Fern.' Adam greeted her, unsurprised by her presence, having heard the exchange at the door. He dried his hands on a tea towel.

She gave him an uncertain smile, her bravado at the front door slipping.

'Have a seat.' He pulled a chair out for her, seeing as Sabrina wasn't going to. 'Can I make you a cuppa?'

'No, ta, I'm awash with tea.' She sat down and looked up anxiously at Sabrina and then back to Adam, who she felt was her ally. 'I didn't get the chance to ask you last night, but are you married?'

'He's me, fella,' Sabrina answered, feeling her face heat up. Adam grinned, not flustered at all.

'We met at the Swan Inn; it's a pub on Wood Street,' he supplied.

'I remember it.' Fern said.

'We've been together seven months.'

Sabrina mentally added, and two weeks, five days.

Fern nodded. She'd warmed to Adam. She sensed he was a good man, and it was apparent from his manner he adored Sabrina and she him.

'Sit down.' Adam took Sabrina by the shoulders and led her to the seat she'd not long vacated.

She'd no choice but to do so.

Once he had the two women settled at the table, Adam announced he'd make himself scarce.

'No, stay, please.' Sabrina flicked a panicked plea at him. She didn't want to be left on her own with Fern.

He looked at Fern, who was fiddling in her purse for a cigarette. 'Stay,' she said, locating the packet and placing a smoke in her mouth; she spoke around it. 'You should hear what I've come to say, too.' Her hand shook as she tried to strike a match, and Adam held out his hand.

'Here, let me.'

She smiled her thanks and handed him the box. He struck the match, and she lit her cigarette, taking a few anxious puffs before speaking. 'I got pregnant with our Sarah not long after Ken and I married. I'd convinced myself by then that you'd have found a good home, Sabrina and I wor worried about how it would affect you if I were to barrel in and rip you from it. I'd have had to have found you first, though, and I'd no idea where to start looking. You could have been anywhere. I already knew there was no rhyme or reason to the timeslip. I could be pulled through and lose Ken forever and still not find you; there was Sarah to think of too.' She looked to Sabrina for a flicker of understanding, but her face was stony.

'All I ever wanted me whole life wor a family of my own, and I never dreamed I'd have two. I didn't think I'd get a second chance after losing you, and I never gave up on you, Sabrina. I want you to believe that. I never stopped wanting you back, but I didn't know how to make that happen without losing everyone else. That's what I came here today to tell you. I put my trust in fate in the end, you see, because it wor fate tore us apart, and I prayed it would see fit to bring us back together. And, it has.'

Sabrina stared at the knots of wood in the tabletop. 'Kenneth doesn't know about me?' she asked after the silence had begun to stretch long.

Fern shook her head. 'No. I could never find the words to tell him. I never changed the story I told him when we first met, and he never questioned any of what I'd said. We don't live in the past, do we, luv? Life propels us forward. It's the way it is.'

That was true, Sabrina thought. Then she asked herself, would she change her life? If she had the opportunity to go back and change everything, she'd have had her mother, but she wouldn't have had Aunt Evie. Sabrina couldn't imagine not having her in her life. And the thing was, you couldn't change what had already been. You could only make peace with it. For whatever reason the future shifted and changed but not the past.

Fern was right life did keep moving you forward. It was a conveyor belt you stepped on the moment you were born, always moving you in the one direction because it didn't go backwards. For whatever reason, however, the future shifted and changed. Fern would vanish from nineteen eighty-three, as would three-year-old Sabrina, never to be seen again. But the past, well, that was set in stone.

Sabrina thought about what Lily had said that morning. Life was short, and it had her standing at a crossroads. If she were to turn one way, then anger over feeling rejected would fester. Or, if she turned the other way, she could accept the separate conveyor belts they'd both been put on and stop asking why.

Adam held his breath, watching as Sabrina raised a tremulous hand. His mouth curved into a smile as she reached across the table and laid it on her mother's.

Fern grasped hold of it tightly.

Adam breathed out. This was what they'd come for. He'd also figured something out, something he wasn't sure he would share.

Fern was aware, right here now in nineteen forty-five of where Sabrina could be found in nineteen sixty-three. Her three-year-old daughter would be outside Cripps wondering where her mother was and why she'd not come for her. There was only one reason why Fern hadn't gone to her when time caught up to the day she'd lost her daughter. It was because she wouldn't live to see her fifty-ninth birthday.

He observed the connection between the two women as they held each other's hands, both finding comfort in finally knowing the truth of what had happened to the other. No, he resolved; he wouldn't mention what he'd figured out. He'd say nothing unless Sabrina brought it up. There was no point. You couldn't change what was written in the stars.

Chapter Thirty-three

Liverpool, 1945

She was a Tubb. Nothing could change that, and the Tubbs were a brave bunch. They had Viking blood running through their veins, Lily told herself. She fancied she could hear the hammering of her own heart over the din the small lads kicking a ball about in the street were making. She scanned their ruddy faces to see if her cousins, *your half-brothers, Lily,* she corrected herself were there in the fray but couldn't see them.

There were no signs of shadowy life behind the net curtains of the front room either, but given the time of day, she'd hazard a guess her aunt, she couldn't bring herself to call her mam, would be in the kitchen. The boys were probably hovering around underfoot with their noses twitching, waiting for dinner. She pictured the familiar scene with Aunt Pat flapping them away with a tea towel.

It wasn't too late, she thought. She could turn and walk away. *No, Lily, you've come this far* and repeating this, she took a steadying breath. Her conversation with Max the night before nudged her on. She'd promised to listen to her aunt's side of things, and this was why she put one foot in front of the other. She climbed the three steps to the front door and knocked. A few weeks ago, she'd have opened the door and barrelled straight in. Today she took a step back to wait.

Thundering footsteps sounded, and the door swung open to reveal Donny. He was nearly as tall as she was, Lily thought. How was it possible for him to have grown in the short time since she'd last seen him, or was it her mind playing tricks on her? She stared at him, thinking how odd it was knowing he wasn't her cousin after all but rather a brother. 'Hello, Donny, is Aunt Pat about?'

'Where've you been then?' Donny demanded, filling the space between the frame as he postured. 'Mam said you'd moved back to the house where you used to live. You made her cry, Lily Tubb.'

His glare was accusatory as he waited to hear what she had to say. Lily would have found the twelve-year-old acting the man of the house amusing if she hadn't been on eggshells about seeing her aunt. She knew Donny clashed with his dad at times over his behaving as if he ruled the roost. Her aunt had explained he'd got used to his dad being away during the first half of the war and had found it hard to relinquish the title of man of the house when he'd returned.

'I know I did, and I'm sorry.' Lily met his gaze steadily.

'She won't tell me what you did.' Donny didn't budge.

'I didn't do anything, ta very much.' Lily was beginning to feel annoyed, and if Donny didn't step aside and let her in, she'd push him out the way.

'Who's at the door, Donny?' Her aunt bobbed out from the kitchen, straightening her pinny. She came to a halt as she registered who her oldest son was talking to. 'Lily!' Hope flared on her face.

'Hello, Aunt Pat.'

'Donny, let the girl in, for goodness sake.'

Donny moved aside reluctantly, and Lily stepped inside, breathing in the familiar scents of the house that had been a home to her when she needed it most.

'Come on through to the kitchen, Lily luv. I've a pie in the oven, and if I don't keep an eye on it, the top will burn. You know how temperamental my cooker is. Donny, round up your brothers and take them outside for a bit, would you?'

Donny bristled but did as he was told.

Lily followed behind her aunt, and as she hovered in the kitchen doorway, she heard a whooping coming down the stairs. She received a much warmer welcome from the littler of the brothers. Charlie wrapped himself around her legs, and Gerald stood grinning up at her. She realised how much she'd missed the boys, even Donny; she knew he was only looking out for his mam. He herded the younger two towards the door.

'Don't bang the door shut,' Aunt Pat called out as Gerald did precisely that. She gave a rueful smile, but it didn't reach her eyes which shone with uncertainty. 'Those lads will be the death of me. Sit down, and I'll put the kettle on.'

Lily would have offered to make the tea. She knew where everything was, but it didn't feel right to make herself at home. So instead, she sat at the table, her stomach giving an involuntary growl at the whiff of pie as her aunt opened the cooker to check on it.

'You've lost weight,' Aunt Pat remarked once she'd righted herself, glancing over at Lily before busying herself with warming the teapot. A cake tin was produced, and she sliced a wedge of carrot cake, all the while prattling on about how Lily would have to cook proper meals once she was wed. 'I'll give you my Lord Woolton Pie recipe. It's the secret ingredients I added to it that makes it tasty, luv.' She slid the cake in front of Lily. 'The war might be over, but we won't see the end of rationing for a while longer. You'll have to learn to be creative in the kitchen. I can write down a few recipes for you if you like?'

Lily nodded absently. She hadn't come here to talk about food as Aunt Pat knew well. However, her aunt was just as anxious as Lily was, and somehow that made her feel marginally better.

The tea-things were set down on the table. 'Get that down yer, luv, before you fade away?' Pat gestured to the untouched cake.

'Aunt Pat, tell me what happened,' Lily said, ignoring the cake. 'I want to know why I was brought up by your sister and her husband.'

'Your mam and dad, Lily Tubb, and don't you forget it. You were luved as much as any child could be. What was done was for the best at the time.' She turned the teapot three times as was the custom. 'That's all any of us can do, you know. Our best.'

Lily nodded but didn't speak because she hadn't come here to butt heads. All she was after was answers.

Pat sighed and poured the tea. 'There's not a lot to tell, Lily. I was only sixteen when I found out I was expecting you. I'd met this fella at a dance, you see. Frank was his name. He never told me his last name. He swept me right off me feet, although when I look back now, I think I was more in luv with the idea of the sweepin' than the actual being swept.' She gave a tinkly laugh, but Lily didn't raise a smile.

'We went out a few times. He took me to nice places. Places I'd never been to before or since. Restaurants with fancy place settings and silver so shiny you could see your face in it. I'd wear me mam's best dress and sneak out of the house feeling so grown up, only I wasn't, of course. I wor a silly child, Lily, whose head was easily turned. I didn't know I wor pregnant until I was nearly four months gone, and when I told Frank, well, he took fright. He arranged to meet me a few days later and then fobbed me off with a handful of notes and the name of a place he'd heard about where I could go to get rid of the baby. It wasn't the fairy tale ending I'd hoped for, and I knew then he wor married and that I'd never see him again. I wor on me own where you were concerned.'

Lily tried to put herself in her aunt's shoes, imagining how frightened she must have been, and she watched the trembling of her hand as she raised her teacup to her mouth.

'I went there, you know, to the place he told me about. It wor down a back alley. Filthy dirty place.' She shuddered. 'The women hanging about were a rough lot. I stood outside that door for an age. I was terrified of what would happen if I went through it and equally terrified of having to go home to tell me, mam and dad if I didn't.'

Lily felt a wave of sorrow for her teenaged aunt as she waited to hear what transpired next.

'I went home in the end, of course, and faced the music.' Her face was clouded. 'I was sent away to me mam's sister's down south where nobody knew me to have the baby. It wor Sylvie who suggested she and Joe bring the baby, you, up as their own. They'd not been blessed, you see, and so it was all arranged. Sylvie thought it better if I didn't see you. She wor scared—'

Lily interrupted, 'Of what. I don't understand!'

'I've thought long and hard about this, and I s'pose she thought you might luv her less if you knew. I lost you and me, sister.' Pat drained her tea and carried her cup and saucer over to the worktop. She stared out the back window at the fence beyond.

Lily sat there absorbing what she'd been told, and it dawned on her then. 'It wor you. All along it wor you.'

Pat didn't turn around.

'My guardian angel.' The woman in the hat she'd seen all through her childhood from afar, it was Aunt Pat; of course, it was. How had she not realised sooner?

'You're not to think badly of Sylvie. I won't have it, Lily. She wor a good mam and a good sister once.' Her back was rigid.

'She was.' Lily ached for a minute more with her mam. She wanted to tell her it didn't matter. She didn't love her any less. She could have told her, and it wouldn't have changed how she felt about her and Dad.

'We've gorra learn. Haven't we, Lily? To move forward and not dwell on the past. Surely that's something this godforsaken war has taught us?' Pat turned around then, her eyes bright with tears.

Lily got up from her seat and took the short few steps across the small space to her aunt. 'We do.' A twin set of hazel eyes stared at one another, and then Pat opened her arms and pulled Lily into her.

'I luv you, girl. Always have, always will.'

Chapter Thirty-four

Liverpool, 1945

The temperamental clouds of the morning had been blown away by the time the newlywed Mr and Mrs Waters left the registry office. Instead of grey skies, it was the sun that greeted the small party who'd gathered on the steps of the building where the couple had just said their vows. They were awaiting their photograph to be taken.

On the pavement below, giving the bride and groom a clap was a huddle of well-wishers. A mix of neighbours, including Mrs Dixon and Mrs White along with people the couple worked with.

Max's friend, a keen amateur photographer, stood centre stage adjusting his camera. He'd been doing his best to tune out Mrs Dixon, who was bending his ear about how she'd known Lily since she was a young girl. 'Wasn't it a shame her poor, dear departed mam and dad weren't there to see her in all her finery today,' she'd said just as the bride and groom appeared, dabbing at her eye with a handkerchief.

He was responsible for the photograph Alice had told Sabrina to guard with her life, Sabrina thought, positioning herself there on the steps for a better view of the bride.

Lily was radiant, far more beautiful in real life than in the picture currently stored in the pocket of her bomber jacket back at Needham Road. A camera could never capture how her dress brought out the creaminess of her skin or how the sun illuminated the intense red of her hair visible through her sheer veil. The dress Evelyn had worked her magic on at Brides of Bold Street to ensure it fitted Lily perfectly was exquisite.

Sabrina had itched to hug her aunt the day she'd gone on her errand to inform her Lily would require the dress to be altered after all. She'd wanted to confide in her all that she'd discovered, and it was only through sheer willpower she kept her mouth shut and her arms by her side. So instead, she'd used the few minutes they had alone in the shop before Evelyn appeared from out the back to scan the space. It had looked sparse with its limited array of fabric rolls and mannequins.

Sabrina knew her aunt well enough to know she was chuffed by the news Sabrina imparted that Lily would wear the beautiful gown after all. She'd found herself being scrutinised by this younger version of her aunt in a rather drab shop coat compared to the technicolour versions Sabrina was used to. People's faces didn't change, though, not really, Sabrina thought. Her face was fuller without the lived-in lines of skin that had weathered the years, but she was still her Aunt Evie. Even if she didn't know it!

'You look familiar,' Evelyn had said. 'I'm sure we've met before. Have you had a dress made here?'

Sabrina had just smiled enigmatically and said, 'No.'

Evelyn turned her attention to Adam then. 'You're not related to Ray Taylor by chance, are you?'

'Distantly,' Adam had replied, equally enigmatic.

They'd made their excuses to get on their way after that, not wanting to fend off questions they couldn't answer truthfully.

Sabrina brushed the tendril of hair away from where it had come loose from the sweeping side do she'd attempted, which was more in keeping with the fashion of the day. Her eyes travelled past Lily to her new husband. Max was beaming from ear to ear with his brother, a burlier version of himself, proud as punch by his side. She moved her attention back to Lily and watched Sarah. The latter was taking her maid of honour role, seriously as she titivated with the bride's veil.

Sarah looked lovely in the dress she'd had repurposed for her best friend's big day. The lilac colour was stunning with her dark colouring. It was on her sister Sabrina's gaze lingered. The sister that would never know she existed. It was best that way, she and Fern had decided.

She'd snatched moments with Fern in the handful of days leading up to today's wedding and felt she had a better understanding of who she was as a person. When she'd let go of her own angst, she'd discovered that ultimately she was relieved to know her mother was happy. That those seconds when they'd been separated, which had turned into years, hadn't destroyed her life. For Fern's part, she'd finally found inner calm now she knew her eldest daughter had been well cared for.

There was still sadness, Sabrina acknowledged as she studied Sarah's profile, that their lives would be played out in different times. It was the way it had to be, though. She hoped Sarah found a man like Max, like Adam, she thought feeling the warmth of his hand in hers. She hoped she would have a happy life too.

Sarah must have felt her gaze on her because her sable eyes flicked to Sabrina, and she smiled.

Sabrina smiled back.

Lily's Aunt Pat fussed with the youngest of her three boy's hair, trying to smooth it down while he squirmed. Then, finally, her uncle told her to leave the poor lad be. He glowered at his other two sons, who were giving one another a sly kick.

As for Lily, she basked in the love she was surrounded by. Her mam and dad were with her in spirit, and she stood proudly beside her husband on the registry office steps.

Lily was ready to embrace married life and all the surprises it would bring.

'Ahright, you lot. If you can hold still and on the count of three, say cheese.'

There was a last-minute kerfuffle as everybody took their places.

'One, two, three.'

'Cheese!'

The camera whirred and clicked, freezing the moment to Polaroid forever, and then the group descended the stairs.

'Look, Lily, mam's over there with our Alfie. They've come to congratulate you.' Sarah waved over at her mam and little brother.

Sabrina hadn't noticed Fern and Alfie in the milling group below. They'd been hidden behind another woman's considerable girth. Fern had a firm hold of Alfie, who was looking eager to be off. Seeing the little boy who was her half-brother fidgeting like so made her smile. He reminded her of the twins, only there was one of him, and from what Fern had said, one was definitely enough!

Adam still holding her hand, pumped it gently. They would go back to Needham Road from here. Then they'd make their way to Bold Street in the hope that the inexplicable forces at work in this pocket of Liverpool would take them home. They moved off to the edge of the gathered friends and neighbours, watching as the bride and groom were met with congratulations and pats on the back.

Fern, aware of their plans to leave after the wedding, made her way over to them, leaving Alfie with his sister. Both looked unimpressed at the arrangement.

She reached for Sabrina's free hand and held it in both of hers, her eyes sweeping over her as she tried to commit every detail of her firstborn to memory. 'I'm going to come right out and say this, Sabrina.' Her gaze travelled swiftly to Adam. 'You'll have to forgive me for being selfish.'

He didn't let go of Sabrina's hand as he waited.

Fern turned to Sabrina once more, desperation lacing her tone as she said, 'I want you to stay, Sabrina, please don't go.'

For the briefest moment, Sabrina felt a tug. She could stay and get to know Fern, Alfie and Sarah, be part of a family she'd not known she had, but then she felt Adam's hand solid in hers and knew what her answer had to be. He was where her future lay. She didn't belong here, and neither did he. She belonged with him, Aunt Evie and Flo.

Sabrina shook her head slowly. 'I can't stay.'

'I know.' Fern's eyes glistened, and her smile was watery. 'I had to ask, though.'

'I'll try to come back,' Sabrina said, not knowing if she would be brave enough to.

'No.' Fern's mouth tightened. 'You've your whole life ahead of you. Don't keep looking back over your shoulder.'

'Mam!' Sarah called out, irritation spiking her voice over something her brother had done.

'Go,' Sabrina said, pulling her into a fierce embrace. 'This is where you belong.'

'I luv you, girl. Always did, always will.' Fern held her close.

'I luv you too.' Sabrina murmured before separating herself and turning. Adam was by her side as she began to walk swiftly away. She didn't want the curious onlookers to see her cry, and she didn't trust herself not to change her mind.

Sarah had watched the exchange bemusedly, as had Lily for whom everything had slotted into place. She picked up her skirts and hurried after Adam and Sabrina.

'Sabrina, Adam wait,' she called.

The couple slowed and waited for her to catch them up.

'You're leaving, aren't you?' Lily could tell by their faces they were. 'Sarah's mam, Mrs Carter, she's your mother, isn't she Sabrina?'

Sabrina didn't say anything.

Lily shook her head. 'It's not my business, and I won't breathe a word, but I hope you got what you came here for.'

Sabrina looked up at Adam. 'We did, ta, Lily. Thank you for trusting us enough to let us stay.'

Adam, too thanked her for giving them a roof over their heads and her help.

Lily smiled. 'I thought you were both a bit touched at first.' She tapped the side of her head, 'but I'm glad I went with my heart and not me head. I wanted to give you something.' She unclipped the dainty pearl earrings she was wearing, 'Will you give these to Alice? From me; they were me nan's, and I want her to wear them on her day.' She glanced down. 'As well as the dress.'

'She'll look just as beautiful as you do, Lily.' Sabrina took the earrings, tucking them away before embracing the red-haired bride. Adam gave her a quick squeeze.

'Be happy, Lily, and have a wonderful life with your Max.'

'The same to you two,' she said, turning back towards her husband.

Sabrina and Adam walked away, and this time they didn't look back.

Chapter Thirty-five

Liverpool, 1982

Evelyn, Sabrina and Adam were seated on chairs that could have done with a tad more cushioning. Adam shifted for the umpteenth time since he'd sat down and tugged at his shirt collar. Evelyn, her face in shadow beneath the brim of her new wedding hat, a delicate peach affair glowered at him from behind her glasses. She'd thawed toward him since he and Sabrina had returned from their sojourn into the past. Thawed, but she was yet to thoroughly defrost.

Mercifully, Sabrina had found the answers she'd so desperately needed in nineteen forty-five and still come back to her. Evelyn knew she'd have withered inside if the pull to stay in the past with her mother, a woman called Fern, had been too strong. She studied the backs of her hands resting on the lap of her two-piece peach suit. They were hands that had given her so much joy with their ability to create beautiful gowns. Sabrina, though, was her most immense joy.

She deserved to be privy to her and Ray Taylor's story, she mused, twisting the small sapphire ring she wore on the middle finger of her right hand. One day soon, she'd tell her, she resolved, feeling Sabrina's arm resting against hers, but not today.

It was just over a week since Sabrina and Adam had said goodbye to Lily and Fern. First, they'd left their borrowed clothes folded neatly on the bed of the room they'd stayed in at Lily's house on Needham Road. Then, changing back into the gear they'd arrived in, they'd made their way to Bold Street uncaring as to the curious stares directed at them. The air had grown soupy within minutes of them beginning to traverse the pavement outside Cripps. Fate, or was it serendipitous? Sabrina was starting to think it was the former which had brought them home to nineteen eighty-two. To where they both belonged and where she planned to stay.

Sabrina nudged Adam to sit still. The chairs with their mean padding had probably been bought with the intention of the backsides gracing them not being sat on them long enough to go numb, she thought. Reaching into her purse to retrieve her Opal Fruits, Sabrina didn't bother offering Aunt Evie the packet. She'd only get a monologue on how false teeth and chewy sweets were a recipe for disaster. She held the tube under Adam's nose instead, and he helped himself, leaving a pink one beneath the sweet he took for her.

She unwrapped the square fruit and studied it momentarily. It was the same shade of pink as her new dress. A colour the shop assistant at Chelsea Girl had described as this season's jellybean pink. She popped the sweet in her mouth and sat up a bit straighter, smoothing the skirt of the pink belted dress with its gold buttons and shoulder pads. Aunt Evie said she'd get stuck going through doorways given the size of them, but Adam had said she looked gorgeous, and when Aunt Evie wasn't looking, he'd pinched her bum.

She chewed away and eyed the windows situated a little over to her left but out of reach with longing. She could feel the beginnings of a headache. By the time they ventured outside, she'd have a headache and a numb bum to boot thanks to the cloying mix of perfumes rivalling for top dog in the small space in which they'd crowded.

The registry office room could seat eighteen, and rows three seats wide and three seats deep were evenly spaced either side of the aisle Alice would soon walk down. Sabrina hoped it was sooner rather than later because her fiancé Mark was jiggling from leg to leg as though he needed a wee. Nerves, she guessed. He was handsome in his army uniform. Her eyes swung to the plump, rosy-cheeked celebrant who looked like she'd be more at home baking cakes than officiating over a wedding. The celebrant leaned over and said something that made him smile. The jiggling stopped.

They were honoured to be here with Alice, having been insistent they come saying it was what her nan would have wanted. She hadn't said she believed Sabrina's long-winded story of having gone back in time to when Alice's nan, Lily was young. Nevertheless, she'd stared at the earrings Sabrina proffered as though they were the most precious gift she'd ever been given. Lily would have indeed been happy the three of them were here today for her granddaughter's special day. Sabrina thought, scanning the room in which every seat was taken.

'That must be Mark's mam,' she whispered to Evelyn. 'Alice said she was put out they weren't having a big do.'

Evelyn looked to where Sabrina indicated a stick-thin woman in an apple green dress with a matching hat she almost needed an entire row to accommodate. Her expression was one of dissatisfaction as she glanced back to survey the small gathering.

'Good on them for sticking to their guns,' Evelyn whispered back. 'It's their day, after all. His mam obviously decided if she couldn't have a big do, she'd wear a big hat. Mind you, she needs something to distract from the size of that nose.'

Sabrina sniggered.

'What's so funny?' Adam asked.

Before she could answer, though, the doors swung open, and the wedding march sounded from an unknown source. Alice stood there poised in the doorway as all eyes swivelled towards the bride, who'd decided she didn't need anyone giving her away. An appreciative murmuring swept the room.

'She looks gorgeous,' Evelyn breathed.

'Stunning,' Sabrina said.

'She looks just like Lily,' Adam stated.

The dress, which had served three generations of Alice's family, brought out the creaminess of her skin just as it had Lily's. Her red hair was pulled back today in a bun and threaded with apple blossoms. In her ears were the pearl earrings Lily had pressed on Sabrina with the wish her granddaughter wear them on her wedding day. The perfect finishing touch. Her hands held a spring posy of peonies, larkspur and love-in-a-mist.

She glided forwards to meet the man who would officially become her husband in a few minutes, and the service that followed was short and sweet. It might have been a no-nonsense affair, but it still saw Evelyn reach for the tissues. Sabrina, too was busy dabbing her eyes when the couple were bent over the table beside the celebrant and two witnesses signing the marriage documents. Adam looked at them both bewildered. Women were a mysterious lot, he thought. Why did they always cry when they were happy?

They got to their feet as the jubilant newlyweds walked hand in hand from the room with family and friends filing out after them.

'I'm starving,' Adam said in Sabrina's ear. 'Can't wait for lunch.'

'You're always thinking of your stomach.' Sabrina grinned up at him, although she was looking forward to the luncheon that was to follow at the restaurant where Alice was an apprentice. It was French, no less.

'I hope they're serving lamb. I like a nice bit of spring lamb,' Evelyn said. 'Although it does tend to get stuck in me dentures.'

'Aunt Evie!' Sabrina admonished. 'Keep your voice down.'

The group gathered on the steps of the registry office under a clear spring sky. Sunlight was dancing off the puddles from the rain shower that had been and gone in the time Alice and Mark had said their vows. A man in an ill-fitting suit took charge, flapping about arranging them just so on the pavement in front of the one-storey, brick building before clicking away with his camera.

'Toss your bouquet, Alice. It might gee our Terry up if I catch it,' a girl around Sabrina's age called out. Laughter echoed about the group, and Alice took her place in front of them all.

She glanced back over her shoulder, 'Ready?'

'Ready!' A handful of eager female voices replied.

Alice tossed the posy high in the air over her shoulder as all eyes were trained on the gentle pinks, purples, blues and whites bunched together.

Sabrina's hand spontaneously shot up and caught the bouquet.

'You're for it now, mate,' someone jeered, but Adam just grinned, and Sabrina dipped her head to hide her pink face as she breathed in the sweet fragrance of spring.

The End